JUST INTUITION

MAKENZI FISK

MISCHIEVOUS BOOKS
2014

Mischievous Books

www.mischievousbooks.com

First Mischievous Books Edition 2014
Cover Design: Makenzi Fisk
ISBN: 978-0-9938087-0-8

ACKNOWLEDGMENTS

I am thankful for my partner Stacey, and daughter Wahnita, who provide me with endless support and inspiration.

Tracey, you encouraged me to write, and I am grateful.

My characters and stories are purely fiction and in no way resemble actual people or events. That said, I have certainly been influenced by quirky friends and relatives, and real life criminals with whom I have crossed paths.

… and thank YOU, for reading.

DEDICATION

I am humbled to have enjoyed the love of many furry companions and I cherish every single memory. Pets have a particular way of weaving themselves into my life and my stories.

I want to remind the reader that no actual animals were harmed in the creation of this book. It's fiction, silly. I hired imaginary stunt animals who were well paid for their contributions and are still living happily in my mind.

PROLOGUE

The bitch is down there. I imagine her skeleton lying with arms crossed, like in the movies. I used to think about the fishes eating her flesh, but I guess she's just bones now. She's probably got her big mouth open and I bet she's still screamin'. *Well, go ahead and scream. No one can hear you.*

I stand on the trail by the bog, my bog, looking at the edge where the moss meets the rocky outcroppings. The bare end of the nearest willow branch easily snaps off and I toss it out, aiming for the pool of open water in the middle. It comes up short and slaps the soggy surface, wobbles and lays like a dead snake. Something heavier will sink to the bottom. I pick up a medium sized rock and consider its weight before heaving it with all my might. It flies past the stick, lands soundlessly and disappears.

She ruined my life and I hated her. She deserved it, telling me what to do and pretending she cared, when I know she didn't. If she really cared, she would have given me what I wanted. But she never did. That day, she pretended we were having a good time, going for a picnic and talking sweet. After a while she started a fight. Like always.

I guess I didn't need to hit her so hard, but the rock was right there, like a sign or something. Blood ran down the side of her head and she fell to her knees, staring at me like she didn't recognize me any more. She tried to get up and pawed at my leg. *Get your hands off me!* I kicked her in the neck. She knew I don't like to be touched. *Don't touch me!*

She grabbed her throat and staggered halfway to her feet so I

1

shoved her as hard as I could. She went over into the bog like a drunken hippo and I remember her face, all squished up and covered with moss and mud. Her eyes opened wide like a doll from a horror movie but I wasn't scared. I wanted to laugh because she looked so funny making such a big deal.

She slapped at the sloppy moss with her hands so I picked up a big stick and pushed her back from the edge. Her head dipped under. She never was a good swimmer, and the muck made it worse. When I was tired of listening to her bawl I hit her on the head. She went under and then it was real quiet.

It was so easy. No one would ever find her. Stuff that sank to the bottom of this bog never came up. If you push a stick through the water and down into that muck, it burps up a rotten stink. That's why everyone calls it loon shit. Already, she was probably sucked down and it's a perfect place for her. I used to dream about this all the time. She was gone. Really gone.

That day, I squatted beside the bog, enjoyed the warm sun shining on my face, and the sound of birds doing whatever birds do. In her purse, I found a pack of Marlboro's and lit one with her disposable lighter. I pocketed the money from her wallet, filled the purse with rocks and tossed it in after her. It sank quicker than she did and I sat back to savor my first smoke in weeks. I wheezed like an asthmatic but it settled after I smoked a few more.

I stayed until the whole pack was gone and I'd made myself light-headed. Suddenly I realized that I was happy for the first time I could ever remember. So, this is what happy feels like, I thought.

I had to do it. I wanted to. I'm glad.

The sun is getting lower in the sky and I stand up, gathering saliva in my mouth. I spit as far as I can, just for good measure. *This is my bog.* I turn and walk up the trail to the little white house at the other end.

The car is gone. Of course. Saturday evening is a no-brainer. Card night with the Lutheran Ladies Bridge Club. The old broad would never miss the gossip. They're like a little gang of whiskey jacks. Always picking through someone else's stuff. Those stupid birds never shut up, just like all them ladies. *Mind your own business!*

It's not even dark yet but I open the gate, walk past the satellite dish on the lawn and right up on the back porch like I own the place. Yes, the key is under the mat. It's so easy. She's so stupid. She must be the only one out here who bothers to lock the door. Better to get a dog but she'd never do that. What if he took a crap on her carpet? She'd have a heart attack. I have to work real hard not to laugh out loud at the thought of a big Rottweiler taking a dump in the middle of her tidy living room. The thought of her keeling over from a freakin' heart attack is even funnier and I can't stop myself. I snort the laugh through my nose and wipe it on my sleeve. Why am I worried? No one is around to hear me for half a mile.

I turn the key in the lock and push the door open, real gentle, and it doesn't even squeak. She probably oils the hinges every week. I hide the key back under the mat now, so I won't forget later. Everything in its place. Hospitals are not even this clean. I check my shoes, she'd spot a single bit of dirt or grass, and close the door behind me. Ah, my second home.

Fresh muffins are cooling on the counter beside the oven. They smell okay and I bet they are still warm but I don't take one because she'll notice that for sure. I've been coming in here for months and by now I've learned where she keeps everything. Stupid jewelry in the old dresser drawer, a bunch of stupid glass dolls and trinkets. I couldn't pay someone to take that crap. But it's sure nice to come relax at my weekend getaway. Nobody is here to bug me.

I look in the fridge out of habit. Friggin' garden vegetables and nasty looking baked stuff. No meat and not even any beer. How can she live like this? Who doesn't drink beer? I peel a slice of cheese from a stack and stuff it in my mouth. I'm careful to close the package and slide it back into place. It's weird white cheese and I choke on it but manage to get it down after I chew it a few times. She'll never spot that. Who counts their cheese? I know there's nothing good in the pantry but I take a peek anyway.

Last time I tried some minty crap in a bottle but it tasted like toothpaste so I spit it in the drain. Shouldn't have done that. She might have noticed.

I sit carefully on the sofa and turn on the TV. The old lady has better channels than home. A Bruce Willis action movie is on and I turn up the volume. That guy knows how to kick ass. Bruce hadn't killed his first dozen when, between gunshots, a noise outside catches my attention. Gravel crunches in the driveway and I jump straight up off the couch. I peek between the blinds as she parks her blue car out front. She's behind the wheel with her seatbelt on, all prim and

3

proper and annoying. What the hell?

She's out of the car before I've hit the off button and brushed the wrinkles from the couch. I make for the back door but there's no time. She's climbing onto the porch and she'll see me for sure. I grab the closest knife from the rack in the kitchen and grip it tight, my feet spread wide. Blood pounds in my throat. Should I get rid of her? Could I do it? What would Bruce Willis do? The tiny paring knife shakes in my hand and I decide that today is not a good day to mess up this tidy kitchen. I race to the bedroom and shut myself in the closet. It smells like mothballs but I can't really complain, can I?

I hear her open the fridge and close it again. There is rustling in the kitchen and then the backdoor slams. She's gone again, as fast as she'd come. I wait until the car pulls away and now I'm pissed. This is my time. My time! She has no right to ruin it! She made me run and hide in the closet like a little pussy. Knife clenched hard in my hand, I shove the door open and step out.

What would have happened if I'd jumped her the minute she stepped through the door? Would she scream? Would she fight? Would she just stand there like a friggin' rutabaga? I examine the little paring knife in my hand. Probably best it didn't come to that.

"Scheisse!" I punch the inside of the closet but it hurts so I swear out loud a few more times "Scheisse! Scheisse! Scheisse!" It occurs to me that this is my favorite cuss.

In the kitchen, I slide the knife back into the rack and open the fridge. The nasty looking baked stuff is gone. The fresh muffins too. That's why she came back. I slam the door, return to the couch, and make a point of sitting my ass down hard to reclaim my space. A pillow bounces off and lands on the floor. I pick it up and rearrange it. My relax time is ruined. I hate her. I flick the TV on, change the channel, and turn it off again. She's ruined everything.

I imagine myself smashing every single thing in this room. *Boom!* Out goes the front window. *Crash!* That's the glass on the cabinet. *Smash! Smash! Smash!* Goodbye to all those stupid little glass dolls. I imagine sitting here in a huge pile of broken glass, glittering like little diamonds all around me.

I stare at the dolls for a minute before I get up and wipe the wrinkles off the couch, like I always do. It's time to leave. On my way past the kitchen stove, I turn every damn one of the knobs all the way on. Gas hisses out the burners and I smile. It will stink to high

4

heaven when she gets home tonight. Maybe she'll light a match. That'll be worth watching. I shut the door behind me and walk the trail around the bog. I'll get myself a beer and be back as soon as I can. I don't want to miss the show.

It takes longer than I planned to clear my head and find a couple of beers. I am so excited that I forget to apply insect repellent and am half eaten-alive before I'm forced to go back for it. Blackflies and skeeters are nasty out by the bog after dark if you don't keep moving. I know the trail by heart and can walk it with my eyes closed. It's a warm evening and I can't wait. I pop the tab on the first can of Budweiser while I walk.

I feel like it's my birthday and something incredible is coming. I have already imagined a half dozen different scenarios. Church Lady will come home and light a smoke. No, she doesn't smoke. She will light a candle. Yes, she'll pour herself a glass of wine and light a candle. Nope, she doesn't drink either. Well, something needs to happen, or I will be forced to make it happen.

When I reach the little white house, I see I haven't missed the show because she's not home yet. I find a spot just outside the picket fence where I can wait. I take a long swallow of my first beer and set the second can in the weeds at my feet. Me and the King of Beers. What a perfect night.

A few minutes later, headlights come up the road and I squat behind the fence when her blue car pulls closer. Excitement bubbles up from my belly and I rock back and forth a little. I just can't stop myself. Church Lady gets out of her car and damned if she doesn't lock her door. Why in hell would she lock her door way out here? To stop thieving squirrels? Like I said before: she's stupid.

I see her plain as day under the moonlight, struggling with her bags. Her stupid old lady shoes trip her on the step before she makes it up to the porch. She puts her key in the lock. I can hear a gurgling sound in my throat and it takes a minute before I realize it's me. She reaches inside for the porch light switch and a flash instantly blinds me. The heat wave follows right after, like I'm at the wrong end of a blowtorch. I am knocked backward so hard that I'm a bit scrambled so I lay still and stare at the sky for a minute. When I sit up, I see what I've done.

The entire back end of the house is on fire and those old lady shoes are standing empty and alone on the porch. Flames curl hungrily around the shoes but there is so much smoke that I can't see Church Lady at all. My imagination fills in the blanks. I must have the sloppiest grin on my face because it just looks so amazing! I jump to my feet and raise my hands above my head like a kid on a roller coaster. I think I'm shouting but don't really know what I'm saying. Just a bunch of words that seem to roll together off my tongue. I have never felt so alive!

After a while I realize that you can probably see the smoke and fire for miles. Someone will be here soon to find out what's going on but I don't want to leave yet. I stay a minute more and then take off running. This was the best night of my life!

I am halfway home before I remember that I left my beer by the fence.

CHAPTER ONE

The first rosy hint of daylight flooded the horizon when Erin wearily poked her key in the lock and turned. She gave it the requisite jiggle, accompanied by a shove from the toe of her running shoe. Making the hundredth mental promise to 'fix that damn door', she wrenched it open with a loud screech. So many things needed repair in this old house. An ancient alarm, the first of its paranoid generation, obediently beeped its warning. She tapped the keypad and the red light switched to green.

A large Golden Retriever dashed around the living room corner and snuffled her pant legs, its tail thrumming a happy rhythm. Erin held the excited dog back with one firm hand, placed her shoes side-by-side on the rack, hung up her jean jacket in the front closet and clinked her keys into the basket on the top shelf. She looped the strap of her leather shoulder bag onto a hook. A baleful yellow-eyed glare greeted her from the back corner.

"Wrong-Way Rachel," she panned, with a half grin to the cat. The cat stared back. "We meet again." She cocked a finger like a gunslinger. "You vindictive little feline."

Rachel turned her back, swished her bottlebrush tail, and ignored her. Erin cringed at the plume of Persian cat hair swirling through the closet and closed the slider halfway.

A glimpse of her own reflection in the hallway mirror startled her. Short bangs drooped over her forehead and she ran a hand through them. Dark shadows created semi circles beneath tired eyes and fine lines were beginning to show at the corners. In a few years they might be crow's feet. She backed up and patted her stomach under her golf shirt. At least she was still in good shape.

At twenty-six, she was the youngest officer, and one of the few on Minnesota's Morley Falls police department without a paunch. She intended to keep it that way. Her compact, wiry build and fast metabolism had not seemed a positive attribute when she was a kid but the benefits kicked in when she reached her twenties. A furry paw nudged her foot and she turned her attention to the warm reception from the dog. She rubbed the retriever's velvety ears.

"It's nice to see you too, Fuzzy Fiona," Erin murmured. Fiona's muzzle was graying with age, but she still had all the vitality of her younger self. The dog flopped onto her side and lifted a front leg to expose her soft belly.

"Yes, you are so easy!" She laughed and patted Fiona's chest. The dog's tail beat louder against the hardwood floor.

"Shhh. You're going to wake your mama."

The dog clambered to her feet and followed her, nose to pant leg, into the kitchen. Despite blindness, Fiona had developed pretty effective ways to get around.

She'd showered before leaving work but Erin still felt dirty inside and out, the stench of smoke and something else less pleasant embedded in her sinuses. She used the plastic bristles of the pot scrubber to scrape the remainder of the black soot from under her fingernails.

Last night's fatal fire had made it a tough shift. As one of the first responders, she assisted on the initial call. The death of a human being stood out as the worst part of her job, traumatic when it was someone she knew. When the attending detective showed up, she'd been unceremoniously relegated to perimeter security. It distressed her to be shut out, hobbled, and unable to help.

She tried to relax and clear her mind before she went to bed, especially when agitated. The fatal fire wasn't the only thing troubling her this morning. Everyone at work was on high alert since last month's bust of a biker carrying a quantity of methamphetamine. Since then, there had been more than one anonymous death threat left on members' vehicles behind the station, and calls for upgraded security cameras. She might be a bit protective of her girlfriend, but this was Erin's life, not the life Allie had signed on for. In a town this size, criminals knew who you were and a cop could never let down her guard.

Sighing, she used the dish cloth to swipe at three dusty footprints on the window ledge. The cat was invisible most of the time but she sure made her presence known.

Fiona watched Erin go about her morning coffee-making routine, tail thumping when she moved between counter and sink. The shiny Italian coffee machine was one of Erin's few indulgences and she thoroughly enjoyed it. Despite the kitchen's dilapidated appearance, no substandard coffee was served here. Only the very best beans from a specialty roaster in The Cities would do.

Erin chose a mug, her favorite with a big hand-painted flower and perfectly shaped handle, and poured coffee to just under the rim. When she was on night shift, she stuck strictly to decaf. She had enough trouble sleeping and didn't need to add caffeine to the mix. When she brought her mug to the table, Fiona lay on her feet, hot breath steaming the toes of her socks. Those adorable doe eyes and eagerness to please made Fiona infinitely endearing. The dog was growing on her. The cat, not so much.

One hand on her coffee mug and the other on her iPhone, Erin opened the News App and thumbed through the highlights. Ever since the horrible events of 9/11, when she'd overslept and awoken to a world under siege, she began and ended her day with the news. She rarely missed a thing.

Her ears pricked at muffled cries and a crashing thud upstairs. Allie! The all too familiar sensation of adrenaline knocking on her skull overtook Erin's exhaustion. The dog startled up ramrod straight and froze. For all her virtues, no guard dog was Fiona. Break in? Did the decrepit alarm malfunction? Why didn't Fiona alert earlier?

Because she had learned to think and move, Erin was at the front closet in a few swift strides. She located the off duty pistol in her leather bag, unsnapped it from its concealed holster and palmed the 9 mm SIG Sauer P220 in one fluid motion. Up the stairs in seconds, she operated on instinct. In a half crouch on the balls of her feet, Erin continued down the hall on silent socks. Her nerves wired for sudden movement.

Bathroom: Clear. Guest room: Clear. Windows: Secure. Nothing out of place. No sign of forced entry.

Finally, she approached the master bedroom and toed the door from the side. The window was open and wooden blinds swayed in the breeze. There was the empty bed, but no sheets, no blanket—and no Allie.

Panic rose in Erin's throat. She tore the window slats aside. Sunlight stabbed mercilessly into every dark corner. Thumbing the magnetic alarm contact on the window frame, confusion roiled in her gut. Why had the alarm not activated with this security breach? She dove onto her belly and peered under the bed, commando crawling behind the armoire. Nothing but a few dust bunnies. One ear against the oak floorboards, she held her breath to listen. The house was eerily still and only Erin's heart thundered in the silence. An unexpected wave of nausea overtook her and she swallowed hard, her face flushed with the effort.

She lay still and tried to calm her breathing but a faint scrabbling noise sent her vaulting over the mattress. With the Sig 9 mm gripped in her right hand, she covered the hall, semi-barricaded by the doorway. Blood pounded in her ears.

Light padded footsteps approached from below and Fiona's timidly inquisitive muzzle appeared at the top of the stairs. The dog proceeded down the hallway, sniffing the air as she walked. She stopped in front of the linen closet, peered with clouded eyes at Erin, wagged her tail once and lay flat. Nose pressed to the crack beneath the door, the dog emitted a low moan. Erin joined her outside the tiny closet, turned the knob and eased open the door.

Her girlfriend curled in fetal position under the shelves of linens. Erin's internal panic reached a new crescendo and she touched her arm. Allie's entire body jolted upright and she smacked her head against the shelf. Mewling like a kitten, she thrashed against the tangle of bedding.

* * *

What woke Allie was the smell. Acrid smoke. Burning stench curled evil fingers into her nostrils. Throat constricted by fiery tentacles, she held her breath, eyes screwed tight. Her skin burned with furious intensity and she tried to kick, but found her limbs immobile. She was trapped in the blaze.

The shadowy figure watched excitedly and raised arms to the sky.

She struggled with all the ferocity of a wild animal. Incessant roaring intensified and descended in an incendiary tornado. Lungs ready to burst, she gulped air like the drowning and her tormented body freed itself.

Hell's inferno opened to devour her.

* * *

"Wake up, baby." Erin's voice cracked.

Allie's dark brown hair splayed across her face. A trickle of crimson ran the length of her eyebrow, drizzling a bloody streak onto the white fabric of the sheets. Fiona whined and tucked her tail between her hind legs.

Erin dropped the pistol and gathered Allie in her arms. She felt hot. A fine line of moisture beaded her upper lip and she was drenched in sweat. Eyes wide open, she panicked and gulped for air. One hand brushed her bloody eyebrow and she stared blankly at the red smear.

"It's okay. You're okay. It's just me." She whispered soothing words until Allie's movements calmed and her breathing slowed. She tucked her face into Erin's shoulder and Fiona's nose intruded to sniff wetly at her cheek. The dog huffed in relief when she reached out a trembling arm to encircle her. Fiona was apparently more of a comforter than a protector.

"What's going on? Are you hurt? Are you having a nightmare?" Erin asked. She brushed disheveled hair from her girlfriend's forehead.

"Burning in hell. Burning alive."

Woven in Allie's hair, Erin's fingers froze.

"Watching fire..." Allie whispered. She stared unfocused toward the end of the hallway.

Erin turned to look. Nothing. Tiny hairs prickled the back of her neck.

"Church Lady is gone..." Allie's whisper trailed off and she sucked in shallow gulps of air. Erin was now thoroughly transfixed.

"Whaddyamean?" It all came out as one word. She made a conscious effort to maintain control. "What-did-you-say?"

Silent for a moment, Allie's breathing changed and tight muscles released. "It's just a nightmare. I'm not crazy, you know," she whispered tersely into the folds of Erin's shirt. She was suddenly awake, aware, and very defensive. She pulled away and met Erin's

11

gaze. Intensity smoldered in her dark eyes. "I'm not!"

"I know. I'm always on your side, remember?"

Allie kicked clear of the snarled sheets. Startled, Erin and the dog followed her to the bedroom. Fiona wagged her body in a semicircle beside Allie, who balanced evenly on both feet and faced the morning light.

"What happened?" The adrenaline kick Erin had experienced a moment ago was making her lightheaded.

"It was just a nightmare." Allie closed her eyes and filled her lungs.

"I was afraid someone had broken in. I could't find you, and the window was open—"

"It was hot last night. I bypassed that window when I set the alarm."

"Oh," Erin took a step toward her. "I didn't know you could do that."

"It's in the alarm interface toolbox." Allie scrunched her eyebrows and stretched to her full five foot nine inches, rolling her shoulders like a fighter. After a few more deep breaths, she shifted gears and made her way out the door.

"Baby, wait!" Erin trailed behind her, snatching a robe from its hook. She caught up to Allie in the hallway.

"You're not going out to slay the dragon in your tightie-whities are you?" Erin grinned. "You'll freak out the neighborhood kids."

Allie grimaced, took the robe and draped it around her white T-shirt and blue polka dot panties.

Erin made more coffee and meticulously buttered two slices of toast in the kitchen. Allie reappeared, her face scrubbed pink and her long hair tied back in a tight ponytail. A small skin-colored Band-Aid covered the corner of her eyebrow and she'd dabbed makeup on the red scrape. Dressed in jeans and black T-shirt with a little red maple leaf in the center, Allie's svelte physique made casual look hot. She was absolutely refreshed. Like someone had punched the restart button on her day.

Fiona head-bumped Allie on the thigh and she opened the back door to let her out. Erin marveled at the blind dog unerringly picking her way down the steps to the yard, nose to ground. Allie sat in a kitchen chair, Android phone in hand, scrolling through her Facebook page. Wrong-Way Rachel appeared and wove a tight figure eight around their legs. The three-legged cat nimbly launched herself onto the table and swished her tail in Allie's face. She reached two fingers out to smooth Rachel's whiskers, which delighted the cat into making a happy chirping noise.

"The cat—" Erin sputtered, "on the table—"

"Sorry hon. You're right. We'll get the hang of this." Allie lifted Rachel and set her on the floor. A light dusting of feline hair marked the spot where she had been and Allie sheepishly swatted at it. With a twitch of her tail, and no farewell, the cat exited for her latest hiding place. Allie resumed browsing on her Android. Her expression was positively serene. Like Buddha.

She suddenly rose and stood by the door where, two seconds later, the dog's happy grin and dangling tongue appeared behind the glass. She let Fiona in and the dog tracked muddy paw prints across the floor.

Erin stifled a sigh and eyed the closet that held the sponge mop. She placed the café latté she'd made on the table for Allie. It was nice and frothy, just how she liked. Without looking up, Allie absently reached over, grasped the handle of the coffee mug and slid it to the right about a foot.

Erin picked up the plate of toast and balanced the butter knife. She remembered to snatch a jar of homemade crab apple jelly from the fridge on her way back to the table. Before she could put it down, she fumbled and the knife lurched over the edge of the plate. It skittered across the table where seconds before the coffee had been. Erin cocked her head and stared at it and then the mug. Uncanny. She reached over and straightened the knife beside Allie's plate.

"Pretty coffee, Honey." Allie smiled and picked up her mug to take a swallow. "Good too." It always made Erin smile when Allie called her that. *Honey.*

"It's Saturday. I don't work tonight so I can sleep later..." Erin began, shifting her weight from one foot to the other. A crazy idea began to form. "Why don't we take Fuzzy Fiona for a walk? She could sure use one. I've been busy. You've been busy with your new job. Fiona deserves it." Erin knew she was manipulating Allie by using the dog, but a spark was igniting in her mind and it stifled her guilt.

Allie's brow furrowed. "You know I have to go soon. I'm meeting the girls from work at Zumba."

"Zumba? Is that even a real thing?"

"Yes, it's a fitness class, and it's fun. Not everyone likes free weights and treadmills."

"Can't you miss it once? Spend some time with me?" she cajoled. Allie hesitated until Erin pointed to the grinning dog. "Look at that face."

That did it. Allie bent, rubbed Fiona's ears and retrieved her jacket from the hall closet. Erin patted the dog, her unwitting co-conspirator. It was simply an idea she had. There was no harm in walking a dog and having an idea. She glanced at the dirty trail across the kitchen. They could go right after she mopped the dog's footprints off the floor.

CHAPTER TWO

"How far into mosquito country do we actually need to go to walk the dog? She likes it fine just going around the block." Allie rolled up her window when the roadside brush threatened to scrape the side of the Toyota Tacoma 4X4.

Erin kept her window wide open, her elbow propped up on the frame, cool wind ruffling through previously tidy hair. She knew Allie liked how it looked when it was wind-blown into disarray but it annoyed her when it whipped her eyes. She ran a hand through to straighten it.

Allie was a city girl, born and raised in Toronto. Concrete and cultivated urban landscapes her home turf. She easily navigated Yonge Street in her black Mini Cooper during Friday afternoon rush hour traffic without losing her cool or spilling a drop of her latté on the leather seats. She knew the best outdoor sight-seeing patios at Church and Wellesley and was most comfortable on a proper sidewalk in a pair of good walking shoes. Allie stifled a grunt when the tires hammered over furrows in the road, jostling her harshly against taut seatbelt. She hunched further down and clung to the door handle.

Warm and clear, the temperature would be eighty degrees by mid afternoon. At least the heat might drive off the majority of hungry mosquitos. They'd driven five miles from Morley Falls, and Erin navigated through a labyrinth of unmarked dirt roads. She pointed out a few squirrels and a raven along the way. Within minutes, Allie was disoriented.

"What kind of animal is that?" She pointed directly ahead.

Erin squinted her eyes. There were deer around here, rabbits and maybe the odd moose. She stole a peek at Allie, whose brows knitted together in concentration.

"Oh, duh." Allie announced. "It's not an animal." A few seconds later a dark willowy shape materialized ahead when a figure emerged from one of the bush paths.

"Who is that?" Allie studied the road, eyes wide. She sucked in a breath. When they drove closer, she let it out. It was a young girl, no more than eleven or twelve. Thin as a reed, she wore a long sleeved gray hoodie pulled up over her head and walked with an odd stiff-armed gait. As they passed, she turned her pale expressionless face toward them and vaporized back into the brush.

"That was Lily," Erin told her. "She's old man Gunther's granddaughter and they live at a little place just in behind here. He's been taking care of her since her mom took off a couple years ago and nobody else wanted her. Quite a few guys liked going ice fishing with Gunther every winter but, in the last few years, he's turned into a hermit. Now he pretty much keeps to himself. Except for his grandkid, of course."

"There's something about that kid."

Erin nodded. Everyone in town felt a bit sorry for Lily, the poor motherless kid practically raising herself. The girl had unusually pale eyes and a thin frame. Her skin was so light, she appeared almost translucent. They rode on in silence, Allie massaging one temple.

"I think I'm getting a headache."

"I'm sorry I don't have any Advil." Erin glanced sideways at Allie and wondered how her girlfriend was adjusting to small town Minnesota life. Sure, there were negatives to being outside a big city, but there were good people here too. Allie had been here a mere few months. Would she miss being away from the Center of the Universe, as outsiders often laughingly dubbed Toronto? This was beautiful country and Erin hoped Allie might see that. She could teach her to navigate the interconnecting lakes by canoe. To find the moose feeding in the bog, to pick wild blueberries, maybe even catch a fish. They could sit shoulder to shoulder on their back porch, breathe pure air and watch sunsets with no suffocating city smog.

Allie glanced back, eyes silently imploring her to slow down over the bigger bumps.

Erin gripped the steering wheel and dodged potholes with easy familiarity, smirking an apology. Despite the deplorable road conditions, she was enjoying the drive. "Around this corner is a nice path we can walk on," she reassured her.

Between them, the dog quivered with excitement, her nose scenting the air through the window. Fiona shared Erin's love of the rough country surrounding Morley Falls and was an eager walking companion. She bounded into Allie's lap with two paws on the passenger door when Erin ground to a halt on the road.

"What's wrong?" Allie blurted.

"We're here."

* * *

Allie cautiously opened her door and helped Fiona to the ground. The dog wiggled her body in circles, unable to contain her excitement. Allie looked up and down the dirt road, hemmed in on both sides by thick underbrush. She could not figure out where 'here' was.

Erin hopped out the driver's side and slung her leather bag across her shoulder, messenger style, before setting off. A few feet in front of the truck, she pointed at a small gap in the brush and waved Allie over. "The trail is here." She disappeared and Allie rushed to follow.

This was wild country and Allie's pulse quickened. The low brush was so thick that she had to hurry to keep up with Erin, already hidden from view only a short distance ahead. Fiona, nose to Allie's pant leg, followed her happily down the narrow trail. Ferns and low growing branches behind the dog swayed when Fiona's magnificent tail swatted them from side to side. With one arm awkwardly extended in front, she brushed a route through overhanging branches that grasped and tore at her hair like claws. Her free hand swiped at biting insects.

Trees blotted out the sky and Allie heard only the buzzing of hungry mosquitoes and the panting of the dog. A branch cracked somewhere off to the left. Allie's scalp tingled. Fiona let out a low growl and planted her tail between her legs.

It was suddenly too quiet, and too dark. The birds had stopped singing. There were only her footsteps and the branches ripping at her clothing. Darkness swirled around her. Humid earthiness of the undergrowth strangled her throat. She glanced over her shoulder. A shadowy presence was following. Watching. Waiting.

She hunched her shoulders and scrambled faster to catch up to Erin, who kept up a jaunty pace ahead, ducking the occasional overhanging branch. Streaks of sunlight pierced the darkness and the phantom vanished. Allie stopped and forced herself to take a deep breath. The dog nosed her hand and prodded her forward. There was no unseen menace, no danger. Was she being paranoid? She patted Fiona's head and hurried on.

A moment later, the trail widened and they approached a clearing where she joined Erin who surveyed a field of moss. The incessant buzzing of mosquitos dissipated when they distanced themselves from the dank undergrowth to stand in the sunshine. Erin touched Allie's cheek, her hand cool against burning skin. Eyebrows squeezed together, she tucked errant strands of hair behind her ear.

"I'm fine." Allie answered the unspoken question.

Erin nodded. She turned and gestured toward the rough green carpet of plant life before them. "It's a floating bog," she announced, hands on hips like a proud land baron. "There's a fairly deep lake underneath all this moss." She pointed to what looked like a jumbled mound of weather-beaten sticks. "Over by the little creek is an abandoned beaver lodge but I haven't seen any beavers around for a few years now. As a kid, I used to be able to paddle down the river from my parents' dock, up the creek and through the culvert under the road to the far side of this bog. There was always a family of beavers slapping their tails at us, and it had a nice clear pool of open water."

Allie smiled at the thought of Erin as a little blonde sunburned waif.

"My brother and I liked to catch minnows all around that far side and sell them as bait to the tourists. It was better money than a paper route. Now the creek is almost dried up and you can't get a canoe in anywhere until you reach the river." Erin looked down at Allie's tidy leather shoes. "Back then, you'd be up to your hips in muck right here where we are standing. Instead of getting your city shoes sucked off your feet, today you're just getting your toes wet. It's amazing, eh?"

"I'm the Canadian here," Allie quipped. She didn't want to ruin her shoes, and retreated from the edge of the mossy shore to more

18

solid footing near the trail. "I'm supposed to be the one saying eh."

Erin laughed. "All the old Swedish geezers in my family have been saying eh since forever. I'm sure we invented it, but you Canadians portaged it back across Lake Superior to claim as your own." She bent down and picked a sprig of tiny green leaves from the edge of the bog.

"Wintergreen." She tore off a leaf and popped it into her mouth. "It will get a little red berry later in the season. Also edible." She handed the sprig to Allie who cautiously tasted it.

"Minty!" Allie exclaimed, putting a couple more leaves into her mouth. "Trés cool." They were surprisingly refreshing. She picked another sprig and put it in the front pocket of her jeans. This was the first time she had ever eaten anything off the ground in the wild and it was energizing.

She heard a veritable cacophony of birdsong, but could not name a single species. Brown, blue, red and black streaked wings flitted from branch to stalk all around her. Then there was a familiar staccato in the distance. Now that she identified as a woodpecker. Even in the middle of Toronto, woodpeckers hammered telephone poles.

Tiny yellow blossoms peeped shyly from the moss near her feet and she bent to smell the moist richness of new plant growth. In the grasses further ahead, dragonflies in dazzling colors zoomed precision loops in the air in pursuit of insects. A gold and white butterfly careened drunkenly between pink, purple and blue petals. Allie exhaled in awe. She never would have noticed any of this had she not stepped off the trail. She followed Erin's careful footsteps around the sodden edge of the swamp.

"Don't try to walk out past this point or zoop! You're underwater," Erin warned. "I did that once on a grade six field trip and my teacher, Mr. Wozniak, pulled me out by my little red backpack. 'First time in the swamp?' he asked me. The other kids teased me for the rest of the year." She laughed and then sobered. "I remember it being kinda scary." Fiona sniffed at the edge of the mossy area and backed away when her paws sank into the water.

Allie relaxed and began to enjoy the walk. It helped having a personal guide. Since she'd been in Morley Falls, her new job consumed her time and there was no chance to sightsee.

"What's going on?" She pointed to a stand of blackened spires across the bog. Occasional wisps of gray smoke still wafted into the surrounding air.

"Uh, I don't know." Erin deliberately evaded Allie's question. "The other side of the bog is close to the highway turnoff. We should go look."

"We could have driven!" Allie frowned suspiciously at her. She had not lived here long, but she knew that if they were near the highway, this would have been a short easy stroll from the paved road. She scratched itchy mosquito bites on her neck and scowled at the smelly swamp water ruining her leather shoes. Erin was being unusually deceptive and she had never seen this side of her. Why all the effort to come in the back way?

Without another word, Erin turned and led the way down the trail skirting the bog. Allie followed reluctantly. They slowed when they could see that the blackened spires were scorched tops of poplar trees and the smoking remains of a house below. Burned nearly to the ground, the brick chimney and the frame of the kitchen stove stood solitary in the wretched carcass of the home.

Allie stopped, feet rooted, and stared at the charred wood that used to be a home. Her face blanched and her gut twisted like she'd been punched. She bent over and gripped her knees to keep from falling.

"I don't want to go there." She backed away, repelled like opposing magnets.

Through the poplars, flashing lights of a police cruiser and an unmarked vehicle blocked the road into the home. A uniformed officer stood with his back to them, writing on a notepad. Accompanying him was a beefy blond man in jeans and polo shirt who casually leaned one haunch on the hood of the cruiser. The blond man crudely gestured the outline of a woman with both hands, obviously telling a dirty joke.

Both laughed and the blond man shielded his sunburned face to light a cigarette. He inhaled, tilted his chin and blew smoke straight into the air. Allie focused on the scene, not noticing Erin discreetly side-step behind an outcropping of brush. Her brain buzzed.

"Watch her burn. Watch her burn!" She exhaled the words as if in a foreign tongue.

* * *

20

Erin snapped her attention to Allie whose eyes opened wide. Face twisted in fear, she pivoted and strode back down the trail. Her stride became a hurried jog and then she sprinted. Swampy muck clung to her shoes and spiky branches scratched her skin bloody. Fiona yelped and thrashed blindly in her terrified wake.

Erin lost sight of them and her throat ran dry. In the woods, brush crashed like a fleeing bull moose. Allie had missed the trail. Following the noise, she tried to parallel their progress from the footpath. With fewer obstacles, she reached the truck first.

Allie stumbled from the trees fifteen minutes later, T-shirt torn and arms bloody. The recently applied Band-Aid had vanished from her eyebrow and a new trickle of blood wound its way along her cheekbone. She pushed past Erin and groped for the truck's door handle. Fiona whimpered and circled her legs.

Erin grappled with the remote key. Too late. She bolted like a cornered rabbit around the truck. Finally she stopped, bent and vomited onto the road.

"I'm so sorry!"

"Stay away!" Allie panted. She clung tight to the truck's bumper, thighs trembling beneath her.

Erin looked into her girlfriend's stricken face. There was only one option now. She had to tell her.

* * *

"Church Lady. Burning in hell. Are you on crack?" Allie sprang from the kitchen chair. She had washed up and changed her clothes but angry red scratches marked both arms. A fresh Band-Aid covered her eyebrow and she had applied more makeup to cover scraped skin. "This whole story is preposterous!" Arms crossed over her chest, she glared at Erin.

"I'm not saying you're some kind of witch or anything." Erin hesitated. "But you react to things before they even happen, you dream about things you can't possibly know, and you freaked out—"

"You watch too much reality TV. This is not rational."

Erin took a deep breath and began again. "I just mean that it's interesting when you move things right before I drop something on the exact spot. You brake before the car in front of you swerves into your lane. You open the door for the dog two seconds before she

21

gets there. You know what's happening before it does. You do it all the time."

"I'm a good guesser," Allie scoffed. "Everyone does that."

"Well, actually everyone doesn't. That's why people break stuff and there are car accidents. Other people don't know what's coming."

"So let me get this straight. You dragged me down a back road donkey trail through a stinking swamp swarming with mosquitoes." Allie angrily gathered her wallet, phone and keys. Snatching up her laptop case, she faced Erin. "And you pretended to be my tour guide, all to make sure your cop buddies didn't see you sneak me to a house where a poor old lady died in a fire!"

Erin swore there were sparks in the air. She nodded contritely.

"Because you think I can magically solve your murder case with my nonexistent superpowers. You are the only one who thinks it's murder, because you say all the other cops think it's an accident!" Allie's angry voice raised in pitch. Fiona circled her and she reached out to reassure the dog.

"It wasn't an accident." Erin clenched her jaw tight. "I looked at the scene this morning before I came home and I've known Dolores since I was a kid. She was extremely meticulous." Allie raised an amused eyebrow.

"More than me," Erin conceded. "My point is that she would never have left all four gas burners on. She wasn't some forgetful old lady. She had specific routines and just because she was in her seventies does not mean she wasn't still sharp as a tack. You can ask her Bridge partners, or any of the ladies she served with in the Lutheran Women's League. She was clear headed and precise. This just does not fly. I know this was arson. Someone murdered Dolores Johnson."

"People make mistakes."

"That's only one piece of the puzzle. Someone had been breaking into her home when she went out. She filed three police complaints in the last month."

"That changes things." Allie adjusted the strap on her shoulder. "What was stolen?"

"Umm, nothing was actually stolen but Dolores was certain someone had been in her house." Erin bit her lip and waited for the inevitable.

Allie sighed. "Reinforcement for the scatterbrained-old-lady theory at the office?"

"If you were as detail oriented as Dolores, trust me, you'd know when someone messed with your stuff."

"Well, that's solid evidence." The sarcastic tone unnerved Erin. A few months into this relationship and everything they had built together crumbled before her eyes.

"But there's your nightmare—"

"Everyone has nightmares," Allie retorted. "I need to go. I can't lose my new job." She wrenched the door closed behind her and left Erin standing alone.

"Not like you," Erin whispered to the empty hallway. She crumpled to the floor and wrapped her arms around the dog's neck. Fiona leaned up against her, nuzzled her cheek and gave her ear a lick. Burying her face in the soft fur, they sat together by the door.

CHAPTER THREE

Minnesota's vibrant wildflowers splashed color on the shoulders of the road in hurried summer bloom. Today Allie drove her car, Erin occasionally interrupting the silence with brief directions.

"Turn right after the third red mailbox."

The black Mini Cooper bumped over potholes that Allie made no attempt to avoid. Erin grunted when the tires shuddered through a particularly large one but Fiona stood her ground on the back seat. The dog dangled her tongue out the open window, grinning enthusiastically. Allie ignored Erin, and the car's chattering suspension.

Was this payback? She would not be so impressed when she dealt with car repairs later. Ah well, she never kept a car longer than three years and could always trade it in.

Allie had met Erin's parents but Erin knew she was anxious about meeting the rest of the Ericsson clan. Although nervous, it was time. At the very least, it had to be better than sitting home for another night of avoiding each other. The future had seemed so beautiful when they first moved in together. Maybe they could fix things.

"Did you remember to bring dessert?" Erin asked. "I'm sorry I got tied up at work, and I didn't give you much notice—"

"Don't worry."

"My family is pretty big on dessert."

"I took care of it." Allie's tone was final.

Erin snuck a peek at her girlfriend and felt a familiar leap in her chest. This was the woman she had fallen for six months ago in

Toronto. They'd met at a party and she had made an ass of herself flirting with the beautiful brunette, thanks to the ubiquitous Jell-O shots she'd too eagerly consumed. Allie didn't have to say a word. She had simply arched one exquisite eyebrow, and the look shook Erin to her very foundation. Really? it said.

She still remembered those exotic brown eyes, flecked with gold and green, locked steady on her own. They looked right into her and she felt naked. Her bravado evaporated in embarrassment when it dawned on her that she'd had too much to drink. Of course, Allie was too grounded to be fooled by inane lines. Too discerning to fall for the clumsy flirtations of an arrogant stranger. In that moment, Erin knew Allie disdained the superficial, the immature, and she was ashamed.

She withdrew and spent the remainder of the night drinking coffee, trying not to look like a stalker. She just could not take her eyes off that woman. It was more than a physical attraction. Sure, she was awed by Allie's athletic beauty, but there was something more. As the evening progressed, she found it harder to resist the overpowering desire to release the hair tie from that tidy ponytail. She longed to set those brunette tresses free, to kiss the curve at the corner of her mouth where it curled into a mischievous grin. She wanted to get close enough to breathe her in. She couldn't really describe what compelled her, an internal vibrancy. Fierce strength and solid confidence swirled around her and Erin was captivated. Hopelessly enraptured.

Over the next months, they'd formed a long distance friendship and Erin was ecstatic when it blossomed into love. She made up for her crass first impression, ten times over, Allie later laughed. Allie was the one who'd made the life changing decision to move all the way from Toronto to rural Minnesota to be with her. Only weeks ago, they moved into their forty-seven-year-old fixer-upper with big plans to renovate it together. That's when the nightmares had started.

When they reached the red mailboxes, Allie jerked the wheel to enter a hidden driveway, at first glance no more than a break in the bush. Wider than it looked, the opening led to a manicured lawn ringed by meticulously tended flowerbeds. A tidy white bungalow and large garage nestled under mature trees. Fifty years of footprints had worn a well beaten path to the river where a red motorboat lay moored to the dock.

A huge trampoline graced the lawn, beside an equally large satellite dish. Two young girls shrieked excitedly, their shoes discarded and dresses twisted by their leaps into the air. Allie parked at the end of the drive and tilted her seat forward to let the dog out. Tail wagging in circles, she bee-lined for the sound of children.

"So glad you made it." The screen door banged shut behind a middle aged woman to whom Erin bore a striking resemblance. Her blonde hair had paled but she had the same compact build, piercing blue eyes and fair complexion. A small boy followed her. He stood on tip toes to peep through the window of Allie's car.

"Did you bring your kitty?" He pulled himself up with the door handle and pressed his forehead to the glass. "I never saw a kitty with only three legs."

"No, Jimmy, but we brought Fuzzy Fiona." Erin messed up her four year old nephew's hair. She had almost forgotten that the cat was missing a leg. It didn't slow her down, but possibly contributed to her evil personality streak. She could jump, crawl and sneak into the most unusual places and scare Erin half to death in the process. It had taken some getting used to when Allie moved in with not one but two house pets.

"Fiona is over there." Allie pointed to the lawn where the dog lay flat on her back, accepting belly rubs from the girls who had abandoned their trampoline. "Go ahead. She loves everyone."

Jimmy peeked once more into the back and whispered. "That's a pie in a box!" He climbed off the side of the car and scurried off toward the other kids.

"It is nice to see you again, Mrs. Ericsson." Allie's face flushed slightly when she retrieved her dessert offering from the floor behind the seat. The brightly colored cardboard box promised Delicious Blueberry Pie. Homemade taste. She handed it to Erin's mom who held the box by the edges.

"Auntie Erin's new friend brought a store-boughten pie!" Jimmy called out, running across the lawn. The girls turned to gape at Allie.

"Well, thank you Allie." Erin's mom politely ignored the kids' chatter. "I'm Ellen. Please don't be so formal. This is not Buckingham Palace. Come in. Come in."

Allie followed Erin and her mother up the steps to the freshly painted porch. A spray of small blue flowers in a pink vase sat on a table just outside the door and a half dozen pairs of assorted footwear jumbled together beside it. She added her stained leather shoes to the pile.

* * *

Inside, it was surprisingly bright and Allie raised her eyebrows at a row of floor to ceiling windows looking out to the river. Fiona ran by outside, tail windmilling behind her, pursued by the two exuberant girls. Jimmy followed on their heels, a stick in his outstretched hand. All three kids were blond haired, fair skinned and pink cheeked.

Erin's mom urged Allie to take over her seat at the table and introduced her to Erin's brother Thomas, and sister Liz. Ellen then made a point of busying herself in the kitchen. Thomas was fair haired like the children but Liz was the only one in the clan with light brown hair. Both regarded Allie with familiar clear blue eyes, the Ericsson family trademark.

Allie noted the playing cards splayed on the table, a game of Cribbage already in progress. Erin shrugged apologetically and headed back to the door where her father, Tom Sr., stood in his navy blue coveralls. He held grease stained hands up like a surgeon and avoided touching anything. She joined him on the porch and the two of them assumed the same casual posture while they examined a mechanical part.

"I think it's a problem with this little jigger here," he told her.

"The impeller looks worn. Did you check the oil seal?" Erin pointed at something and he squinted at it, furrowing his eyebrows. They spoke for a moment, alternately inspecting the part and then walked off toward the garage.

"The boat motor is kaput," Thomas explained to Allie when they'd gone. "Dad and I tried to fix it earlier but Erin's always been better at engines. I'm a computer guy. We don't like to get our hands dirty."

"You'll have to take over for me." Erin's mom pointed to the cards on the table. She turned to the open oven and poked at a large turkey partially covered with shiny foil.

"I'm afraid I've intruded," Allie said. "I don't know how to play Cribbage." Thomas and Liz exchanged a veiled look.

"Don't worry, we'll teach you," Liz said. She shot another of those indecipherable looks at her brother. "Mom!" she called over the whirring of the stove hood fan. "Where's the blueberry wine you made last fall?"

"Erin says you're an IT Tech?" Thomas chose three glasses and poured the wine his mom had produced. "Is that how you are allowed to work in the States so soon after moving here?"

"Something like that," Allie said. "My work permit was expedited when my company offered me the position. They had no local applicants with the requisite skills and I had to give them a copy of my diploma, of course."

"I do graphic design so all that techie stuff is alien-speak to me. I just make the front end pretty."

Allie noticed that he had poured her an extra generous amount. She took a cautious sip. It tasted delicious. She took another. "We are installing a new EVPL for the Health Region to integrate into the existing network and take advantage of an upcoming fiberoptic opportunity." Allie stopped when she was met with blank looks from both Thomas and Liz.

"EVPL: Ethernet Virtual Private Line Service," she explained.

"Graphics and pretty picture guy here." Thomas laid a manicured hand on his Hugo Boss clad chest. "Liz's boy Jimmy is only four years old and I swear he knows more about computer programming than I do."

"And I'm a mom who works part-time at the window factory, has three little brats and a husband on perpetual night shift." Liz raised her hand like a kid in school. "No computer techie speakie understood here." She laughed, a spontaneously melodic sound.

Allie grinned back. Like their parents, both siblings exuded warmth and were immediately likable. She sat forward and took another sip of blueberry wine. She had never been much of a drinker but this was quite good. With brief instruction, Cribbage proved to be fairly straightforward. It was all about fifteens and thirty-ones, and not getting stuck behind the dreaded Skunk Line.

"Fifteen-two, fifteen-four." Liz counted while she laid down her cards.

They neared the end of their game and dinner was nearly ready but there was still no sign of Erin or her dad. The kids marched through their second excursion of the kitchen, dog in tow, looking for pre-dinner snacks. Fiona's nose twitched as she air scented. A tiny hand snatched a piece of cheese from a tray and it soon disappeared into the dog's waiting mouth. Fiona had her ways. With her soft brown eyes, she often took advantage of children and little old ladies. As a result, the wily canine had devoured the lion's share of pilfered treats. Allie grinned. She had lost count of how many times Thomas had refilled her glass and the room seemed much warmer than when she had first sat down.

The girls stopped their sneaky kitchen foraging long enough to circle the table and examine their mother's cards. Allie could see them counting on their fingers. Liz introduced them as Sophie and Victoria.

"Mama named me after Auntie Vicky because she saved her from a grizzly bear when she was a baby." Victoria stretched her hands over her head like bear claws and assumed a dramatic tone. "All Auntie Vicky had was a butter knife and her big brave voice and she fought the bear all by herself!"

"And I'm named after a Swedish princess!" Sophie said. "She was the most beautiful in all the land and I look exactly like her!"

Liz laughed and shooed the kids away from the table with a wave of her arm. Thomas smirked and palmed the girls candies from his pocket when they ran past.

Jimmy stood on his toes and peeked at the box on the kitchen counter with Allie's pie. He clucked his tongue like a serious old wife. "Is that store-boughten pie made out of cardboard like mama says?"

Liz shushed him too late and she avoided Allie's eyes, concentrating on her cards.

"I know where you can pick blueberries to make a real pie for next time," he whispered earnestly, patting Allie's shoulder. "Don't worry, I'll show you."

"I'm not much of a baker," she whispered back with a forgiving wink to Liz, "but maybe we can pick blueberries some time."

Jimmy leaned on Allie's arm and examined the cards in her hand. "Are you gonna get skunked?"

"I don't really care," she confessed. "It's a good game anyway." Thomas surreptitiously poured more blueberry wine into her glass and she playfully frowned at him.

Jimmy pointed to the Seven of Hearts, the Five of Clubs and the Three of Spades in Allie's hand. "That should help." He nodded approvingly when she used the cards to make a couple of points and then draped himself across her lap.

"You sure must fish a lot." Jimmy inquisitively touched the skin on her arm.

"I've actually never been fishing. Why would you think that?"

"Well, you have such a dark tan!"

"Jimmy!" Liz leapt from her chair and reached for her son.

"My tan!" Allie laughed. "I work indoors, in front of a computer all day long and I certainly don't have a tan. I was born this color."

"You don't have to—" Liz's face turned purple.

"It's okay," Allie said patiently and Jimmy twisted in her lap to peer at her face. "My mom was Irish and my dad was Ojibway. I have brown skin like him."

"Okay." The four year old twisted back over and let his arms dangle to the floor. Sometimes it was as simple as that. Fiona curled up beside her chair and he brushed his fingers back and forth across her fur. The dog snuffled appreciatively. There was an undeniable sense of warmth and comfort surrounding her, and she liked it.

"Why don't you girls go outside and play until dinner is ready?" Ellen chided them. She stopped one more little hand from snitching a crouton. It was beginning to dawn on Allie that they weren't only sisters, but twins. They weren't dressed identically, as mothers of twins often do, and they had very different haircuts.

"There's too many blackflies out tonight!" Victoria hovered close to her mom and blinked wide blue eyes. "If blackflies can eat a whole moose, don't you think they would eat me too?"

Thomas laughed out loud.

"It's gonna get dark soon!" Sophie exclaimed.

Outside, the sunset painted the sky with pastel hues of pink and orange. Most of the daytime songbirds no longer flitted through the bushes outside the window and the breeze calmed. There was a stillness that had not been there when she'd come. As if the woods knew the day was winding down, it tucked in its little ones for the night.

"I don't want the Bog Monster to get me!" said Victoria. Wide-eyed, all their earlier precociousness evaporated and they crowded toward their mom.

On her lap, Jimmy's body stiffened too. Allie patted his shoulder in what she hoped was a reassuring manner.

"Who scared you with that old swamp tale?" Liz put down her cards and scooped the girls together as one.

"Uncle Thomas did!" Two little fingers pointed directly at Thomas.

"Lots of folks around here say it's true." He shrugged innocently.

"There's nothing in that bog except Johnny Fiddler's four wheeler that he sunk when he was a teenager. It's probably sitting underneath the old beaver lodge and their little kits ride it for fun." Grandma Ellen winked at Jimmy and his sisters, who all mirrored the same incredulous expression. "Why don't you kids go watch the Disney Channel until dinner?" She turned and pointed a stern, silent finger at Thomas whose impish grin evaporated. The children did as they were asked and the blaring TV provided a layer of background noise.

"Once again, Uncle Thomas traumatizes my kids." Liz waggled a finger at her brother in a startlingly accurate imitation of their mom.

"You have to admit," Thomas said, "weird things happen near the bog."

"Is that the place they call the floating bog?" Allie's head spun and her chest tightened at the memory. She clenched one hand around her glass to mask the trembling.

Breathe.

A burning lump ignited in her throat and she gulped a mouthful of wine but inhaled instead. She gasped and choked for a long moment before she could calm herself and breathe normally again. Thomas and Liz were polite enough not to comment.

"People say it's haunted," said Liz, after Allie had composed herself. She leaned conspiratorially forward in her chair and shot a sideways glance at her kids who were enthralled with whatever was on TV.

"Erin took me there last week," Allie said flatly. Liz stared at her and Thomas spent an inordinate amount of time shuffling the cards before he looked up.

"Sure it's pretty, but that would not be my best spot for a romantic date." He slowly and deliberately dealt out the cards. "Erin hasn't any sense. No one goes out to the bog unless they must. Everyone in town believes it is haunted. Now look what's happened to Mrs. Johnson! The only other person foolish enough to live near there is old man Gunther, but see what it's done to his life? He might as well be dead too. Something evil is out there. It howls on summer nights—"

"That's enough of that old story." Mr. Ericsson stood on the porch outside the screen door, wiping his hands on a rag. "There is no bog monster and that's no kind of conversation for Erin's new friend." He came into the kitchen, and Erin loped in after him.

"We fixed the boat motor," Erin said, her confident posture signifying satisfaction. She took the rag from her dad. Giving her hands a wipe, she frowned at dirty fingernails. "Dad says he's found a good fishing spot up on the big lake. Maybe we can go next weekend." She headed for the bathroom to clean up. Her dad swiped a piece of cheese from a tray on the counter and popped it in his mouth. Then he gave his hands a quick wash in the kitchen sink.

Mrs. Ericsson turned out to be a fantastic cook. Allie enjoyed every mouthful of roasted turkey and twice-baked potatoes. It reminded her of home cooked dinners growing up with her foster parents and Allie was beginning to want to belong to this clan too. Although a little shy on the outside, the inner warmth of these people was enchanting.

When dessert time came, Erin's mom slid a fresh baked fruit cobbler to the rear of the fridge and brought out Allie's 'store-boughten' blueberry pie. Everyone took a piece and no one made a single face while it was consumed. The kids smothered theirs with mountains of fresh whipped cream.

They said their good-nights and Erin shepherded Allie down the walkway to the car. Allie's blueberry wine buzz had diminished after Erin returned and figured out what her siblings were up to, but she was still fuzzy. Erin squeezed the exhausted dog into the backseat and took command of the driver's door.

"I'll drive," she stated, fetching the extra key from her leather bag. Allie held two palms up in supplication.

CHAPTER FOUR

Erin navigated the end of the driveway and was past the mailboxes before she managed to find the Mini Cooper's headlight switch. Twin yellow beams efficiently illuminated the dirt road ahead. She gunned the engine and aimed the car straight down the middle, picking up speed and dodging memorized potholes. A sliver of moonlight trimmed the tops of trees and thick brush became a blur on either side.

Allie was not used to such darkness. In the city, there was always ambient light from somewhere and nights were never this dark. She did like being able to see so many stars. She had no idea there were this many. The Milky Way splashed across the sky and she now appreciated how it had earned its name. Somehow, she was calm and secure for the first time in years. She had not drunk alcohol for a long time and was unaccustomed to the fuzziness it produced. The sky was so beautiful, so vast.

"Those are the cutest kids I ever met," she mused. "Your aunt Vicky must have been pretty tough to fight off a grizzly bear!"

Erin puckered her eyebrows. "What?"

"And I suppose the part about you being descended from Swedish royalty was made up too?" Allie gave her a wink. "It would have been quite a feather in my cap to be dating a Princess!"

She burst out laughing. "I can't believe they were telling you the old family tales. My family loves to make up fairy tales to entertain the kids. There are no grizzly bears around here and our ancestors were farmers and maids, not royalty!"

Allie smiled. The royalty claim was pure fun, but the story about the grizzly bear really had her going. She knew alcohol made her much too gullible. "I don't care. I love those kids. Especially little Jimmy. He says he will take me blueberry picking."

Erin eyed her suspiciously. "I don't think I've ever seen you drunk before. What are you talking about? You hate kids."

"I don't really hate kids. I just never met any I liked before. I always had snot-nosed foster brothers getting into my stuff and little foster sisters stealing my socks."

"That hardly sounds like a federal crime worth hating all children for." Erin dodged another pothole. Allie didn't bother bracing herself for the abrupt maneuver and bobbled along with it.

"You're right. I think I was a bit spoiled by my foster parents. They treated me like their own from the beginning and I must have been jealous of their attention. Even though they were never able to adopt me, I knew I belonged and was loved. I guess I was a little brat. I doubt I made it easy for any of the other kids who came and went."

"I'm sure you weren't all that rotten," Erin said, "otherwise how would you have grown up to be so wonderful?"

Allie sloppily punched her arm. "Yeah, I love you too." Sobering, she squinted at Erin. "But you better be honest with me from now on. None of that cloak and dagger crap. I don't like being manipulated."

"If you'll give me the chance to prove it, I promise you'll never have a reason to mistrust me again."

Allie suddenly groaned. It was as if the pressure in her skull literally strained at the cranial sutures. Hunched over, she dropped her head into her hands, hair twisting through fingers. Unbidden, disturbing images writhed their way into her brain. She struggled against them, but finally weakened and could no longer resist.

A crescent moon winks down through the tangle of angry steel and dead branches. The shadow figure growls like a feral animal, rolling a boulder against the jagged metal shapes. Crouching behind for one last swallow from a shiny can. Rocking back and forth in malevolent glee and tossing the can into the pile. Red and white. Red and white. Find it. The shadow dissipates into the trees like smoke, dripping evil residue in its wake.

* * *

34

"Are you going to be sick?"

Allie squeezed her eyes tight and locked her lips in a grimace of pain. In the subtle glow of the dashboard panel, her face drained of color. Erin knew something was wrong when she struggled to release her seatbelt.

"Do I need to pull over?"

Allie pushed her door open and extended one leg.

"Stop!" Erin reached out. Her hands faltered on the steering wheel and the car swerved violently, skidding sideways when she stomped the brake pedal to the floor.

Already in motion, Allie landed before they had fully stopped. She stumbled to one knee, then righted herself.

"Wait!" Erin yelled. She jammed the shifter into park but Allie was already walking purposefully up the road. Fiona squeezed out the open door and raced to block her path. She changed direction to outmaneuver the dog and continued on. Fiona followed, bumping her thigh with her body. She reoriented herself and kept walking, the dog circling and bumping every time she took a step.

Erin disentangled herself from her seatbelt and punched the button for the car's four-way hazard flashers. Lesson One at the Police Academy was to protect the scene and yourself. It would make the situation worse if another car smashed into theirs on the dark road.

"Where are you going?"

Allie did not answer, continuing toward a tight bend. Erin sprinted to catch up and took her by the arm. Dark brown eyes reflected the night sky. Her expression was placid, like a sleepwalker, and there was not a flicker of recognition. Allie turned her face and Erin's eyes followed her gaze. Just on the other side of this blind corner was a grotesque pile of rubble that had not been there when they'd come. She looked back at Allie's widened eyes and understood.

They approached the haphazard barricade cautiously. Old tires, twisted metal from long deceased farm machinery, mounds of brush and deadfall, and a medium sized boulder were jumbled together in the middle of the road. It would have taken a fair amount of time and effort to assemble this junk heap and Erin gave a low whistle. Damage to the Mini Cooper, and to them, would have been substantial if they had not stopped.

Allie stood in front of the pile but looked beyond. "Watching us.

Waiting." Fiona made a guttural canine sound halfway between a growl and a whine, tucked her tail and ducked behind Allie's legs.

"Who's watching? Who's waiting? What is going on?" Erin squinted into the dark. She backed toward the car, where her pistol lay in her bag. There was not a sound. Not a snapped twig, not a rustle of wind in the leaves. They had left the headlights far behind them at the corner and only inky blackness lay ahead. Adrenaline coursed through Erin's veins. She clenched her fists.

Sharp pain between her shoulder blades stunned her and a small rock skittered to the road at her feet. She whirled around, enraged. Not a single branch stirred and she could not make out a thing. The dog stared ahead, body rigid, hair on end.

"Who is out there? This is not funny! You could have caused an accident!" Silence mocked her. "This is a criminal offense!" She almost laughed at herself. Her voice in the darkness sounded so pathetic. She chose a substantial looking stick from the ditch and gripped it in her hand. It made her feel better.

Keeping the stick nearby, Erin heaved items from the barricade off the road. Anger boiled up and, swearing vehemently under her breath, she pitched them as far as she could with each throw. It was strangely gratifying to hear them crash into the undergrowth.

She kept one eye on Allie who, still a little dazed, rummaged through the pile of rubble like a raccoon. To get her attention, she nudged her shoulder, but Allie kept searching. She picked up an item, discarded it and picked up another. Finally satisfied, she wordlessly held out a beer can to Erin like a prize.

"I think you've had enough tonight, baby." Erin gently took the can from Allie and guided her by the shoulder. "I guess this is why you so rarely drink." Erin tossed the can with her other hand, and the red and white label glinted when it spun in the moonlight. It clattered on gravel.

They walked back the way they'd come, Erin steering Allie like a disabled shopping cart with the dog trailing timidly behind. Fiona yelped involuntarily at a faint crackling in the brush and hair bristled down her spine. All of Erin's senses on high alert, she scanned the brush in the direction of the noise. The stillness was absolute. Erin gripped the stick more firmly and prodded Allie to quicken her pace.

They finally rounded the corner but no reassuring lights greeted them. The car was a silent black shape. Erin was sure the engine had been running and even more certain that she'd left the four-way flashers on.

She approached cautiously and opened the passenger door. The keys were gone from the ignition so Erin used the interior lights to look for other signs of tampering. The dog grumbled and circled the car nervously, before hopping up and wedging herself into the rear. There did not appear to be anything else awry. Erin heaved a sigh of relief to see her leather bag stowed behind the driver's seat. She snatched it up and knew from the heft that her pistol was still in its concealed holster. She jammed it into the front of her jeans and was immediately reassured.

Then she helped Allie into the car and buckled her seat belt. This was the safest spot for her while Erin conducted a quick search of the area and she had a modicum of undeserved confidence in the security capability of the dog. Fiona was not a reliable bodyguard, but Erin rationalized that her canine senses might be a useful alert if anyone approached.

She searched the area and noted scuffs in the gravel as well as a few freshly broken branches on one side. Someone had recently passed on foot. There was no one here now and it did not appear that they had left anything behind, except the barricade. She settled into the driver's seat, took a breath, and leaned over to double check that Allie's seat belt was clipped securely.

A sharp thwack on the back window crashed through the stillness like an explosion and Erin leapt from the car, pistol instantly in her hand. She scrutinized the brush, gun automatically following her sight line. At first there was no sound and then the soft whipping of branches. Someone scrambled quietly away. Erin pursued but found the brush nearly impassable without knowing where the trail was. Brambles scraped at her, snaring her legs. By now, the assailant was long gone. There was no hope of catching him this night.

She returned to the car and saw a solid bulls-eye crack in the back window. A palm-sized rock lay nearby and she angrily kicked it.

"Ouch!" She winced at the intense pain in her toe and got into the car. Soft-soled running shoes were not made for punting rocks. Her heart pounded in her ears and she punched the wheel a couple of times in sheer frustration. Allie stared back at her, eyes clear at last, but a look of confusion on her face.

"What's going on? Why did we stop?"

"Everything is okay." Erin squeezed each syllable through clenched jaw. "I need you to give me your keys. Right now. We'll talk when we get home." She hit the automatic door locks.

Abruptly sober, Allie handed her keys over. Erin started the car and, with one more glance in the rear view mirror, shifted into drive.

* * *

I have a smile on my face as I take off like a panther. That's right, I'm a badass panther and this is my territory. I am jogging on soft cat's feet and I can still hear that stupid cop thrashing around like a snared rabbit. She's makin' so much noise that I wanna laugh. The stick she was wavin' didn't scare me, but the gun from the car sure got my attention. Even a panther knows when to bail out. I hit the trail before she started popping off shots like Stallone in The Expendables. But not before I chucked a big rock at their frickin' car. Right smack in the middle of the goddamn back window. A perfect throw, if I do say so myself.

Bitches! Both of 'em. I've always hated that interfering cop and now she has a zombie girlfriend. Every time I've seen her, she's just plain weird. And her dog is some kind of useless. When they came snooping around my bog, their stupid mutt walked past me without barking or anything. I wanted to jump out and slap its tail out from between its legs. I imagine what would have happened if I'd done it that day, and it's funny enough to simmer me down some.

That was their first mistake. Trespassing on my bog. Poking around my business. Mind your own business. The bog is mine.

I wanted them to smash into my roadblock tonight and I can't figure out how they knew it was there. It would have been great to see the car burst into flames. I would have danced around the bonfire like a wild savage. That would have taught them a real lesson. The brand new crack in their back window should be a good reminder.

I stop and take the set of keys from my jeans pocket. Balling them up in my fist, I throw them in a nice high arc. With so many leaves on the ground, no one will find them for a hundred years.

In the dark, I nearly miss the fork in the trail and sink to my shins in the swamp. By the time I get to town I'm cranky, my shoes are muddy and I'm thirsty. I could use a beer but this whole damn place closes at 11p.m., which was hours ago. I'm also out of cigarettes so, when I see a pack of smokes sitting on the dash of a parked car, I try the handle. Of course, it's not locked and I help myself.

When I flip open the Camels, I'm surprised to find a fat little doobie snuggled right in there, alongside the remaining half pack of cigarettes. Never tried one of those before and it feels like tonight's the night. Millions of dope-smokers can't be wrong so I stop by a fence and light up. It tastes weirder than it smells but I inhale and hold the smoke until I'm ready to burst. For the life of me, I don't feel a damn thing. I grind it into the gravel with my shoe and light up a real cigarette to get the taste out of my mouth. I don't care what brand I smoke; it's all the same to me. I suck in a lungful. That's what I wanted in the first place.

The streetlights on this part of the avenue are out. Have been for a while. I guess that's why I like coming this way. I like walking past the little cemetery at the end. That cemetery is old as dirt and no one gets buried there any more. You can barely read the names on the gravestones and nobody ever visits. They say it's haunted, but don't they say that about every cemetery? Isn't that the point, really? I've never seen a single spook and I've spent a lot of time here. All I know is that it's a good spot to sit and think without anyone getting up in my face. A good spot to walk around.

I take a shortcut through and pause to bend down and read my favorites.

Mathilda "Hildie" Johannson 1898-1962 Loving Mother

Below the name is a picture of an angel that looks like she is blowing her nose. Runny Nose Hildie, her friends probably called her. Cracks me up every time. I read a couple more and come to a freakishly tall one that is familiar.

Harold Woods 1902-1955 Millwright

There's no picture on this one, but it's the tallest one in the row and always catches my attention. I put my shoulder against it and give a good shove. I'm pretty sure I've shoved it over at least twice before but it just won't stay down. One more push and it topples backwards. Scheisse! I jump out of the way before it lands on my foot and then I boot over a couple other easy ones.

Past the cemetery, right across the road, sits a large metal dumpster. I'm done my last cigarette so I hold the glowing end to the empty package until it ignites. When I toss it in, I aim for a pile of newspapers. Too lazy to recycle? Time to pay the price.

It's already smoldering and flames will be visible soon. Awesome.

I wait around a few minutes until I see a steady line of gray smoke. Spreading cheer everywhere I go, I'm like freakin' Santa Claus.

The car is three blocks up, where I left it and I retrieve the keys from under the floor mat like everyone else in this town. I drive down the back alleys, park the car and toss the keys back under the mat. I've been driving since I was eight but sometimes I want a set of wheels that no one knows. The old guy here never notices, as long as I leave it in the same spot. I'm good at that.

It's a short walk to my place but it's almost dawn when I get home. I still need a beer so I go into the shed and grab one from the little fridge. A nice cold Bud is a luxury I truly enjoy. I park my ass on a wooden stool by the work bench and the first few swallows go down real nice.

It's been a long time since I did any work in here so I pull a drawer open and look at the scalpels, fleshing blades and shears. They are still as shiny as the first time I held them in my hands. A metal cabinet holds fiberglass forms for a bobcat and a fox that arrived mail order a long time ago. A tight row of taxidermy chemicals lines the top shelf and I face all the labels to the front so I can read them. The newer ones in plastic bottles are clearly labeled and I run my finger along the acids, degreasers, and deodorizers. There are a few dark glass bottles with labels long worn off and I've forgotten what they were. Maybe I never knew in the first place. They intrigue me and I open one to take a sniff. It smells like always and burns my nose a little. I put it back.

The mounted head of a five-point white-tail deer stares through glass eyes down at me from its permanent spot on the wall. It's not a bad job but not my work. I avoid looking at the dust-covered muskrat in the corner. That one was mine. The face is distorted, the eyes are all wrong, and I hate that thing but I can't bring myself to throw it in the burning barrel.

I remember when I tried to skin a squirrel at the age of six. It seemed like a good idea at the time. I'd found it already dead by the road and thought I was doing a great job until I caught holy hell for it. In hindsight, it was a pretty pathetic attempt. I've done a few critters since then but I don't think it's really my thing. Maybe I don't have the patience, or maybe I'm too lazy, and things never worked out. I still like to come out and make sure everything is still here, just in case.

I finish my beer and trudge over to the house. If I get my ass to bed, I can probably still catch a few hours of sleep. As I drift off, my mind goes back to those bitches. They had better keep their noses out of my business.

CHAPTER FIVE

It took quite a bit of convincing on Allie's part for Erin to go to work today. She was fine. Really. Just had too much to drink. Didn't want to talk about it. She would curl up with the pets on the sofa and relax. Fiona had been overly attentive to her and that was probably the best thing. Before she went to work, she promised to go to yoga and recharge her batteries.

Last night, Erin had lain awake alone in their bed for a long time before she fell asleep. She'd slept but she sure didn't feel rested this morning, even after her coffee. She set and then double-checked the alarm before she left the house. She stretched her shoulders against the new bruise directly on the point of her scapula. It had been a bright red welt when she'd seen it in the mirror. Someone had a pretty good arm.

Erin tossed her lunch bag into the coffee room fridge beside a large blue Tupperware container marked CZ. Every shift a new container appeared, sometimes more than one. Who had such an appetite? She would have to ask Officer Chris Zimmerman about that.

She left her off-duty pistol in her locker and changed into her uniform. Tightening her belt with the .45 cal Smith & Wesson around her waist, she emerged from the locker room mentally changed as well. Today she would sneak back out to Dolores Johnson's house and examine the scene again. It didn't matter that everyone else considered it an accident, she knew otherwise, and Dolores deserved better.

She sauntered into the briefing room at ten to seven, chagrined to see Lieutenant Derek Peterson leaning against the sergeant's desk. Derek had been in plainclothes long enough to appear uncomfortable in the too-tight uniform he now wore. More at home in jeans and golf shirts these days, his belly sagged a few inches over the top of his belt buckle. He adjusted his duty belt self-consciously, sliding his sidearm and lock-blade knife further back.

As a high school football player, he'd thought highly of himself and so did most of the cheerleaders. Erin never figured out why, but he had butted heads with her since their senior year. A grade ahead of her, he had joined the local PD fresh out of high school and she joined after college. On the number of occasions she had worked with him, she'd learned not to trust him one bit. He made his own rules when it seemed fit, and his inflated sense of entitlement annoyed her.

"Sergeant Berg away on his course?" she queried, skipping the customary greeting. It was no secret that the sergeant had been campaigning for a computer crimes course for years. He'd finally persuaded the administration to send him to Quantico to 'learn from the big boys' as he put it. He would spearhead a new subsection within the Criminal Investigation Unit specially designated for solving computer-based crimes like child exploitation. Since these crimes had no geographical boundaries, he would liaise with other units across the continent and around the world. A family man with small kids, he was driven more than most cops, and one of the few who wanted to bring the PD's technology into the current decade.

When Sergeant Berg finished his course, he would take Derek's place and Derek would take the Sergeant's position on Erin's crew. Good for the Criminal Investigation Unit. Bad for Erin. Right now, Derek merely reoriented himself to life in the Patrol Unit.

Derek nodded but did not look up, frowning at a sheaf of papers in his hands. She got the distinct impression that he enjoyed making her wait. He ran a hand through shaggy blond hair and continued reading. She could swear he was sucking in his gut and wondered how long he could hold it.

"Where is the rest of the crew?" Erin sat uneasily at the conference table, the focal point for morning briefings.

"Z-man won't be in until ten, because he had to take his mom to the doctor. Jake is home sick with probably the same flu as Z's mom, and I sent Ryan and Mark off to an early call. Right now, it's only us here."

"What's the early call?"

"Mark's assisting the fire department down at the end of Ash Avenue with a dumpster fire." He paused and looked back at his papers. "Ryan is with him."

"Two guys sent to a dumpster fire?" Erin raised an eyebrow.

"Are you questioning me as your supervisor, Officer Ericsson?" Derek tensed his shoulders in exaggerated surprise.

"Cut the crap Derek." Erin met Derek's pale green eyes. "Nobody is here for you to impress." Even in high school this had been the only way to deal with him.

He looked at her for a moment and then he snorted. "You always were such a shit. A little firecracker."

She stared back at him. "Do you have anything useful to tell me today or should I go find out for myself?"

He dipped his head and said, "I dunno. I just picked up these papers from dispatch and haven't had a chance to go through them. I sent both guys on that call because there was vandalism to headstones at the old Ash Ave cemetery and I thought they could share the paperwork since the fire and damage are probably related."

"So, is that it?" Erin rose to her feet.

"Yup," he grunted. She was about to scurry past him when she reconsidered, and stopped.

"Sooo," she said again, drawing the sound out unbearably long. He looked up, surprised, and more than a bit suspicious.

"What are you after, Ericsson?" His brow furrowed and his lips pulled back against his teeth.

"I wanted to tell you that I heard Ryan and Mark talking the other day and they are really looking forward to you being transferred to our crew." The lies cemented the end of her tongue like grade one Papier-Mache paste.

"Really?" One side of his grin nudged higher. "And what about you, Erin?" He came up to his full height in front of her. "Are you excited?"

"Couldn't be happier." A little piece of her shriveled inside.

He held her gaze a moment longer and his frown relaxed. He settled his weight back onto the side of the desk.

"Now that we're all happy here, whaddyawant?" Sarcasm slithered underneath his words.

"I hear you've closed the Peterson arson case already," she said.

"Arson, nobody said arson."

Unfortunately, Derek was not only her supervisor for the day, he was also lead investigator on the Dolores Johnson case and Erin wanted information. She remembered that she needed to tread lightly with his high-school-football-star ego.

"That was really fast work." She stretched out the adjectives. Running a hand slowly through her hair, she tilted her palm toward Derek.

He took the bait. His eyes moved to her hand and then predictably downward, lingering on the soft skin at her throat and the curve of breast beneath her shirt. Every professional interviewer worth her salt knows this as a palm flash, but Derek still fell for the feminine distraction like a teenage boy. Not that she often used it, but she had to admit it worked. She angled her head slightly and the effect was complete.

"Yeah," he said. The edge dropped off his attitude and he sucked his gut in another inch.

"How did you do that so fast?" she murmured. "You must know all the right people at the crime lab. Did the tests come back already?"

"Uh, I didn't see the need to—"

"Really? Are the forensic guys all done? There were no signs of accelerants? No forced entry?"

"Fire guys said no accelerants, but the whole place was burned to a crisp—"

"The stove was tampered with. Was the gas line checked?"

"The old lady musta left it on." His tone was dismissive and she backed off. She did not want to be so assertive that he withheld information.

"What about the autopsy? That could not be complete yet."

"Nope. In case you haven't noticed lately, the Medical Examiner's Office is as cash-strapped as we are. They won't spring for unnecessary procedures. Absolutely nothing out there says it wasn't a tragic accident, so there was no need for an autopsy. The remains were released to her family yesterday and they are going to cremate her today. She was already mostly cooked anyhow." He stifled a laugh, puffing out a bit of air in the process, and his belly drooped back over his belt.

Erin's narrowed her eyes at him. He caught her look and his grin disappeared. Graveyard humor did not apply to people you actually knew.

"I get that you liked her, but she was a nutty old broad," he said more softly. "She'd been phoning in reports of phantom intruders for the last three months and there was never a shred of evidence. Seriously, once she reported someone broke in and stole two slices of cheese. That's whacked. She was clearly losing her marbles. Maybe her kids should have put her in a home."

"Did you do a full search of the surrounding area?" She knew she was pushing her limit.

"Search the bog? That's impossible. What goes in, stays in. We were at the scene for six hours. You don't think we are bright enough to notice anything unusual? I told you there was absolutely nothing out there."

She remembered seeing Derek the day she took Allie to the bog. With one ass-cheek on the hood of the patrol officer's car, it didn't look like he was doing much of anything useful. He probably didn't even do his own paperwork.

He leaned close to her face and spoke clearly and slowly, as if talking to a child. "In case you missed it the first time, the case is closed. C-L-O-S-E-D." The hard edge back in his voice, he rolled the papers in his hand and squeezed them in one tight fist. "Leave it alone, Ericsson. It's my case, and it's done."

He walked out and left Erin alone in the briefing room. She felt dirty somehow, complicit in the murder of Dolores Johnson. Storming from the building, she seated herself in the front of her cruiser and gripped the wheel of the white Dodge Charger. Like a mobile office, it was tricked out police style with lights, siren, augmented suspension and a compact Plexiglas shield for prisoners in the back. Usually she loved to drive it but today she was having trouble appreciating the perks of the job.

Two fender-benders consumed most of her morning. The sheer number of car accidents in this town continually amazed her. How in the world did one manage to hit the only car for blocks, or back up into the only other car in the grocery store parking lot? It was nearly noon by the time she had freed herself from the paperwork, the inevitable tracking down of insurance and licensing information, and the dismayed owner of the parked car. The Big City PDs didn't even bother with this stuff. They merely told the drivers to come in and fill out their own paperwork for the insurance companies to battle out. *Not here. We still pride ourselves on service to our community.*

Eager to get back to the Johnson property, Erin pulled into the station to grab her lunch first. She stopped abruptly at the entrance to the coffee room. Derek sat polishing off the last of her chicken salad sandwich, the Ziploc bag she had packed it in sitting in silent accusation. Surprised, he brushed crumbs from the table.

She glared at him and opened the fridge where her crumpled lunch bag sat. The only thing left inside was her apple.

"What the hell, Derek?"

"What?" he said innocently. "Ain't no big deal. I was hungry."

"Are you the immature bastard that has been stealing my lunch all summer?" It had been especially infuriating to come in and find her lunch ransacked nearly every week. He never took the fruit, but always ate her sandwich, and the little cheese sticks were the first to go. "Why is it always my lunch you're stealing?"

"Have you seen what Z-man has in his Tupperware?"

"No!" Unlike him, she did not snoop in others' lunches.

He snorted and waved a dismissive hand. "Anyway, you bring the best stuff."

She wanted to punch him. They gave this man a gun and trusted him to serve and protect. He was a petty lunch thief! And was that her lost ballpoint pen peeking out from his pocket? She snatched it back before he could protest.

"You've got more money than me," he said. "You can go buy lunch. I have a starving wife at home to feed." He shrugged and attempted a belch but it came out as more of a defiant squeak.

"And a big house and a brand new waterski boat!" she finished. "Unbelievable. You owe me."

"But the bank owns those…"

Stalking out of the coffee room, she stepped around the eavesdropping janitor in the hallway. She felt a modicum of guilt over the dirty looks she'd been wrongly directing at him. Right now she was too angry to stop and apologize.

Gas pedal to the floor, she drove aggressively over the bumpy road to the Johnson property. Beside her, a plastic wrapped ham sandwich from the Sportsman's Stop 'N Go bounced on the seat.

The fizzy burn from a bottle of Coke helped soothe an angry lump in her throat.

At the end of the driveway, she parked and mentally mapped out a grid pattern. Her starting point would be the ominous mound of soot and debris. She began by snapping a few general photos with her iPhone. There had been no basement in the old bungalow and she stepped over a short concrete foundation that now served as the perimeter for the charred remains.

She looked at her boots covered in ash. The kitchen had been here, at the rear of the house. A gas stove now sat cockeyed at ground level, having fallen through the floor where it had buckled. She brushed soot off the front end with her bare hand and examined it. A nefarious scenario played out in her mind as she took close-up photos of the ends of the burner tubes. The plastic knobs had melted off but it was patently obvious that all four control valves had been in the full open position.

Metal legs of table and chairs poked up, everything covered in a thick layer of black soot. There wasn't much else to see and she couldn't differentiate one blackened shape from another. She did remember something about fast fires creating a hump-backed charred phenomenon called alligatoring on burnt timbers. The effect is more severe closer to its origin. That confirmed that this explosive fire started in the kitchen. The gas stove. She wished she'd paid more attention to arson investigation during her classes at the academy.

The rest of the house had been reduced to ash, except the blackened brick chimney, which still stood tall. She scraped debris away from the front and took a peek inside, but didn't really understand what to look for. Surely she'd know it when she saw it.

She stepped back over the foundation wall and wiped her boots on the grass. Soot had powdered her uniformed pant legs nearly to her knees and they would need to go directly into the washer at end of shift. A few steps away from the house, she considered the framework for the back porch. The angry lump resumed its position in her throat.

Someone had turned all the gas burners on. It was dark. Dolores didn't have a chance. The moment she hit the light switch, an electrical arc was created when the circuit was completed. This spark had ignited the gas and the whole place exploded in flames. Derek had told her earlier that they had found Dolores' charred shoes standing on the top of the step, as if she'd just stepped out of them to put on her slippers. The shoes were in an evidence bag somewhere down at the station but the mental image left behind was eerie. Erin hoped the end had come fast, for Dolores' sake. She took a deep breath and swallowed the jagged lump.

Bordering the drive, a stand of mature poplar trees stabbed blackened tops skyward. Below these ominous sentinels, she searched a tight pattern back and forth across the yard. Every piece of debris, every discarded wrapper flying on the wind was examined. With no outbuildings, it was a straightforward process.

Around back, a small raised garden bed still held vegetables. Unwatered for days, they withered in the summer heat. So sad and untended, Erin was compelled to water them, but there was no garden hose and no water. An old hand operated water pump sat nearby and Erin pumped the handle a few times but was met with a grating screech. The well, dried up years ago, had been kept around for sentimental or decorative reasons.

The back gate on the white picket fence hung open, but it was hard to tell if someone had passed through recently, or if the emergency crews had simply left it that way. Dolores would have kept it latched to keep out animals intent on her vegetable patch. She exited the gate, walked along the well-beaten trail that skirted the bog and doubled back following the fence line. Tufts of grass and brush bordered the fence on the outside, while inside the yard, the grass was trimmed as neatly as a golf green.

Was Derek right? There was nothing out here but mosquitoes and weeds.

She was on her way back, only a few yards from the open gate, when a metallic glint in the brush caught her eye. She used her boot to separate tall grass and dropped to one knee at the side of the trail. Concealed in the brush sat two shiny beer cans, one upright and sealed, but the other keeled over, almost empty. Red and white Budweiser cans. In a flash, she remembered the can Allie had spent so much time looking for at the barricade. The can Erin had unceremoniously tossed into the ditch, glinting red and white in the moonlight.

From her position, she found herself with a perfect view of the charred back steps to Dolores' house through a gap in the brush. The weeds lay flat in a semi-circle at her feet. Someone had spent time here, and had planned to spend more time before they were interrupted. She unfolded an evidence bag from her pocket and carefully retrieved the cans. This was something. Better than the nothing Derek had come up with.

On her way back in the gate, she made sure to latch it securely. As she walked to her car, she slapped vigorously at her pant legs until soot clouds rose around her and crusty black particles rained down. With ash in every pore, she wiped the back of one hand across her brow to staunch the flow of sweat stinging her eyes.

She had just placed the evidence into a box in the trunk when another patrol car pulled up beside her. The crewcut young officer behind the wheel rolled down his window and hailed Erin.

"You are walking a thin line, my friend." Chris Zimmerman, known as Z-man, or just Z to his friends gave her a conspiratorial wink. "I didn't think you could resist mucking around out here the first chance you got," he said. "You are like a dog with a bone, but you should learn to keep your theories to yourself at the station. This is Derek's investigation and he's convinced the rest of the crew you might be a little bit insane." He pinched air between index and thumb.

"I know what I'm doing out here, but what are you doing out here?" she countered.

"I'm your wing man, girl." His baby smooth face broke into a wide smile and then his expression melted to a more somber one. "Besides, I knew Dolores too, and I'm not buying it that she was a forgetful old fool who died accidentally. I think there's more to this story."

"Are you sure you want to get mixed up with me and my crazy theories?"

"Game on." He winked at her again. "Have you found any evidence Derek missed?"

Erin had been on the same patrol crew with the slightly quirky Officer Zimmerman since she'd been hired on the department. Despite his eccentricity, they had always worked well together. He was intelligent, loyal, hard-working and a solid investigator. She had implicit trust that he would watch her back.

"I'm not sure," Erin said, "but I think someone has been watching the house from the bog side. I found a little spot where the grass was flattened and I picked up a couple of beer cans. Maybe Kathy in

Forensics can get some prints." She sure hoped Kathy was working today. Dave was the only other Forensic Tech, but she had less faith in his skills.

"Interesting." Zimmerman, steepled his fingers and squinted his eyes in a parody of a comic book character. "Anything else, my little sidekick?"

"No, you're the wing man this time, remember?" She loved the wacky repartee they had. It made working together so much more rewarding. "That makes me the superhero."

"Foiled again," he quipped. "No, seriously, Superchick, what else you got? Someone drinking beer out by the swamp is not quite enough for a murder investigation."

"It's Wonder Woman, and I also took some close-up photos of the gas stove. All four burners were cranked wide open. That did not happen by chance when the stove fell through the floor. Someone turned them on deliberately." She handed him her iPhone and he zoomed in on the pictures.

"Dolores was totally obsessive-compulsive," he said, startled. He handed the phone back. "She checked things two or three times. She never would have left the house with the gas on, let alone all four burners on high!"

"Exactly."

"Compelling evidence, but still not much to go on. What can I do to help?"

"You've got confidential informants out there," she said slyly. "Can you keep your ears open for any info on stalkers? Whoever did this likes to watch. Somebody must know something about this guy."

"Will do." Zimmerman rolled his window up halfway. "But keep your head down, Wonderpumpkin. You don't want to get on Commandante Derek's bad side."

"Too late. How's your mom doing, by the way?"

He rolled his window back down and leaned his elbow on the frame. "She's fine. She was having a meltdown thinking she was allergic to my new pet, but the doc says it's a garden variety flu. I built her a command center in front of the TV when I left. She has juice, snacks, a Stouffer's lasagna for the microwave, and her purple fuzzy blanket. It's only a few steps to the bathroom and it's the best I can do for now. She's convinced that she has the plague but she will be fine in a few days."

"You're a good son," Erin told him facetiously. "How many lizards did you bring home this time?"

"Just a cute little veiled chameleon I named Picasso." He cupped his hands as if holding a tiny bird and his eyes had the sloppy look usually reserved for babies or puppies. "He's an awesome dude but man does he eat like a monster! His tongue is twice the length of his body and he can snatch a cricket from your fingers before you know it! He totally creeps my mom out with his independently moving eyes but that is unquestionably his best feature."

"Yeah, I'm sure your mom is impressed."

"She'll get used to him. Picasso is a lot nicer than my first pet. When I was about twelve, a guy sold me a Green Iguana that grew to like four feet long! He took over our house and I always had cuts on my hands from his sharp spines and talons. Iggy terrified my mom."

"Iggy?"

"Yeah, Iggy the Iguana. Give me a break, I was only twelve. Anyway, one day Iggy escaped and started a fight with Princess, the neighbor's Schnauzer. Princess was tougher than she looked and that was the end of Iggy. I cried my eyes out and my mom made me a special dinner that night. I thought she was trying to console me, but in retrospect, I think she was celebrating."

"That's hilarious!" Erin's sides shook and she struggled to stifle a laugh. "I mean, so very, very sad for you."

"Yeah, laugh it up, Captain Lizardhater." He put his foot on the gas pedal. "Reptiles are the misunderstood souls of our world."

"See you later Zeeeeeee!" she cheerfully called after him, but he was already rolling up his window.

Back at the station, Erin tossed the wilted ham sandwich from her car into the garbage dumpster. Sweltering in the blazing afternoon sun on the front seat of her cruiser, it was probably teeming with potentially fatal bacteria by now. And it looked gross. Hunger gnawed at her but she was too tired to care. She descended the back stairs to the small Forensic Lab and swung open the metal door.

"Anybody tell you that you look like a chimney sweep?" A white-coated woman emerged from the computer lab and met her beside two spotless white-topped evidence examination tables. She plucked an antibacterial hand wipe from a dispenser and dabbed at Erin's face. It came away blackened.

"Funny, I just talked to Z-man and he didn't mention that." He'd probably been laughing about her soot smeared face for the last fifteen minutes.

"Can I make one guess where you've been?"

Erin eyed the forensic technician with a tired smile. "Kathy, I have had a weird day." She held out the evidence bag.

"Well, what has my favorite girl brought me?" Kathy Banks, a short bubbly redhead with an impish smile and a face full of freckles, was the most cheerful and optimistic person Erin knew. Kathy was gleefully in her element when crawling around a filthy crime scene on her hands and knees in a white biohazard suit.

"I need these checked for prints, and maybe - DNA?"

"DNA?" Kathy laughed. "Not a chance! Do you have any idea how much that costs? There is no way I can squeak that through." She looked steadily at Erin. "Since that fire was Lieutenant Peterson's file, and it was closed yesterday, I am assuming you want this off the books?"

"Please?" Erin was ashamed that it came out a little whiney. With the stress at home and wading around soot and weeds all afternoon, she was feeling the lack of sleep from the night before.

"Don't worry sweetie," Kathy patted her shoulder. "Of course I'll check it for prints." She took the bag by the top corner and studied the contents through the transparent plastic.

"I wish it had been you called out to the Johnson fire. Dave is okay, but he's just not—well, he's not you." She knew that Dave spent more time honing his social skills than he should when he worked a crime scene. In her estimation, that meant more chances to miss things. She turned to leave but Kathy called her back.

"I have a few free minutes. Why don't I have a look at this right now?" she said.

Erin's heart raced. She matched the forensic tech's jaunty pace back to a room informally known as The Powder Lab, a separate room with melamine and wire grid topped tables equipped with down draft vents. Kathy snapped on a pair of latex gloves and gingerly retrieved the two cans from the evidence bag. She adjusted a dust mask over her mouth and nose and flipped open the top of her dusting kit, selecting a plump brush and metallic gray powder from the row of little bottles. Erin bent into a half-crouch to observe. She was always fascinated by Kathy's skills. It was like watching a magician make the impossible appear.

"How is your new girlfriend liking Minnesota? She seemed so sweet when I met her at the grocery store. I bet you two are as happy as a couple of newlyweds."

"Okay, I guess." Erin didn't talk much about her personal life at work, but Kathy was different. She didn't feel like merely a work associate. She felt like a real friend. "I think Allie misses the convenience of the big city," she said evasively.

Kathy glanced up at her and then back to her work. "Well, these cans have been handled a lot, in hot sweaty fingers. Most of the prints are overlapping but I'll grab them anyway."

Erin's optimism deflated and she stood to leave.

"Don't write this off yet," Kathy reassured her. "I'm good, remember? I'll have a better look after I enhance and enlarge it on-screen. There might be something I can work with."

Erin nodded but the optimistic adrenaline burst evaporated and fatigue returned.

"I'll let you know if I come up with anything, and you can make me one of those super-lattés you are famous for."

Derek was waiting for Erin outside the dispatch office at end of shift. "Where have you been all afternoon?" He stopped, studied her pant legs and his neck turned a mottled shade of red. "I should write you up for insubordination."

"Go ahead, you immature lunch thief." She defiantly met his eye, but he stared through her, like she was a mere housefly. Then he turned and brusquely walked away.

Erin took her time in the locker room, carefully stuffing uniform pants into a plastic bag. Wisps of soot wafted out the top of the bag and she quickly knotted it closed. Her stomach gurgled and she gathered her things. When Derek assumed permanent command of her crew, she could always put in for a transfer. Maybe she would apply for the Forensic Identification Unit. Dave was nearly burnt out and would be leaving soon. It would be pleasant to work with the effervescent Kathy. She was still mulling over her options when she spotted her truck in the parking lot.

The Toyota 4x4 sat at an odd angle and Erin swore when she saw that both tires on the passenger side were flat. Sharp punctures marred the sidewalls. She bent and traced the damage with her fingertips. She didn't need Kathy to tell her they were made by a one and a half inch blade. They would match the knife on Derek's duty belt. Bastard! The surveillance camera mounted on the side of the main building was out of range. She made a mental note to park right up front from now on.

Pulling her cell phone from her bag, she punched in the direct line for dispatch and informed them of the damage to her truck. As she hung up, she noticed Derek's cherry red 1973 Ford Mustang idling on the street in front of the station. It sat for a moment and then drove off, with a sharp chirping of rubber on asphalt. Her eyes, like two angry red lasers, followed until his tail lights disappeared.

Then she called Allie.

CHAPTER SIX

Erin slid into the passenger seat when the little black Mini Cooper arrived behind the police station. Allie drove fast, barely slowing for corners She was getting to know her way around the streets. Allie concentrated on the road and waited for Erin to speak first.

"How was yoga?"

"Unpleasant. There was a new instructor who was messing with my Qi," Allie said.

"Your what?"

"My Qi." She pronounced it chee. "You know, my life force, my energy, my soul." A small grin tugged at the corner of her mouth. "I'm kidding. I'm teasing you because you think all that stuff is crap."

"No, I don't. I'm not a total Neanderthal."

Allie reached over to touch Erin's sleeve. "I know you're not."

"I'm sorry you left work early," Erin apologized. "I could have waited."

"Not a problem."

"I had a shitty day. I solve the mystery of who has been stealing my lunches, and then the asshole slashes my tires. I want to punch Derek Peterson in his smug face!"

"Another cop slashed your tires?" Allie asked incredulously. "Are you sure? Did you report it?"

"I'm sure Derek's unstable enough to do it but I can't actually prove it."

"So you can't actually accuse the guy. You deal with bad guys on a day-to-day basis and not many of them are happy with you. It might have been any of them."

"And the asshole knows it!" Erin wanted to punch the dash but held back. "I don't know what his problem is!" Her stomach flopped over, feeling like it would devour itself.

"Well, don't take it out on me."

"I'm sorry. I don't mean to. I spent the afternoon out at Dolores' house and it was unbelievably hot, and I didn't have lunch and—do you have an antacid?" Erin asked meekly.

"The Sportsman's Stop 'N Go is up ahead. I'll pull over and you can get some." Allie pulled into the lot with the bright yellow illuminated trout and parked out front.

"I'm going to wait in the car," she said. I'm getting a wicked headache all of a sudden. It must be that silly fish sign." She attempted a small grin and laid her head in her hands.

"Okay, be right back." Erin shoved open the store's glass doors and immediately sensed that something was wrong. There was no one at the counter. Robbery? Medical problem? A quick peek down the aisles revealed the closed office door. She approached and heard a thump. A firm woman's voice behind the door told someone to sit down.

"Everything okay?" Erin knocked lightly and sidestepped so she wasn't right in front of the door. "Do you need a hand?"

The door opened abruptly and Gina, the store clerk, looked out. She laughed, a gravelly noise deep in her throat.

"Little Blondie come to save the day." The corners of her hazel eyes crinkled in delight at the old joke. The long brown hair she'd always prized was disheveled around her flushed face. Behind her on a wooden straight-backed chair sat Lily, as skinny and pale as ever. Head down, tears drizzled slowly down her cheek. She wore the same gray hoodie, pulled up over her colorless hair, and her jeans were torn at the knees. The young girl hunched with legs twisted and one foot over the other, battered blue sneakers looking like they'd been to the city landfill.

Erin knew Gina from way back. Gina was two years older and, held back a grade in school, had always played the tough girl. Gina's belly and square jawline looked a little softer than they used to, and a few gray hairs straggled down over her forehead, yet she was not even thirty. She wore a faded pair of jeans and similarly faded black Harley T-shirt that practically screamed Don't mess with me. They had lived in another world when Erin had stolen her first real kiss from Gina behind the soccer field in grade five, but the earth rotated on its axis that day.

Gina had gone on to publicly date most of the boys on the football team, and secretly a few of their girlfriends, but she always saved a private wink for Erin. The years had not been kind to Gina and their lives could not have turned out more differently.

"Don't worry about it," Gina told Erin, closing the door partway behind her. "I caught her shoplifting again."

"Did you call down to the station?"

"I phoned a while ago," Gina said. "Then I called her grandpa. Gunther was supposed to be here fifteen minutes ago. Lily didn't want to wait and nearly bit me trying to take off." She paused, brushed at a reddened spot on her tattooed forearm and blew out an exasperated sigh. "But I'm not worried about that little pipsqueak."

Behind her, Erin could hear the heel of Lily's running shoe thrum anxiously on the tile floor.

"Are you sure?" Erin asked her. "I'm off duty, or I would take care of it."

"I don't think a little package of lip gloss is worth all this hassle, but the rules are that I have to report all shoplifters. I probably would have given it to the kid if she'd told me she had no money. A girl's gotta look good, doesn't she?" Gina turned around and directed that last comment to the hunched over girl whose foot tapping immediately stilled. She leaned in and handed Lily a phone number written in black marker on the back of a cash register receipt.

"It's the number for the Kids Help Line. Don't be afraid to phone if you need to." Her tone was sympathetic.

"Oh, here comes the cavalry now!" Gina said, peering out the front window. Erin's jaw tightened when Lieutenant Derek Peterson parked his red Mustang directly in front and sauntered through the doors.

"On my way home, heard the call on the radio, and thought I'd stop by to take care of your little problem," Derek volunteered, breezing through the front glass doors. His eyes took in the scene and he acknowledged Erin with a curt nod. "Unlike some people, I'm never really off duty."

Erin stood stock still, eyes like flint.

"Where's the kid?" He circled Gina like a mongoose wary of a cobra. She held out a finger toward the office.

Derek sternly gestured and the girl meekly followed him. She had left the piece of paper with the Kids Help Phone number behind on the desk. Standing on the sidewalk, ragged blonde hair spilled out the front of her hood. She hung her head and compliantly sat in the front of his car. He opened the glass doors to the store, spoke in low tones to Gina and then left. When he had gone, Gina shrugged and turned to Erin.

"He said he's gonna drive Lily home." She shook her head. "Told me to pretend this never happened. That's kinda weird."

"Yeah, weird," Erin said.

"Oh, look who came after all. A day late and a dollar short," Gina drawled. Gunther parked his Ford truck cockeyed out front, stepped out and left the door hanging open.

Under the illuminated sign, Allie still sat in her Mini Cooper, head in hands. The yellow glow made her look positively sallow but Erin wasn't comfortable about the situation and didn't want to leave yet. She reviewed the expiry dates on the sandwiches in the refrigerated display case and decided maybe she wasn't that hungry after all. There was bread at home and she could have a few slices of toast. She picked up a package of Tums and then snatched up a bottle of Advil for Allie's headache. Nonchalantly lingering by the front door, she placed the items on the counter.

Gina stepped outside to talk to the old man but Erin could not hear what was being said. Gunther waved his arms angrily, his face turning from pallid and sweaty to absolutely apoplectic. She wondered if he was going to give himself a heart attack right there. She leaned casually on the door but backed off when he blustered through.

"Scheisse!" he growled in German. "Shoplifting again!"

"Gunther!" Gina pleaded. Her hands reached for him. "She's already gone!"

"Git yer hands off me!" he bellowed, pulling his arm away so violently that Gina shrank back. She nervously tucked a strand of brown hair behind her ear. His reaction had definitely rattled her.

"She is schlecht, that one," he hissed through yellowed front teeth. Sweat trickled down his stubbly cheeks to his throat. "She's so bad." He edged over to the panel of refrigerated beverages and deliberately plucked a can of Budweiser off the wire shelf.

Gina looked pointedly at the beer in his hand and his brow furrowed.

"You owe me," he said, tucking it into his jacket pocket. "Leave it alone, or you'll regret it." Gina averted her eyes from his penetrating glare.

Erin stepped forward and Gunther swiveled to level his jaundiced and bloodshot gaze at her. It gave her pause because she could not smell a whiff of alcohol on him.

"Achten," he grunted. "This is a family matter." He backed out the door like a prizefighter unwilling to turn his back.

On the sidewalk, he viciously kicked the metal garbage can, spilling its contents. He stalked around the trash and into his truck. Erin and Gina wordlessly watched him back out and head home.

"Don't worry about it." Gina peeled a couple of bills off a crumpled wad in her pocket and placed them in the cash register. She busied herself polishing a glass topped display case. Erin handed her a five dollar bill for her purchases and Gina took it without comment. No change was forthcoming and Erin shrugged off the sixty-five cents. "Happens two or three times a month."

"Why do you let him do it?"

"Gunther Schmidt is the reason my grandpa survived the Vietnam War," Gina said dismissively. "That's an old family debt that can never be repaid, and that's just how it works."

Erin gave a shrug. "I don't think he's drunk but he doesn't look right. Is he sick or something?"

"Yeah, I wondered that too. He's been getting worse every time I see him. He never used to be such an asshole. He used to come in here before I closed up at night. I think he was lonely. I'd buy him a beer and we'd both sit out back and shoot the shit. Now he takes his beer To Go. Maybe I did something to piss him off. Maybe it's old age dementia. My grandma had that, only she wasn't so friggin' pissy about it."

Gina flashed a grin at Erin who suddenly noticed that she was standing a lot closer than she had a moment before. Gina was taller and Erin felt warm breath on her hair. She retreated a half step.

"Aw, an occasional stolen Budweiser won't be the thing that kills him. He has a free beer from time to time. I write it off or cover it myself. It's no big deal because I'm the manager now." Gina stood taller, and her jaw jutted out a little.

60

"Congrats, Gina," Erin said sincerely. Gina had worked for her uncle at the Stop 'N Go since she left high school and this step up was overdue.

Gina glanced out the window. Allie had perked up and was using the rear view mirror to smooth her hair. "She's cute. She pick you up from work today?" Her voice was smoky. "You know I wanna take care of you like that."

Erin didn't answer but rolled her eyes in that *oh give me a break* look.

"You come see me sometime," Gina said, eyes twinkling with amusement. "You can bring your new girlfriend and maybe we'll all get matching tattoos on our hineys."

"I'll keep that in mind." Gina played this game every time, ever since grade five.

"You look a lot better than you did a few minutes ago," Erin told Allie when she climbed into the driver's seat. "You were a little green around the gills. I bought these for you." She handed over the Advil, and Allie returned an embarrassed grin.

"Yeah, I get these weird sudden headaches sometimes." Allie changed the subject. "Was that the same kid we saw out on the road the other day?"

"Right. It was Lily Schmidt," Erin said. "Derek, of all people, answered the call. That was bizarre. I would have thought he'd say such a minor offense was beneath him. The old man was Gunther, her grandfather."

"That old guy's quite intimidating," Allie said. "I heard him shouting, but I didn't see much. My head was pounding like a hammer drill."

"Ooh, nice mechanic simile snuck in there," Erin teased, poker-faced. "You have been listening to me and my dad talk shop."

"I try to connect with you on your own level," Allie quipped and then her tone became more serious. "Has anyone called Children's Services? That young girl should not have to be stuck with a man like that!"

"I don't remember him being such a belligerent guy. Gunther used to be a decent man. His dad was a fisherman and a trapper, back when people actually traded furs. He was pretty attached to him and I guess that's where he gained his reputation."

"I can imagine. He must have sounded like a ghoul to the other kids."

"On the contrary," Erin said. "Think way, way back, City Girl. Think Davy Crockett cool. Gunther was living it for real. He grew up to be the most sought after fishing and hunting guide in the area. They say he never wasted a bullet and always dropped a moose with a single shot. He also landed the largest Sturgeon ever caught in the big lake. I'm sure his record still stands. You can go out to any fishing lodge and hear stories about Gunther Schmidt. He was a legend."

"He was?" Allie asked.

"Yes, was. Past tense." Erin said. "He used to hang out at the Veteran's Club with his buddies from the Vietnam War but he never was the same after his daughter Tiffany, Lily's mom, disappeared. He sold his boat and doesn't go fishing any more. Doesn't even go to the Veteran's Club. The guys at work say he keeps to himself and it looks like he's drinking quite a bit. Lately, the guy does not look well. And now he's taking care of that kid on his own."

She read Allie's humorless expression and knew her concerns would not go away until she was reassured.

"I promise I'll call a social worker I know and make inquiries."

Allie sat back, satisfied. "Who's the brunette drooling over you?" They had not moved from their spot in the parking lot and Gina was indeed watching them through the dusty front window of the store, although pretending to sweep the floor. She noticed them looking and put extra effort into her broom.

Allie backed out and turned around, spinning a rooster tail of gravel along the shoulder of the road. Erin didn't comment but reached for her seat belt and snugly fastened it.

"Aw, that's just Gina," she said. "We go all the way back to grade school."

"Old girlfriend?" Allie teased and then her eyes widened. "She is!"

"If you must know," Erin deadpanned, "Gina and I were something of an item. She really rocked my world." She paused briefly for effect. "In grade five!"

She laughed. "Your first kiss with a girl?"

"My first kiss with anyone," Erin told her. "I never kissed any boys. I guess I always knew who I was."

"I bet all the other ten year olds teased you to death."

"Nah," Erin said. "It's hard to imagine, but Gina was very discreet."

"A discreet ten year old? Impossible!"

"Eleven," Erin corrected, flashing her a lopsided grin. "Gina was eleven and before you say it, yes, I always liked the older women." Her comment was a familiar jibe about Allie being a mere year and four days older.

Erin grabbed the armrest when the car whipped around a corner, squashing her against the door.

"I will get worried if I find you prowling around the Senior's Center."

They both laughed and it was good to release some of the tension they'd held. Allie tossed the Advil into her glove box for another day. Erin was not so fortunate and popped a double dose of antacid tablets into her mouth.

Erin unlocked the front door with the usual jiggle and shove, and punched her code into the alarm control box. She opened the closet door, ready for a cantankerous cat paw to swipe at her but it was empty. She hung her jacket on the hook and headed to the kitchen.

"You smell like a forest fire," Allie told her. She opened the back door and Fiona happily wagged her way out. "Go have a shower and I'll make us omelets."

"That sounds so—" Movement caught Erin's attention and she was unnerved when the bottom cupboard door vibrated. It eerily swung halfway open.

"What the heck!" She leapt back, startled. She'd seen this in a movie once and it did not end well. Suddenly a fuzzy paw emerged and, claws extended, narrowly missed swatting her leg.

"Goddamn cat!" Erin shouted. "It's like I'm living in a horror film! I never know where she's hiding and she's always attacking me!"

Allie tilted her head and raised an amused eyebrow.

"Seriously, she's only a playful cat. She doesn't have a murderous agenda."

The cat exited the cupboard and the door closed with a dull thump. She innocently wound her way around their legs and Allie picked her up. Wrong-Way Rachel chirped and affectionately bumped foreheads.

"How could anyone not love this adorable kitty?" Allie cooed.

Over her shoulder, Erin swore the cat winked one evil yellow eye. "I don't trust that feline, and she hates me." She let the dog back in and Fiona galloped past her, wiggling her hind end at Allie in joyful welcome. "You too? What am I, chopped liver? I let you in, you ingrate." Her faux anger disappeared when Fiona wheeled around and slathered Erin's hands with happy dog slobber. She gathered the dog close. "Sorry buddy. I had a rough day. I know you love me." What was it about dogs? She could not resist that cheerful grin and waggly tail.

"Oops, we have no eggs." Allie looked blankly in the fridge. "There are no eggs. We need eggs."

"Can't we have peanut butter sandwiches?" Erin's stomach viciously gnawed at her. Fiona whined and paced nervously back and forth between the two women. "Or maybe we can thaw out the leftover lasagna in the freezer? I don't even care any more."

"No, we must have omelets. We need eggs." Allie's voice rose and her tone was uncharacteristically terse. "You need to go to the Stop 'N Go. Hurry!" The dog's whining intensified. Allie put a hand out and caressed her behind the ear.

"Fine. I'll go buy some before Gina locks up." Erin grumbled. She glanced back at Allie's intense stare and headed for the door.

* * *

Cat draped over her shoulder, Allie absently pushed a carton of eggs to the back of the fridge. She shut the door and turned to the window, holding one fist up to a furrowed brow. The dog nosed her pant leg but she remained motionless. She closed her eyes and Fiona leaned against her.

She is suffocating, limbs bound and immobile. Brain pounding in agony, body trapped in darkness. Outside, the shadow figure growls, smelling of gasoline and hate. The shadow lingers nearby to watch the fire feast and then vanishes into the trees.

CHAPTER SEVEN

It is half an hour before closing time when I arrive along the trail. Amongst the trees I watch through the window while she pulls boxes out of the back and empties them onto the shelves. Straightening the potato chips like Dominoes on top, she works her way from one display to the next and stands back to see the big picture. After she is done, she walks up and down each aisle to check everything again. She always does. She's got this whole routine before she finishes for the night, and I've taken advantage of it more than once for the sheer thrill.

Usually I wait until she goes to the bathroom. She'll be in there for at least five minutes. I come through the back door, or even the front if I'm feeling extra bad-ass and I slip in like a panther. Before she comes out, I am gone. I don't care what I take, and I don't need any of this shit, but it gives me some sort of satisfaction to go where I want, take what I want, and be invisible.

Like I was invisible when I went into the parking lot of the police station and slid my knife into that other bitch's tires. It sliced in smooth as butter. One-Pshhhhhh Two-Pshhhhhh and then I slipped away out of sight of the cameras. I wish I coulda seen her face when she came out! That would have been a laugh. Next time, maybe I'll count to Four-Pshhhhh. I'm getting a little bit excited remembering the tires, and thinking about what might happen tonight. It feels so good when it starts like a tickle in my belly and my heart beats faster.

Finally, inside the store, she's done her routine with the displays and when she grabs the squeegee for the front windows I know it's time. She is going to the bathroom for paper towels and Windex, and to do her makeup or whatever else she does in there. I head around back quick, and damn if the door isn't left unlocked, just for me. Luck follows me. I can't help it. It's been that way as long as I can remember.

I squeeze in the back door and slide around the corner by the counter. Then I spy the metal fire extinguisher. It pops so easily out of its bracket and I start to get a whole new plan. I go back, grab the little red gas can and give it a shake. It's nearly full.

I am smiling like a kid at Christmas and my heart pounds. It feels amazing. My entire body vibrates and I rise up on my toes, like I will float. My heart is going to burst from my chest like the creature from *Alien*. I am so alive.

I kill the lights so Gina can't see me when she opens the bathroom door. I am a phantom, hitting her with the canister in that sweet spot right behind her ear. She grunts and crumples, a slow motion pile of rags. Her head hits the floor with a wet smack. I toss the fire extinguisher down the hall and it pings off the tile like a .22 caliber bullet.

This doesn't look how I imagined so I watch her for a few minutes. Maybe an idea will come to me. I lean closer to make out her face in the dark. Her eyes are closed, her jaw twitches and a little puddle of blood forms on the floor under her head. She isn't croaked yet because her chest is still movin' up and down. Well then, I better tie her up in case she wakes up and causes me any trouble. Like they did in The Watcher, I swipe a roll of duct tape from the shelf and wrap her wrists and ankles.

When I'm leaning over, I am close enough to smell her. Shampoo and cleaning detergent. It surprises me a little. What did I expect her to smell like? Motorcycle oil? I personally prefer chlorine bleach and gasoline. Chlorine reminds me of household cleaners, which I like, and gasoline reminds me of—well—of danger and fun.

I look down at her lips moving in a whispery shush shush sound so I wind more tape around her head to cover her big fat mouth. It's not too tidy, but it works. I kick her shoulder with my shoe and now she doesn't make a peep. *Yeah, that's right, you're going down, sucker.*

I don't feel the least bit sorry for her. Anyway, she kind of has it coming, doesn't she?

* * *

Still grumbling to herself, Erin drove down the deserted tree-lined streets of her neighborhood and out onto the equally deserted main road. It was less than a ten-minute drive to the store but this provided her plenty of time to grouse out loud to Allie's car. The muted dashboard lights winked back with her speed displayed in rapidly changing digits. Pulling up in front of the Stop 'N Go, she parked Allie's Mini Cooper in the same spot as before, right under the fish sign. She truly was a creature of habit.

The lot was deserted, no teens looking for late night snacks and no procrastinating parents coming for last minute supplies. Just her, hungry as a skeeter before a storm, and cranky as a bear sow separated from her cub. She grimaced. Crap, even in her mind she was starting to sound like Auntie Vicky with her crazy swamp stories! Give her another ten years and she would be a mirror image.

Erin was so distracted that she failed to realize that the lights were out until she looked up. The store was cloaked in darkness. She checked her watch. It should still be open, and Gina was always punctual. An audible bell spiked sharp prickles of alarm up her spine.

The front door swung easily and she stepped inside. Smoke stung her nostrils before she saw it, dark curls billowing up from behind the counter and rolling across the ceiling tiles in a noxious fog.

"Gina! Anyone here?"

Erin covered her mouth and nose and surged forward, breathing in shallow whiffs. She was sure she smelled gasoline fumes and understood how the fire was spreading so quickly. Smoke wickedly stung her eyes and she fought to keep them open, to see anything through the thick haze now blanketing her.

"Gina!" Erin coughed when toxic smoke burned her throat. She dropped to her belly and wriggled behind the counter where she remembered seeing the fire extinguisher. Feeling her way up the wall, she discovered the empty bracket hanging open. Intense heat from the flames shot toward her, mere inches from her skin. She retreated as the fire leapt and, with a howling whoosh, threatened to engulf her. Shielding her face in her sleeve, she crawled back to the entrance and lay stock still on the hard tile. Beyond the roar of the fire, she swore she heard tapping.

"Gina?"

She risked a few more seconds, straining her ears. There it was again! Skittering like a lizard, she squeezed her eyes tight and navigated across the floor by memory. She passed the open office door and continued to the back of the store. There was no sound for a moment and then she heard it again.

"Gina!"

Erin blindly crawled a few more feet and abruptly smashed her head against a hard object. A quick grope around revealed a wooden chair jammed under the bathroom doorknob. She flung it aside and wrenched open the door.

Like a jumble of discarded clothing, Gina lay inside, trapped. Erin prodded her and was answered with muffled cries.

Pop! Pop! Pop! The display of cigarette lighters at the checkout exploded one-by-one as the fire intensified. The ensuing loud crash probably meant the ceiling had collapsed above it. They needed to get out. Now.

She grabbed Gina by the legs but was kicked back with panicked violence. Stunned by the blow, she let go. "Easy, easy," she rasped. "It's me, Erin." She tore at the duct tape around Gina's ankles but her efforts in the dark were useless.

Gina calmed and Erin again grasped her firmly, pulling as hard as she could. Halfway down the hall, she bumped into the fire extinguisher on the floor. It was too late for that now. She sucked fiery air in tiny gasps. By the time they reached the rear exit, it took all her strength to reach up and shove the door. With the new influx of oxygen, the fire shrieked and flames leapt ever higher, like a voracious creature.

Through the open door, Erin scented the promise of fresh air and it rekindled her waning energy. She grabbed her by the pant legs and hauled. Gina's T-shirt slid up and Erin winced when bare skin scraped, jarring down each and every ruthless concrete step.

Gina groaned in pain but they could not stop until they had reached safety. Muscles protesting and lungs burning, she dragged Gina across the alley to the edge of the woods. She collapsed in exhaustion, chest heaving. Her raw throat screamed in protest. On her back, she tried to refill her raging lungs with ragged breaths.

Beside her, Gina moaned in pain and wriggled against her bonds. Erin rolled over and held her face gently, peeling the duct tape as carefully as she could. Gina let out a surprised yelp when the tape ripped out her hair. More tape bound Gina's hands and feet but she would need a knife for that. She fell back to the grass, wheezing from the effort.

"Sonofabitch!" Gina blinked repeatedly, her eyes unfocused.

Erin examined red blistered forearms and hands. She checked Gina and discovered a trail of blood down the back of her neck below a dark mass of sticky hair. A sizable lump behind Gina's ear seeped blood and she pressed her palm hard against it, Gina moaned again but lay compliant.

Energy consumed, Erin slumped heavily against her in the prickly grass. She kept her hand pressed to the wound and rested her forehead against Gina's shirt to try to calm herself and breathe. Gina smelled of fresh laundry, with an odious overtone of smoke and something metallic. Blood from scraped and torn skin soaked the fabric. She thought of her iPhone in the console of the Mini Cooper. It might as well be a hundred miles away for all the good it did them now.

"This is not what I had in mind when I said I wanted time alone with you," Gina croaked.

Erin was too weary to respond. The smoke in her lungs was oppressive, like slow asphyxiation. She became aware that the piercing wail of the store's alarm had ceased but still heard no sirens. There were no fire trucks. No squad cars. There was only the screeching of the fire, and an occasional ping or crack while it ravaged the building. She watched smoke swirl angrily above, obscuring the stars with its roiling black cloud. Sparks soared through the roof like a vortex of enraged fireflies.

"Hello?" A strained voice called through the dark. "Anybody out there?"

Erin knew that voice. She tried to answer but only managed a cough, so she raised an arm as high as she could into the air and waved it back and forth. Suddenly a worried face appeared above her, like an apparition against the night sky. Erin had never been so happy to see Kathy Banks, her favorite forensic tech. She sank back down and gave Kathy a moment to take in the scene.

"Omigod! Omigod! Omigod!" Kathy exclaimed, hands fluttering as though she would take flight.

Lightheaded, Erin squinted at Kathy through swollen eyes, and idly noted that fire backlit her hair like a halo. The last thing she remembered was Kathy's red hair bouncing against the flames while she shouted into her cell phone.

* * *

Forty-five minutes later, Allie sat beside Kathy in the hospital emergency ward. A nurse stood at the end of Erin's bed, writing notes on a clipboard. In the adjoining cubicle lay Gina, who looked like she'd been in a car accident. Her T-shirt had been replaced by a pastel hospital gown and tubes snaked out to an IV pole. Blood still seeped through the gauze dressing covering her ribs and soaked the side of her gown.

"I'm so glad you called me," Kathy said to Allie. "My phone was right by the window and as soon as I went to get it, I saw the smoke. If you hadn't called..." She let the thought hang.

Allie shrugged noncommittally.

"I think Erin's going to need a little more time before she's up for company, don't you agree?" asked Kathy.

"Company?"

"When you called, you said something about dinner and then I saw the smoke! The rest of the conversation all went to hell!" Kathy's hands animated her speech, gesturing smoke trails in the air like a sculptor.

"R-right. Dinner." Allie recovered quickly. "Of course, dinner. We'd love to have you and your husband over for dinner." They both looked at Erin lying miserably on the bed, dirt streaked and blood smeared, with oxygen tubes affixed to her nostrils.

"As soon as Erin is feeling up to it, of course," Allie added.

"That sounds lovely. I'll bring a hot dish."

Allie brushed her girlfriend's bangs back from her forehead. Erin's face looked badly sunburned and a fringe of hair on one side had withered to wiry corkscrews against her scalp. All the fine blonde hairs on the back of her forearms were singed and her skin, judging from its appearance, suffered first and second degree burns.

Dislodging the oxygen sensor from her fingertip, Erin tried to sit up. She had already attempted to remove it several times so she could go home but the silver haired nurse was having none of that.

"You've been a brat as long as I've been a nurse." She chided her good-naturedly. "You leave that alone." Her tone was kind but she stood firm, blocking any escape.

Erin fell back, wheezing and coughing.

The nurse gripped her chin and readjusted the oxygen cannula. "For once, you are going to listen to me and stay until the doctor has a proper look at you." She shot a warning glance at Gina who lay motionless in the next bed. "You too, Missy."

Head wrapped in layers of gauze, mask securely attached, Gina showed no sign of rebellion. She looked barely conscious, but her eyelids flickered open when she was spoken to and a tiny smile at the corner of her mouth hinted at amusement.

When the doctor finally appeared, it didn't take long before he ordered both women admitted to the second floor. Two porters arrived minutes later for the transfer.

"You're lucky enough to get a shared room so you can talk about your adventure all night." The nurse paused long enough to gently squeeze Gina's shoulder before they were rolled out.

On the second floor, a beefy looking man waited outside the door to their new room and the porters brushed past him to transfer their patients. With curt nods, they left them in the care of the nursing staff and hurried out.

The beefy man fidgeted in the doorway until the nurse had left and then slowly entered. Worry creased his brow and he literally wrung his hands together. He tentatively touched Gina's forearm and she opened two swollen and bloodshot eyes. They wavered and then focused on his face.

"Gin..." he began.

She closed her eyes and turned away.

Beside her, Kathy respectfully cleared her throat and rose to her feet. "I better get on home and get supper for my hubby," she said. "He'll be ordering pizza by now and that's not going to do his cholesterol any favors."

The brawny man sat in the empty chair and avoided looking at Allie. He tore his plaid jacket off, fidgeted with it and then put it back on. He sat back in his chair and then sat forward. Finally, he inched over until he was beside Gina's bed.

"I promise you," he sputtered. "When I rebuild the store, I'm gonna get a brand new security system. State of the art alarm, fire sprinklers, the works. You're gonna get a promotion."

"Uncle Darryl," Gina mumbled. "You already gave me a

promotion."

"I'm gonna give you another one." He rose to his feet so hastily that the chair clattered backwards. He grappled and managed to get it upright. "And a raise. I'm giving you a raise."

"And you promise to pay the alarm monitoring company?" The words grated over her dry tongue.

Erin grunted and narrowed her eyes at him, although he was also avoiding looking at her. She now understood why no emergency vehicles came to the scene until Kathy called it in.

"I will never let that happen again! I swear on my sister's grave!"

"You better not piss off my dead mama." Gina pointed a shaky finger at him.

"I won't! I won't! I swear to God!" Red-faced, he fumbled his way around the cockeyed chair and made his hurried escape.

"Ha." Gina closed sleep encrusted eyelids and her breathing slowed to a deep, even pattern as the oxygen supply hissed.

Allie reached over and pulled the bedcover up around Erin, who had also fallen asleep. She didn't see it, but sensed the dark shadow flit past the entrance to the hospital emergency. Cold fingers squeezed her chest and she caught her breath.

CHAPTER EIGHT

In the morning, Erin was eager to get going. Her parents had delivered her truck, but it took some coaxing to get her to agree to sit in the wheelchair for the ride out. Pride be damned, it was hospital policy, the nurse said. Her tone ensured there would be no argument on that matter.

Her mom gathered her things from the bedside stand, meticulously folding and stuffing them into a plastic bag. Allie stood at the foot of the bed, holding a brightly colored package in fidgeting hands while Erin's dad hustled to retrieve a wheelchair.

Erin gingerly tucked her fresh shirt into the front of her jeans and made her way over to say goodbye to Gina. With a serious head laceration and concussion and painful scrapes down one side of her body, Gina would stay in hospital a while longer. Erin placed a hand gently on her shoulder, and she startled awake.

"It's you," Gina said, creaking her eyes open to puffy slits. A smirk lazily wound its way to her lips. "My teeth are wearing fuzzy little sweaters and I would give my right nipple for a toothbrush right now. I also have wicked road rash, thanks to you." She paused a moment for maximum effect. "It took them four hours in Emerg last night to pick all the gravel out of my skin."

"I'm so sorry. I'm sick to my stomach over that but I had to—"

"I'm just messin' with ya," Gina interrupted her with an awkward wink. "I want to thank you for pulling me out of there." Her voice softened, sincerity moistening her eyes.

Erin's neck felt hot and Gina's cracked lips widened to a toothy

73

smile.

"I'd be cooked like a Bavarian sausage by now if you hadn't!" Gina laughed. "What pisses me off is how much of my hair they had to cut off to get the duct tape out!" She coughed and a hoarse rattle sounded in her throat. She held up one bandaged hand to her roughly shorn locks. "Used to be past my shoulders and now I look like a diesel dyke!"

Erin involuntarily snorted at the unexpected reference and felt the heat spread to her ears. She shot an apologetic glance to her mom, who conscientiously stared at her shoes.

"You owe me a beer for the road rash," Gina rasped.

Erin's dad returned with the wheelchair and she reluctantly sat down so her father could maneuver it out the door.

"Thanks for fixing my truck." She craned her neck around while he pushed her down the hospital hallway. Crow's feet at the corners of his eyes seemed deeper than before and he still wore his navy coveralls with grease stains on the sleeves.

"I had to replace those two tires. Slashed right through the sidewalls. It was lucky Gus's had them in stock." He was quiet for a moment. "Your mom and I worry about your job—"

"Dad—" Erin stopped him before they rehashed that old issue. He nodded imperceptibly.

"And I changed the oil."

"Thanks Dad."

Allie trailed behind Erin's mom, who marched ahead of them out the doors and into the parking lot. She carried the small bag with Erin's belongings and a loaf of fresh baked zucchini bread that was still warm. Wrapped in brightly colored cellophane, the baking was topped with a big red Get Well bow. It smelled divine.

Erin's mom ran to fetch their car and her dad helped her into the passenger side of the Tacoma.

"I'm sure I don't need to tell you to drive safe," Erin's dad said when they left.

"Don't worry. I'll take care of her." Allie slid behind the wheel and started the engine. She took an inordinate amount of time adjusting the seat and rear view mirror.

"I can hardly wait to get home and take a shower," Erin declared. "I'm sure I still have soot in my ears and all the little hairs in my nose burned." She held out a gauze-covered arm. "Under this, I look like a

74

boiled chicken! All I smell is smoke and burnt hair—"

"I'm ready to talk." Allie said.

"Oh, your car—" Erin looked at her hands.

"I wanted to—" Allie tried again.

"Listen, I will pay for repairs. I'm sorry about parking it so close to the fire. The hood is all heat blistered by the fire, and the sign came down—"

"I'm not worried about the paint job," Allie interrupted and then backtracked. "What? What about the sign?"

"The nightshift crew visited me last night and told me that the fire guys backed their pumper truck into the sign and it fell onto your car. The big fish crunched right through the sunroof."

"Oh."

Erin tried her lopsided grin but Allie was looking out the front windshield.

"I don't care about the car. I wanted to tell you that I'm ready to talk."

Erin's eyes widened. "You mean *talk* talk?"

"Yes." A minute passed. "I'll start and the rules are that you are not allowed to laugh, or make fun of me in any way, or I stop." She looked over at Erin, tension straining the corners of her mouth.

"Of course." Erin sat ramrod straight in her seat.

There was another long pause before Allie began. Her voice trembled. "For as long as I can remember, I just knew things. Not big things, just things. Like when I was little, I always knew when my mom would be home. She worked odd hours as a waitress so her shift often changed. I'd be sitting home with my babysitter, watching cartoons or something and I'd turn the TV off, put away my toys and get into my pajamas. It wasn't something I consciously thought about. There was no moment where I was like, oh mom's coming home now and I better get ready. I did it without thinking. I'd sit by the door and a couple of minutes later, she would walk in and say 'Hi sweetie. It must be time to tuck you into bed.' I assumed everyone could tell when their mom was coming home."

Allie waited tentatively for Erin to nod encouragement. "When I grew older, I realized that sometimes I knew what was going to happen right before it did. Most of the time it was only like a two-second warning. I'd be standing there in the kitchen and my focus would totally zoom in on something and I'd think: someone is going to come in and knock that knife off the edge of the counter, right about—NOW. At the point where I got to NOW, someone would come in and knock that knife off the counter and I'd think, wow, why didn't I do something about that? Sometimes they'd get hurt and I'd feel guilty so I started my preventive strategy."

"Preventive strategy? You have a plan?"

"Not really. Yeah, sort of." Allie shrugged noncommittally. "If I feel I need to do something, I do it. If I don't, it nags at me until I do, or until I regret that I didn't. I've been doing it for so long that I don't know if everyone around me is clumsy and I like to pick up after them, or if I really am helping them avoid all those little mishaps throughout the day. Maybe it's obvious and I notice when there's an accident waiting to happen."

"I think it's more than that. Is that what happened when you sent me to the store to buy eggs last night?"

"That was a little bit different. I usually don't get such strong feelings. I didn't know what was happening. I felt that we needed eggs. It was absolutely imperative that you go and get them from the Stop 'N Go right away."

"Well, you were right on with that premonition," Erin said. They arrived in the driveway of their home and Allie turned off the engine but neither made any move to leave the truck.

"After you left, I don't even remember calling Kathy Banks," Allie said. "I only met her the once but I suddenly thought that she was a super nice lady and I should invite her and her husband over for dinner sometime. I needed to call her right that very minute."

Allie opened her door and Erin followed her up onto the doorstep. Fuzzy Fiona greeted them in her usual enthusiastic manner, and spent extra time sniffing Erin's bandages before she allowed them to pass.

"Oh, so now I'm interesting," Erin quipped to the dog. She ruffled the fingers on her good hand through Fiona's fur. The fickle cat was noticeably absent but Erin kept vigilant on her way to the kitchen. She was dying for something cool to drink, and something solid to eat. Opening the refrigerator door, she gaped at the carton of eggs staring back at her from the rear of the middle shelf. She turned a questioning look to Allie, who shrugged without explanation.

"Cheese omelets, it is!" Erin announced, retrieving the nearly full carton, and a package of cheddar. She poured herself a glass of apple juice and downed half of it in a couple of swallows.

Later, thirst and appetite sated, Erin reclined on the couch and rested her head against the pillow. She was tired, but this story intrigued her more. Curled up on the carpet in front of her, Allie turned her back. "I can't have you examining my every expression and interpreting my body language like an interrogator."

"I won't."

"When I was nearly eighteen I started getting headaches," Allie told her. "A horrible pressure builds up in my head and I can barely keep my eyes open. I don't understand what makes it come or what makes it go away. I think it happens when I'm near certain people, or places. Like they give off shock waves or something and I have to get away. If I get too close, I feel like something terrible is going to happen. I feel nausea, and sometimes there are these flashes."

"Flashes? Like visions? Like the day I took you past the bog to Dolores Johnson's house?"

"Yeah, like that, but usually not so intense." Allie took a deep breath. "I wouldn't use the term visions. That's way too dramatic for me. It's more like a flash of lightning with an image. Kind of a quick snapshot."

"Okay, flashes."

"This is so hard to talk about." Allie's voice cracked. She drew her knees up to her chest and buried her face. "I've never spoken these words aloud to anyone in my life."

"It's all right," Erin said. She reached over and laid her bandage-wrapped hand over Allie's. There was warmth in her touch. Allie unwound herself but her body remained tense.

"It's usually not so severe. It's mostly an aversion to a certain person or place. Like magnets with similar poles repelling each other. If I don't get away, it becomes a physical pain spreading through my whole body and it makes me want to throw up, so I am motivated to avoid the situation."

Erin threaded her fingers through Allie's and she breathed a long sigh.

"I guess that's why I like animals so much," she said. "I never feel anything weird. They are what they are. If I close my eyes, I imagine I see their energy. They travel around like little glowing fuzz balls of warmth."

"Glowing fuzz balls?"

"I don't have a better description for it," Allie said. "You promised not to laugh at me."

"I'm not laughing. I'm trying to picture what's in your head."

"Fiona is special. She has the warmest glow I've ever known. I had recently gone through a breakup and needed company so I drove down to the Toronto Animal Shelter. This overweight golden retriever with a big plume of a tail nuzzled my hand. She was only six years old but they told me the dog was too old and blind to be adoptable. Her owner had passed away and no one had come forward to take her. As soon as I touched her, I could feel her energy. So open, so trusting, and so happy to be alive. I knew right away that we needed each other. The staff at the shelter didn't know her name, so I called her Fuzzy Fiona."

"You pick interesting names."

"That's a whole other story," Allie grinned like a Cheshire cat and Erin felt her eyelid twitch.

"What about people?"

"People are not so easy. Their energy is so convoluted and frankly, confusing at times." She looked directly into Erin's eyes, stripping her heart bare. "That's what I liked about you when we first met. You were straightforward, honest with your emotions, self confident. You were so terrible at the suave sophisticated approach and it was easy to tell it had never been your thing."

"Yes, I totally embarrassed myself."

"It was adorable how bad you were at it." Allie laughed and Erin returned a sheepish grin. "When I closed my eyes, I imagined you shining like the sun's reflection across water. I knew how you really were inside. I trusted you right from the beginning. There was no deception between us until that day at the bog."

"Until that day." Shame rose like putrid lava from Erin's core. Allie may have forgiven her, but it would be a long time before she forgave herself. This was a solid reminder to make good on her promise.

"You grew up without talking to a single soul about this?" Erin gave a low whistle and Fiona, sprawled at Allie's side, perked up her ears. "That must have been a heavy burden for a kid."

"I tried not to think about it." Allie said. "My foster parents helped me but it took years. We learned that I couldn't make the feelings go away but if I concentrated hard, or distracted myself enough, I could ignore them so they didn't bother me. I thought it was under control and had almost convinced myself I was normal. Until you came along."

"Me?"

"When I met you, it all crashed back. The two-second premonitions, the feelings about people and places I blocked out before. I can't hide when I'm with you. I feel like a satellite receiver and I'm wide open and taking in anything that comes my way. It's been difficult. The headaches and the nightmares I fought so hard to get rid of are back. I can't catch my breath and my life is spinning out of control like when I was ten."

* * *

"What happened when you were ten?" Erin lightly touched her shoulder. Allie's eyes grew dark and she pulled away stiffly.

"My mom died." She rose abruptly and wrapped her arms around herself. "I don't want to talk about it. I have to get ready for work." Fiona nosed Allie's leg and followed her upstairs.

Erin sank back into the couch. She was so tired she decided to forego a much-needed shower in favor of a nap. There were so many layers to Allie and she fell asleep knowing she wanted to discover them all.

Allie's kiss on her cheek awoke her and she was startled to find Wrong-Way Rachel sleeping in the crook behind her knees. The cat's fluffy tail was tucked tightly under her chin and she purred contentedly. Erin froze, so as not to incur any clawed feline wrath. Her throat was still raw and she was relieved to spy the glass of ice cubes Allie had placed on the coffee table. She reached a hand out and tried to hook it over the top of the tumbler without disturbing Rachel. Allie shook her head and moved the glass closer. Erin smiled, popped an ice cube in her mouth and let it melt.

"Your mom's zucchini loaf is in the fridge and I made you Jell-O for later," Allie said. "I'm taking your truck so call if you want. Don't do anything silly today, okay? Just rest." She kissed Erin again and headed out the door, jingling the keys in her hand.

Erin slept until well past noon and was astonished to find the cat still curled up with her when she woke. At some point, Rachel had moved from the crook of her knee to below her chin, and the rumbling purr reverberated against Erin's sore throat. It was strangely soothing to have the warmth of the cat snuggled against her. She edged away, careful not to disturb her. This unexpected good will could only last so long.

"Truce?" she said aloud.

Rachel awoke and languidly stretched herself out, head all the way down to luxurious tail. She yawned lazily and hopped off the couch, landing feather light on her three legs.

CHAPTER NINE

After an awkward shower, keeping bandaged arms dry with elastic strapped plastic bags, Erin was pleased to shake off most of her fatigue. She was almost herself again. Aside from a sore throat and persistent cough, she actually felt pretty good. She grabbed the dog's leash and headed out the door. Some fresh morning air would be perfect for both of them.

Excited to be out, Fiona strained against her leash and Erin trotted behind. Despite her vision impairment, Fiona kept to the center of the sidewalk, not veering right or left except for an occasional sniff at shrubbery. Less than two blocks later, Erin doubled over, wheezing. Her lungs burned like ignited jet fuel. She had not yet caught her breath and was still bent over with elbows on knees when she became aware of car tires pulling alongside the curb. Fiona's body stiffened beside her, ears pricked and nose scenting the air. The dog let out an excited bark and leapt forward, nearly bowling Erin over.

"Easy, easy, dog." Officer Zimmerman's voice. "Are you okay, Erin?"

"Fine," she wheezed, "I'm fine."

"You will do just about anything to get a day off, won't you?" He waited patiently until she was able to breathe normally and straightened up to look at him. By then, Fiona leaned heavily against his leg, tongue lolling out the side of her grinning mouth. She wetly nosed his hand and her tail whipped vigorously. Zimmerman reluctantly patted the dog twice on the top of her head and tucked his hand into his pocket before she could nose him again. She wiggled with glee.

"I don't quite get dogs," he said, backing off a step. "They're always all over me, and they slobber." Fiona took the step with him and lovingly nuzzled her face on his knee.

"Well, dogs get you," she answered. "What are you doing here?"

"I saw Kathy Banks down at the station. She told me what happened last night, and it's all over the local radio. They are calling you a real honest to God superhero."

"Nah, it just happened and I did what I could," she said humbly.

"Kathy also said she talked to your girlfriend. They thought you were likely to do something silly today, and she asked me to check on you. And here you are. Were you seriously out jogging?"

"Uh, it didn't start out that way. I wanted some air and then the dog was excited for a walk and then—"

"You were headed to the Stop 'N Go weren't you? That's miles away. Are you trying to kill yourself?"

She breathed in and out, slowly and deliberately, before she looked him in the eye.

"Get in," he said, and her eyebrows shot upward. "But the dog rides here." He jerked the back door open so she could guide Fiona in.

"You don't have a leopard gecko in your pocket, do you?"

"No, Merlin is at home. I'm just happy to see you."

Erin laughed hoarsely, slid in front and buckled up. She edged away from the unyielding angles of the onboard computer's mounting bracket. Behind them, Fiona bounded from one window to the other.

"What the heck happened last night?" He hit the power switch and gave the dog enough room to stick her head into the breeze. Her tongue waggled from the side of her mouth, canine nose happily twitching.

"I guess I went to the Stop 'N Go at the right time." Erin deliberately omitted the part about Allie's premonition sending her to the store. She gave him a condensed version of what happened after she discovered the fire.

"Holy frijoles, Batgirl," he said. "Gina's a bit raw around the edges but she's an exceptionally sweet girl. Who would want to hurt her?"

"I can think of one belligerent old hermit," Erin said through clenched teeth. "He was there last night, and I heard him threaten Gina."

"Who?"

"Old man Gunther Schmidt. He was furious when came to get his granddaughter Lily after Gina caught her shoplifting. I was in the store and he sounded threatening."

"Was she upset about it?"

"No, she seemed more sorry for the guy, but I had a bad feeling about it. He has a blowup at her store and an hour later the place goes up in flames. Coincidence? I don't think so!"

"Did Gina see anything?"

"Gina has been mostly out of it since the fire," she told him. "I tried to talk to her at the hospital, but she was too concussed. I think she was hit with the fire extinguisher because it was missing from its bracket and I'm pretty sure I passed it lying in the back hallway on my way out."

"So, Gunther comes in when Gina is in the washroom, grabs the fire extinguisher, waits and clobbers her. He ties her up with duct tape and traps her in there by wedging the office chair against the doorknob. That's methodical, and sadistic."

Erin nodded. "This is a pretty small town and everyone here knows Gunther from way back. He can be a cantankerous old bastard, but he didn't strike me as someone capable of such calculated cruelty toward another person. I guess you never can tell."

"Sounds like he knew Gina's routine and it was easy for him to take advantage. He must have been watching her."

Erin nodded again. "Just like someone was watching Dolores Johnson and knew her routine."

"And someone likes fire." He knitted his brows in concentration. "Hey, wasn't there a fire by the cemetery recently?"

"Could Gunther have done all this?"

"Ryan and Mark were on that call. They said some witness thought it was kids. It's possible that it's not even related."

"Well, there sure are a lot of fires around here lately," she said. "That can't be all coincidence."

"I'm not sure it's wise to connect the dots just yet, but it sure feels tempting to link all these together. Is it reasonable to assume that an old guy like Gunther is traipsing about the bush at night, drinking beer in the swamp behind a widow's house?" He lingered at a stop sign long enough to punch an inquiry into the computer. A second later he looked up. "Gunther is squeaky clean. Not even a parking ticket in the system."

"Don't forget that he used to be an outdoors guide. He knows this area like nobody else. I'm sure he still remembers all the bush trails between his place, the bog, and the Stop 'N Go. It takes a while to drive all the way around by car, but it's probably quite efficient if you know the short cuts through the bush by heart."

"What about motive?" he asked. He tapped two fingers on the steering wheel for emphasis. "What could possibly be the motive for Gunther to go after Dolores, or Gina?"

"I'm still puzzling that out. Gunther served with Gina's grandfather in Vietnam. She said her family owed him. There might be something he's holding onto from the past."

"What about Dolores?" he countered. "Why would he want to hurt her?"

"Like I said, I'm working on it."

The fire investigator's unmarked car and the forensic van were parked out front when they reached the Stop 'N Go. The infamous fish sign lay crashed on its side in the parking lot and police tape was strung from corner to charred corner of the building's remains. Kathy was outfitted in a white suit, glowing like a Christmas ornament against the soot covered wreckage of the building. Camera in hand, she photographed the scene. The fire investigator followed her, nodding occasionally while she spoke. He held a metal canister and stooped to pick up a sample and place it inside.

They parked in the alley at the rear and left Fiona to pace in the backseat.

Erin walked around and stood in front, Zimmerman standing behind her in silent support. Where there were doors, now there was broken glass, twisted metal and half of the front wall caved inward. She closed her eyes and remembered the shrieks of fire devouring combustibles and the noxious smoke filling her lungs. She remembered the sickening feeling of Gina's skin scraping against concrete when she dragged her outside. She remembered struggling to breathe, staring at the sky, and watching smoke and sparks swirl against the stars. She remembered Kathy's halo, and finally waking up in hospital with an oxygen mask on.

"I didn't think you'd be able to keep away from here," Kathy said, her voice sounding muffled inside an N95 particulate mask. She had loomed up before Erin registered it, and stood right in front of her, white mask matching her white protective suit and booties. The only splash of color came from her electric blue nitrile gloves. She pinched the mask from her mouth and nose. She was smiling. Kathy was always most happy in her element.

Behind her, the fire investigator used a flat trowel to clear debris from the floor where the store's front counter used to be. He carefully scraped back layers and viewed each as he eliminated it. When he reached bare floor, he set the shovel aside and made notes. He picked up another burnt sample and placed it in a metal can.

"I knew you'd be itching to get here." Kathy wagged a finger at Erin. "So I asked Chris to pick you up." She smiled at Zimmerman. Kathy was the only one, besides his mom, who called him by his real name, and he shuffled his oversize feet like a schoolboy.

"I only wanted a look," Erin said sheepishly.

"A chronology of this incident might be useful," Kathy said. "Why don't you walk me through it?"

Erin took a step forward but Kathy blocked her way.

"Metaphorically speaking, of course. I don't want your shoes in my crime scene. Just verbally walk me through the sequence of events."

Erin told her the story, as best she could remember, pointing here or there to describe where she stood, or where she crawled. Kathy nodded and took notes. While she talked, Erin noticed something catch Zimmerman's eye and he followed it over into the ditch on the far side of the road. Soon, he was poking in the moist earth with a stick. He returned a few minutes later, clutching a dirt-filled plastic Ziplock bag. Erin raised her eyebrows in query but he merely shrugged. When she was finished describing the events of the fire, Kathy picked up a cardboard box marked Evidence and showed Erin the contents.

"What is it?" She peeped inside but the reddish melted plastic was unrecognizable.

"It used to be a red plastic jerry can," Kathy told her. "Ring a bell?"

"Nope."

"Gina's uncle Darryl said they kept one by the back door, for customer emergencies. She'd lend it to people who'd run out of gas or he'd use it to fill the lawnmower tank once a week. Do you remember seeing it?"

A memory sparked. "There were fumes when I first came into the store. I can't be positive but it sure smelled like gasoline."

"We're investigating the probability that an accelerant was used here. The fire investigator has debris samples and we'll send them off for confirmation. Unfortunately the plastic on this container is so melted that we won't get a print off it."

"What about the fire extinguisher?" Erin asked.

"I already seized that as evidence," Kathy told her, "but same story. There isn't a whole lot we can do to retrieve fingerprints when heat like this vaporizes everything. We might find other trace evidence."

"It sounds like a whole lot of bad news."

"Not all bad news. Dave was working last night and he seized a fairly large quantity of duct tape that was used on Gina. There's an excellent chance of developing prints from that using Gentian Violet."

Erin's face was blank, so Kathy explained. "It's basically a dye we use because it reveals latent fingerprints on the sticky side of tape."

"Oh," Erin said. "What you and Dave do is pretty much alchemy to me, but I sure appreciate the results."

"You know how Dave is," Kathy continued. "He's not in a hurry for anything, so I'll check up on him later and maybe I can motivate him to get it done." She stopped. "Speaking of getting things done, I did see a possibility on that thing you talked to me about at the lab."

"You don't need to speak cryptically," Erin told her. "Z-man knows. He feels the same way I do."

"Well, then," Kathy said. "Those two Budweiser cans were a sweaty, smeary mess but I did get a partial print off the unopened one. Do you have a suspect? It could save time."

Erin almost blurted her latest theory. She bit her tongue. Kathy would think that suspecting such an old man was a wildly ridiculous notion.

"No. No one yet," Erin said, and Zimmerman's face involuntarily twitched at the omission.

"Okay," said Kathy slowly, narrowing her eyes slightly. "I'll send them off to NCIC as soon as I have a batch. It'll be easier to slip them in unnoticed that way."

Erin's expectations sank to a new low. What were the chances that sweaty, smeary, partial fingerprints could be matched by the FBI's National Database? The person's prints would already have to be on file related to a criminal conviction. It was doubtful that Gunther was in the system.

Kathy took in Erin's burnt face, bandaged arms, and sizzled hair, her gaze penetrating and a little bit uncomfortable. "You look like you've been staked out in the hot desert for a week. You need to go home now." She turned back to her investigation, leaving Erin to Officer Zimmerman.

"You heard the lady, Cinder Princess," he said. "Let's get you back home and tucked in. If you want, I'll set you up a little old lady command post like I did for my mama." He guffawed and slapped his knee at precisely the same moment Erin cuffed him on the shoulder.

"So, what's in the bag, Zeee? You find evidence across the road?"

His Adam's apple bobbed before he answered. "Bugs. I found a few nice fat mealworms in the ditch." He patted the plastic bag in his breast pocket. "I thought my little buddies might appreciate a treat."

"So, Picasso is the speckled frog and Merlin is—" she teased.

"No," he interrupted impatiently. "Merlin is my veiled chameleon and Picasso is a leopard gecko." He looked at her, suddenly realizing she was teasing. "I guess you knew that. They're very hungry," he added in his defense.

He dropped Erin off at home and she headed up to the front door, Fiona happily following as if she'd actually gone for a walk. It was after noon and she had only a few hours left to make good on her promise to Allie. She thumbed the screen on her iPhone as soon as the door closed.

"Hello, Children's Services. How can I help you?" The voice on the phone sounded bored and not eager to help at all. Erin decided to sound business-like and see if she could wheedle a few snippets of information out of professional courtesy. To her surprise she was soon chatting to the supervisor. Joan Watson said she was a distant relative, and how was her mother? Go figure. Erin knew her family was big, but she had never bothered to keep track of who begat who. She should pay more attention. There might be vast untapped investigative resources to which she was oblivious.

Joan turned out to be quite a nice lady, but a terrible gossip, which pleased Erin. During the half hour conversation, she learned that a number of social workers had been out to Gunther Schmidt's house over the last two years after Lily's mom ran off. At first, they had considered placing the child up for adoption, but Gunther had stepped forward. As her grandfather, he'd committed to raising her himself and nine-year old Lily wanted to stay. He only had his pension to live on, so they arranged a monthly stipend to help with costs, provided the social worker checked up on her from time to time.

He was testy about the whole situation but tolerated it for about a year. After that, he became increasingly paranoid. He said he was tired of social workers going through his stuff all the time, and told them he didn't want their money after all. The stipend stopped and since then, no one had officially been allowed on his property.

That's when the Lutheran Ladies took up the cause. They delivered baked goods weekly under the guise of doing their Christian duty for the old widower. He ate their pies and their cakes and their Nanaimo bars until one day, they suggested his place wasn't good enough for Lily. They told him Lily needed a mother and would be better off in a God-fearing Lutheran home.

The ladies later reported to Children's Services that Gunther went nuts. He yelled that they could all burn in hell and chased them off his property. The story varies about whether or not he had his shotgun, but the Lutheran Ladies never returned.

Joan said she had gone to the school to check on Lily herself, but the girl told her she was fine. Said she liked living with her grandpa. Her school attendance was satisfactory so there really was nothing else they could do.

Erin made notes while Joan talked. When they finished, she sat back and read through them again. She underlined the word paranoid and then she underlined Lutheran Ladies. She was pretty sure Dolores Johnson belonged to that group. She wrote a $ sign and circled it. Where was Gunther getting the money? A senior's pension was not enough to pay for beer and raise a young girl. Is that why he took it from Gina's store? Why would he want to hurt her if she didn't make him pay? What secrets did he keep?

Erin closed her notebook. She needed to talk to Gina.

CHAPTER TEN

I walk straight in through the main doors and nobody notices me at all. I'm not sure why I came. I don't even have a plan. They were making such a big deal on the news yesterday, and I guess I'm curious.

The people that I pass look through me like I am invisible, or like I belong, which are really the same thing. I must be here to visit a relative. Everyone is going somewhere and they just can't get there fast enough. A red-faced nurse brushes past me, her attention on an old man who's making his big getaway in a wheelchair.

"Mr. Stevenson! Mr. Stevenson," she calls. "No, dear. You can't go that way." In a few hurried strides, she catches up to him and takes hold of the handles. He sits there like a potato. Suddenly he flaps his arms around.

"No! I have to get on the train!"

The nurse dodges his poorly aimed punch. Unfazed, she briskly pivots the chair around. She doesn't even glance toward me. Not once.

It would suck to be a nurse chasing forgetful old guys around in your multicolored cartoon character pajamas all day long. She's telling him he can get on the train tomorrow, but now it's time for his medicine. He's still pissed and is grumbling loudly, but he can't do anything about it. Stupid old man. I'd kill myself before I ever let that happen to me. As they pass, I turn to closely examine a poster on the wall about hand washing. I wait until the nurse has wheeled him away and avoid the elevator to take the stairs up.

Halfway down the hall on the second floor I slip inside a little kitchen when no one is around. There is a sink and a coffee maker with a stack of insulated cups beside it. There is also an ice maker and a fridge. I open it, of course, and see the shelves lined with juice boxes, cans of ginger ale, and plastic wrapped sandwiches. I take a random sandwich and pocket it. I swipe a ginger ale too, popping the top right away. It's nice and cold.

I am starting to enjoy my visit. All the activity and the smells, and so many people to watch. Downstairs, the visitors are agitated. There is lots of pacing and checking the clock and tense faces. Up here, they are relaxed, sitting around in the patient lounge watching TV or staring out the window. It's like the worst has already happened and there is nothing more they can do but wait it out.

I pause by a laundry cart in the hallway and consider stealing a lab coat or something but I decide there is no need. No one has noticed me. I walk past and keep going. Lots of people hate the smell of hospitals but I don't mind at all. It smells like antiseptic and cleaning products, and who doesn't like that?

Finally, I see Gina's name on the whiteboard by the nurse's station and walk down to Room 34B. Outside, I stop for moment with my hand on the door, and almost change my mind. I take another sip of my ginger ale and swallow slowly. My heart pounds quicker when I think about what I might find inside. That's more like it.

In case she has a visitor, I open the door real slow. She is alone. There she is, lying on the bed. She looks dead to me. Her hair is squashed all flat under white gauze dressing that wraps around her head, but short choppy hairs are poking out the sides. She has one tube in her vein, one in her nose, and her face is swollen up like a jack 'o lantern. I hold my hand out in front of her mouth and remember how she looked with the duct tape. I rise up on my toes and my body begins to vibrate. I realize I am feeling a little intoxicated thinking about it. Maybe I should have brought more tape.

I grin and bend close to her for a better look. She doesn't smell like shampoo any more. She looks like shit and smells like hospital. I can't believe I accomplished all that with one tap from the fire extinguisher and a half roll of duct tape. It was so easy, and so worth it.

Her eyelids are shut tight but they start twitching and I wonder what she is dreaming about. Dying? I back out and quietly close the door behind me.

* * *

Erin tentatively entered room 34B. Gina was asleep. Her eyes were swollen and she would have a couple of shiners to show for a while. The small basket of flowers Erin had purchased at the hospital's gift shop seemed so inadequate. Erin slid her offering onto the tray table and sat in the plastic visitor's chair, tapping one foot.

She watched Gina's vital signs displayed on the monitor, heart rate steady at seventy-five and blood pressure one-twenty-four over seventy-two. That, at least, was completely normal. The occasional bleep of medical equipment, the ticking of the clock and the whisper of the oxygen feed were the only sounds in the room. She fidgeted in the veritable vacuum of activity. Acutely aware of the large-faced analog clock grinding away each minute as it passed, she straightened the flower basket on the table. Then she aligned it with one edge. She straightened it once more before she was satisfied.

Someone had carelessly dropped a magazine beside the bed, so she picked it up and rifled through. She was pretty sure it wasn't being read for the articles about motorcycles. The object of interest was probably the cover image of a scantily clad blonde astride a shiny Harley. Nearly half the pages also featured young women wearing bikinis. Erin placed it onto the table and straightened it too. Then she jumped to her feet to pace. Sitting still was not something she enjoyed.

Twenty minutes later, she sat down in the plastic chair and reconsidered the merit of the motorcycle magazine. She had already fetched a plastic tumbler of ice water, placed atop a carefully arranged napkin on the side table. The straw had been bent to a perfect ninety-degree angle. Erin thumbed halfway through the magazine and then returned to page twenty-three. That dark haired girl with the tool belt had amazing abs.

"You like my motoporn mag?" Gina tore the oxygen tubes from her nostrils and rolled over, grunting in the process.

She stood up so quickly she almost toppled the table. Like a kid caught snooping through adult TV channels, she hastily closed the magazine and put it back. "I was just reading—" Erin cut short the clichéd lie.

One corner of Gina's cracked lips pulled upward and she focused a pair of amused but bloodshot eyes on her. Lying in stiff wrinkled sheets, swathed in gauze bandages, Gina looked unfamiliar, for the first time truly vulnerable. Erin was unsure of how to proceed. She held the straw in the glass of ice water while Gina drank.

"Page twenty-three is my favorite too," she said after sating her thirst.

Erin placed the tumbler back on the table, squarely in the middle of the napkin. She flushed when Gina's lips curved upward again.

"You're cute when you blush." Gina's eyes took in Erin's bandaged forearms and singed hair. "But that's not why you're here."

Erin shook her head silently.

"You want to know what I remember." Gina sighed and leaned back on the pillow. "The nurse said that your boys already came but I don't remember what I told them."

"Detective Williams is investigating the fire and the attempted mur—what was done to you." Erin paused for a second but Gina's eyes did not stray from hers. "I talked to him this morning and he said he came by to see you about three o-clock yesterday afternoon, after I'd already gone home. He took your statement but you weren't making much sense. He's going to come see you again later."

"I sort of remember weird stuff."

"Weird how?"

"The nurse said I was ranting about an evil troll stalking me." She held two fingers to her lips.

"Maybe it was the medication," Erin offered.

"Yeah, maybe it was the drugs, but I still feel creeped out, and a bit paranoid, because I felt like I was being watched that night too."

"After I left the Stop 'N Go, what do you remember about that night?"

"Your girlfriend is really cute." Gina tried to waggle an eyebrow under the bandages.

"Stay on task here."

"Fine. I remember being pissed about how Gunther treated me. Yeah, he's a piece of work, like me," she snorted, "but he wasn't really a bad guy. I already mentioned that he used to come in once in a while when I was closing up for the night. We would sit on lawn chairs behind the store, slap blackflies, and talk for hours. He told me all about fishing and hunting, but he didn't hunt much any more. He liked to go out and watch the animals. Any time of day or night, he knew where they were feeding, or where they bedded down. Sometimes I'd be putting out the garbage at the end of shift and I'd see him appear out of the bush across the road like a ghost. Then he'd see me and he'd get this goofy smile on his face. He'd come over and greet me like family." Gina motioned for the water and Erin passed it to her. She sucked through the straw before continuing.

"Anyway, after you left that night I remember doing the cleanup, washing the floors, restocking and facing all the shelves. That's when I got the heebie jeebies, like someone was watching me, but there was nobody around."

Erin nodded without interrupting.

"I went to the bathroom where I keep the supplies and I cleaned the mop in the utility sink. I remember grabbing the window cleaner because I wanted to get all the slimy handprints off the front glass doors but I don't remember actually cleaning them. There's like a gap in time there. Then I remember hallucinating about us laying outside together looking at the stars." Gina looked to Erin who neither confirmed nor denied.

"I dunno," Gina said finally. "It was a nice hallucination. Better than the troll. Anyway, the next thing I remember was when the nurses cut duct tape out of my hair in Hospital Emergency."

"Do you know who did this?" Erin asked her point blank.

Gina raised a hand to cover her trembling mouth. "I think I was closer to him than my own dad. I can't believe he would—"

"You think Gunther did this?"

"Don't you? He was so angry that I barely recognized him." Gina twisted her body under the wrinkled sheet. "Who else would it be? He's suddenly not the guy I know. If he's capable of this, what is happening to Lily?"

"Omigosh!" Erin bolted for the door.

CHAPTER ELEVEN

"That was awesome coffee, Erin, but you can keep Princess FluffyPants here," Zimmerman said. "I prefer my pets quiet and much, much less—um fluffy." He slid his uniform coat off the back of the kitchen chair and bent to brush tufts of Persian hair from his trousers. After he'd finished, Wrong-Way Rachel made one more pass around his legs, depositing a fresh batch of fur. He exhaled loudly.

"Aw come on, Z-man. She's not so bad. She has ninja moves that would make you jealous." With one socked foot, Erin scooted Rachel away from his uniform. Was she really sticking up for that infernal cat?

"I promise I will keep looking until I find the kid. I've tapped all my sources and everyone is out looking, but nobody has seen hide nor hair of Gunther or Lily since the fire. I was out to his place today and there is no one around. His old truck is in the driveway but they are gone." Dodging the affectionate dog in the hallway, Zimmerman made his way to the front door, where his enormous boots stood side-by-side like two soldiers in the entrance. "I will check to see if his boat is missing. He might be out fishing and this is all a big misunderstanding." He jammed oversize feet into his boots and stepped onto the front porch.

"Yeah, a big misunderstanding. I hope you don't think he took her fishing so they can spend quality time together!" Erin said sharply.

"I was being facetious. You know me better than that. This whole thing stinks and I promise you that I am on it." He scratched at the back of his scalp with a hand commensurate in size with his humungous feet. Erin's nose wrinkled in amusement. He was like an overgrown puppy, all paws and angles, but immeasurably adorable, and she was as fond of him as a brother. "Almost forgot to tell you, Kathy wants you to call her when you are back."

"I'm going nuts, Z-man." Erin wheedled. "I need—"

"Sorry, but I have to side with Derek Peterson on this one. He's our Acting Sergeant right now and I know you think he's a jackass, but have you looked in the mirror lately? You truly are not ready to come back to work, SuperFairyNinjaPrincess—"

"You're overdoing it and it's not geeky cute anymore," Erin held up a stern finger to silence him and he stopped, surprised.

"RoboWonderGirl!" he finally blurted, chortling.

"That's it! I'm not wasting any more good coffee on you. From now on, you can drink that swill down at the station and call me on the phone." She frowned, and stood with hands on hips until his tone softened.

"Please, Erin, give it a little time. Besides, right now you can't hold a service weapon in that blistery paw of yours. I will find that old man and I will find the kid. In the meantime, I promise to tell you everything."

She backed off a half step and gave a curt nod.

"You're not going to accomplish anything dragging your sorry self around town." He turned to go but couldn't resist a parting shot. "Even Iggy the Iguana, rest his scaly soul, knew when it was time to hole up somewhere until he was done molting." Walking back to his cruiser, Zimmerman did a smug little hop when Erin's front door slammed.

* * *

The patrol car pulled away from the front of the house right before a black Mini Cooper zipped into the driveway. A large piece of cardboard was affixed to the roof with bright red plastic tape and the crack in the rear window had spidered all the way from one edge to the other. Allie exited and retrieved her computer case from the trunk.

"Honey, I'm home!" she called out, blustering through the door. The pets immediately love-mobbed her and she dropped her bag to snuggle both of them into her lap. "I missed you and yeah, I missed you too, pumpkin." The dog gazed at her with complete adoration and the cat crawled onto her shoulder to greet her with a cheerful chirrup.

"When you are done making goo-goo noises at the pets, I could use a hand in here," Erin called back.

Allie got to her feet and gathered her bags to join her in the kitchen, pets trotting happily behind her. She dropped her packages on the counter and stifled a laugh when she saw Erin. With one handful of wadded up gauze, and an unattended tube of antibiotic ointment oozing itself onto the table, Erin was clearly losing the struggle. Allie gently took the gauze from her and expertly rolled it up.

"This must be the wrong stuff! I can't believe it's the wrong stuff!"

"It works better if you roll it up first," Allie suggested, hiding her smile. "I told you I would help you when I got home. You need to be a little more patient, hon." Erin meekly watched while she efficiently dressed her wounds and made sure the gauze was not too tight on raw blistered skin.

"This is driving me crazy!" Erin sounded whiney and stopped herself. "I'm sorry, this is difficult for me. I don't like being helpless. With everything bandaged, it's hard to do things. Even making coffee is a chore that takes forever! I'm trying but I'm not good at being useless."

"I rented us a movie."

"Is it subtitled?" Erin's tone bordered on petulance.

"No, it's in English, but I can't guarantee they won't use big words."

"Does it have the word triumphant in the reviews or on the cover?"

"Noooo," Allie responded, sarcastically dragging out the vowel.

"Does stuff get blown up? Does at least one person die?" Erin smiled.

"Yes, dozens I'm sure."

"Is there a parental warning on it?"

"Yes."

"Are you going to hate it, but you'll watch it anyway, to be with me?" Erin's eyes twinkled in merriment.

"Maybe," Allie said, kissing her cheek. "I'll make the popcorn."

* * *

Two hours later, Erin nudged her girlfriend's knee. Curled up on the other end of the sofa, wearing fleece pajamas with a kitty cat pattern, Allie looked as innocent and pure as a sleeping child. She could watch an agonizing three-hour foreign language drama with not so much as a blink, but always fell asleep during action movies. Brown hair tumbled around her shoulders and Erin wanted to smooth the errant locks with her fingers.

"The movie's over," she said in a soft voice. Allie woke with a start and sat straight up off the sofa.

"I know where she is!" Allie announced.

"Who? Lily?"

"She's at home. Right now! She is standing outside Gunther's workshop, shivering all alone in her little nightie."

"Did you dream this?" Erin met Allie's eyes. Then she rose to her feet and paced the living room floor purposefully.

"I don't know if I dreamt it. I just know." Allie said quietly. Erin noticed her change in body posture as she began to curl into herself.

"I believe you," she told her, more gently. "Let's go."

"Now?" Allie dubiously looked down at pajama clad legs.

"If she's there now, we need to go now," Erin said firmly. She flung open the front closet and gingerly pulled her denim jacket on, snapping her leather bag over one shoulder. The familiar weight of the pistol inside reassured her as the bag slapped against her ribs. Allie was right behind her, pajamas and all, pulling on a sweater and a pair of loafers.

At the sight of the little car in the driveway, with its cracked window, heat blistered paint, and cardboard covered sunroof, Erin stopped. She pursed her lips and appraised it for a moment before she fished her keys from her bag.

"Good idea," Allie said simply, without an accusatory tone. "It runs fine but it's pretty noisy, and I keep finding sharp bits of glass in the seat fabric."

Erin drove quickly and a little bit recklessly toward Gunther's place. The Toyota truck bounced over the uneven gravel road which narrowed to a single lane as they neared their destination. They rounded the final bend and, thanks to a pale wash of moonlight in the cloudless sky, the house became visible through the trees.

Gunther's Ford truck was parked in front of the old clapboard bungalow which rested, dark and desolate, in a small clearing between the scrubby brush and the river. Tall grass grew up around a faded green fiberglass canoe and an aluminum fishing boat, which lay overturned against the side of the shed.

The door hung halfway open and Erin snapped to attention when a tiny spark of light emitted from within. She strained her eyes into the darkness, but the flash did not come again. At the last moment, she stomped the brake pedal. Tires bit gravel and the Tacoma came to a stop in the driveway behind Gunther's Ford. She twisted the key to shut the engine off, but kept the headlights on.

She sat immobile in her seat, looking at the dark shed and then the equally unlit house. Alarmed, Allie mimicked her, attention fixed on the shed. Perhaps the flicker of light Erin had seen was only a reflection of the moon in the window pane. Perhaps not. Two sharp metallic pings from the engine stirred her to make a decision. The shed first and then the house.

She leaned across and retrieved a Xenon Mini Mag flashlight from the glove box and motioned for Allie to wait in the truck. Quietly getting out, she swore there was a muted thud the same moment she closed her door. She stood still but could not locate its source. Cautiously approaching, she took a quick peek in Gunther's truck. A squashed beer can lay in the truck bed along with rocks, grass and organic debris. Inside the cab, crumpled pieces of paper and fast food containers littered the interior floor mats. There was nothing that piqued her interest, and she turned to the shed.

Ignoring her signal to stay in the truck, Allie exited and swung the door shut. The heavy clunk reverberated through still air. Erin winced at the careless noise and assumed a protective position. The sound of the truck approaching would certainly have been audible, but a slamming door seemed inappropriately loud. Her senses heightened. She instinctively transferred weight to the balls of her feet and stepped in front of Allie. If she insisted on coming, she must remain behind her. They reached the gaping wooden door and Erin directed Allie to the side. There was no need to make themselves targets, silhouetted against the entrance.

Erin took a couple of quick peeks around the doorjamb with the flashlight. Nothing moved so she shone the light inside. Empty. It was a basic rural outbuilding, like a million others in the county, constructed of uninsulated plywood with a bare electrical bulb hanging from the ceiling. She found the switch and flipped it on. Cheerless yellow light flooded the single room and she stepped lightly onto the old wooden floor. Brittle boards creaked so loudly Erin feared they might be heard as far away as the house.

Inside was a sturdy work bench and stool, carefully hung hand tools, basic shelving, a battered metal cabinet, and a preponderance of neglected and forgotten items. One wall held rows of hooks festooned with boat nets, spinning rods, a hand cranked ice auger and other assorted fishing equipment. Each item was arranged in a determinedly logical manner with random junk later piled underneath.

She noticed a pair of old beavertail snowshoes above the door, like another man might hang a lucky horseshoe. As she looked around the shed, it was apparent that Gunther had once taken pride in, and tended to the organization of his belongings. Somewhere along the way he had lost interest and now the shed had become a repository for unwanted household goods.

"This is so creepy." Allie stood in the doorway, mouth downturned and nose wrinkled in distaste. Erin followed her eyes to the white-tail deer head mount hanging on the wall. It had collected dust over the years, which dulled the tawny hair and dimmed the brightness of its glass eyes. Nonetheless, it still bore the mark of expert craftsmanship.

"Relax honey. It's only taxidermy," Erin said, although Allie was now avoiding looking at it. "Lots of old guys used to do it for a hobby when I was a kid." She spied the little refrigerator under the counter and opened the door. A six-pack of Budweiser took up the middle shelf, a half loaf of bread and a stack of plastic wrapped cheese slices below. The shed was apparently not as abandoned as it first appeared.

"I'm sure it was different for people who grew up in urban centers," Erin told her. Auntie Vicky might have said tree huggers. "Taxidermy was common around here, it's part of the fabric of the country. My dad still has a set of moose antlers hanging in the garage."

Allie took a small step and placed the toes of her shoes onto the wooden floorboards of the shed where she stopped, rooted to the spot. Her eyes widened and her nostrils flared. Moisture misted her eyes but she did not move further in, nor did she back out. "It feels creepy in here. Creepy and angry. Like the whole place is covered by a dark smelly blanket and I don't want to be here."

Tears streaming down her face, Allie turned and bolted out the door. She kept up a brisk walk until her sweater and fleece pajamas were starkly illuminated by the truck's headlamps in the middle of the graveled driveway. In the harsh light, Erin could see her bend and place her hands on her thighs, panting.

Erin caught up to her and rubbed a hand across her back. "Are you ok?" For the first time, she realized that she had not given Allie time to change from her kitty cat pajamas.

"In my dream, I saw her standing there." Allie pointed her index finger toward a spot halfway between the house and the shed. "Right there." She paused until Erin prodded her to continue. "She was wearing a light blue nightie and she was alone." She stopped and clutched at her temple. "I feel a bit sick and I'm getting a headache. I'm going to wait in the truck."

"You stay there while I go check the house." Erin had barely started off toward the house when there was a tiny skittering noise beside the shed. She froze mid-step and waited. There it was again. Could Lily be afraid and hiding? She stepped carefully so as not to make a sound and homed in on the origin of the noise. The overturned fiberglass canoe. She crept up and, with one hand on the canoe's gunwale and the other holding the flashlight, she flipped it upright in one swift movement.

A panicked flash of white escaped, startling Erin backward. She righted herself in time to watch it thrash an erratic path through the tall grass and into the denser underbrush of the riverbank. She almost laughed out loud in relief and embarrassment. It was nothing more than a frightened jackrabbit. Lifting one end of the lightweight aluminum fishing boat, she peered underneath that as well. There were no other creatures in residence. She returned both boats to their original positions.

Satisfied, she continued to the house where everything was locked up tight. She shone her powerful flashlight through the windows and all appeared perfectly normal. Nothing moved in the yard. With no valid reason to break and enter, she climbed back into her truck.

In the passenger seat, Allie doubled over miserably, clutching her head. "I'm sorry," she whispered. "I was so sure she was here. I thought... Maybe I really am crazy."

"Maybe it was a mistake or maybe she's already gone," Erin said firmly, "but you are not crazy. She started the engine, turned the truck around and headed out the driveway.

* * *

After the truck's tail lights disappeared, a trap door in the floor of the shed tentatively creaked open, emitting a soft yellow glow. Two small pale hands grappled to prop it up with a stick and Lily emerged, tearing the bottom seam of her light blue nightgown on the latch in her haste. She crawled from the hole, agile as a fox, and plucked at the torn threads.

Dirty bare feet padding on the wood floor, she stepped lightly over to the refrigerator and withdrew a can of beer, popping the tab to take a tiny sip. She opened the metal cabinet and lifted one dark bottle from the top row of unlabeled chemicals. Sloshing the contents back and forth in the half empty bottle, she set it onto the workbench and reached to the rear of the shelf for a Hershey bar. She smiled. Her secret stash. She replaced the bottle and closed the cabinet soundlessly.

"Wo ist mein Bier?" A guttural voice made her jump and she quickly palmed the chocolate bar.

"Dummkopf! Hurry up and close the door!"

Beer in hand, candy hidden under her gown, Lily nimbly scurried down the ladder. The yellow glow beneath the floor winked out when she thumped the hatch behind.

CHAPTER TWELVE

It was nearly midnight and Allie, still too unsettled to go to bed, snuggled with the cat to watch a classic movie. Exhausted, Erin decided to try to get some sleep. She brushed her teeth, up and down in perfectly straight lines, rinsed her mouth and placed her toothbrush back in its holder. Nail clippers neatly nipped off the corkscrew ends of her singed bangs and she washed them down the drain. Her blistered arms gave her less pain now and she unwound the gauze bandages to examine them. Blisters oozed and she decided she'd better keep them covered a while longer. She rummaged under the vanity for the bandaging supplies and headed down the stairs for Allie's expert help.

Halfway down, she heard voices in the living room. Company? So late? Was something wrong? She cautiously padded down the hall and was surprised to see Allie slumped in front of her laptop computer. Although Erin had only met her once, she immediately recognized the woman on the other end of the video call. She stopped in the doorway, unsure if she should be invading her girlfriend's privacy.

Allie swiveled around at the sound of footsteps. "The dreams and premonitions are kind of freaking me out so I told my foster mom," Allie whispered. "We're just talking it through." She pulled over a second chair for Erin, who nudged the stubbornly sleeping feline from the cushion and sat. Erin waggled her fingers at the computer screen and Allie's foster mom smiled warmly back.

"Nice to see you, Erin," Judy said.

"It's nice to see you too," she replied politely. "How is Marcel?"

"He's good. He's working a lot lately." Judy brushed a hand through unruly bangs and sighed. "He wants us to retire in two years, you know, Freedom 55 and all that."

"That would be nice," Erin said, and Judy smiled.

The pets always gravitated to Allie. Under the desk, she had her toes tucked under Fiona, who sprawled end to end. The dog sighed contentedly.

She discreetly touched a hand to her girlfriend's elbow and whispered, "coffee?"

Allie answered with a nod, mouthing "decaf," then she and Judy continued talking as if they'd never been interrupted.

* * *

Allie turned up the computer's volume when the coffee grinder in the kitchen squealed. "I thought it was over." She shouted to Judy above the noise. "Pardon? I said that it's been such a long time that I thought it was all over." She lowered her voice when the grinder stopped. "I'm not sure if I can go through it again." Her shoulders deflated. In the background, the espresso machine hissed while it steamed milk.

The cat hopped up onto the desk, furry body blocking the webcam. Allie smoothed the hair between the cat's ears and deftly scooped her onto her lap. Wrong Way Rachel circled once and then settled. With her view cleared, she leaned forward toward the screen, as if the proximity was not merely virtual.

"You were always an amazingly strong girl, Alyssa," Judy consoled patiently. "Now you've grown into a wonderful woman." She paused and took a slow breath. "Do you remember that when you first came to our home, you used to have nightmares every night, and sometimes you'd panic during the day? You wouldn't even ride in a car for three months, and then you wouldn't let us drive on the highway for about a year!"

"And do you remember that stupid psychiatrist who didn't have a clue?" Allie retorted. She slouched in her chair like a surly adolescent. "He had such an annoying voice and he didn't understand a thing about me."

"Doctor Winkler did have quite an annoying voice," Judy conceded. "And he didn't see how amazing you are, but do you also remember that the nightmares went away after your sessions with him?"

Allie sat up straight and stared at the image on the computer screen. "I grew out of it! Are you seriously giving him credit for that?"

"Well, it's you who deserves the credit. I wondered if you ever realized that all the hours spent dreaming up ways to ignore his annoying voice helped you learn to control your own extraordinary mind. You taught yourself to focus your thoughts and to block out the disturbing images that plagued your sleep."

Allie nodded meekly, but her body again drooped in the chair, hands propping her chin on the desk. "I don't even like to think about it. It feels like it's still so close to me. Like there's a specter waiting in my peripheral vision and, if I turn my head to truly see, I'll be terrified all over again."

"When you were young you learned how to block things out of necessity because you needed to grow up like a regular kid. Now you're an adult and you shouldn't block that part of yourself forever. You might be missing an important piece of who you are. You are exceptionally intuitive and it can enrich your life if you learn to let it."

Allie frowned but she was listening.

"Instead of feeling cursed, maybe you need to consider it a gift. Other kids drew pretty pictures, or were able to spell the alphabet backwards in their heads. You, on the other hand, always knew what you were getting for Christmas, and surprise birthday parties—forget about it!" She laughed and Allie grinned reluctantly. "You found all the neighborhood's lost puppies and kittens and your friends came to you for dating advice because you could always tell them if they were seeing the Wrong Guy. You were responsible for saving a half dozen of your little foster brothers & sisters with your two second warning. Unfortunately, you also were sensitive about bad things that happened and that's what was so hard for you as a small child."

"Two second warning?"

"That's what Marcel & I used to call it." Judy hid a tiny embarrassed giggle. "He figured it out first. He noticed that you'd blurt out something random, and two seconds later it would happen. When he heard you say stuff like that, he'd yell, *Judy! Two second warning! Go check the twins!* You remember those busy three year olds who got into everything? I'd run to their room, and sure enough those little guys had snuck out of bed. I'd catch them plugging the toilet with toys, or trying to climb out the second story window for an adventure. Who knows how many Band-Aids we'd have gone through if you hadn't been around!"

"I do remember," Allie said thoughtfully. "And I remember the time I told you someone needed to go to the neighbor's house right away but I didn't know why. I had been trying to do my homework but I couldn't concentrate because I kept thinking that the most important thing in the world for me was to hurry and tell you. After I told you, I could go back and get my homework done."

"Yes, I did what you asked and found that Mrs. Christie had fallen and needed to go to the hospital," Judy nodded. "If you hadn't told me, it might have been even more awful for her."

"I never realized..." Between thumb and forefinger, Allie pulled thoughtfully at her bottom lip.

Erin reappeared beside her and slid a steaming cup of coffee onto the desk. She took Allie's hand and her tone was serious. "What you know is important. You can help people. Gina would have died in that fire if you hadn't sent me."

"I don't know how to do this," Allie breathed.

"You were only a scared child when you figured out how to block things to protect yourself," Judy answered. "Now you are a grown woman with such strength and resilience that I am continually in awe. It's time to stop hiding and believe that you can take control of this gift of yours."

"I have confidence in you too," Erin said, squeezing her hand. Allie stared at their intertwined fingers for a moment and then turned back to the computer screen.

"I'm afraid. What if I'm wrong?" Her forehead puckered. "I was wrong tonight. I thought I knew where to find the missing little girl."

"Sometimes it took a while for you to understand what you sensed, but you were never wrong. You should try again," Judy urged.

"I will. You always know what to say. You've been a good mom." She let that last word hang in the air, and it was a long time before her foster mom composed herself enough to respond.

"You've never called me that before." Judy dabbed misted eyes with the corner of her sleeve.

"I meant to. I'm sorry. I should have." Allie terminated the call before her own tears streamed down. She buried her face in Erin's shoulder. Between them, the cat wiggled from Allie's lap and stalked across the desktop. The dog stayed put, guarding her warm feet.

"I need to tell you about my other mom," Allie murmured. "My mom before I went to live with Judy and Marcel."

"Oh." This topic had always been strictly off-limits. She practically held her breath, afraid that, like a wild forest creature, any movement would stop the words that needed to come.

"I never knew my dad," Allie began, edging tentatively into her story. "When I was little, my mom told me that he was a musician. She said they met in Winnipeg when she snuck into a bar with her underage friends. Lee Fisher was barely 18 but already on the road with his band. He was exciting, mysterious and so very unlike anyone she had ever met."

Allie adjusted herself nervously in her chair. "They were young and foolish and he had gone to the next gig before she found out she was pregnant. By then, she understood that she really didn't know much about him so she decided not to tell him about me. He was an Ojibway from Northwestern Ontario and she always told me he was the most handsome guitar player she'd ever seen. She said that I got my good looks from him, because I sure never inherited mom's strawberry blonde hair."

Erin waggled her eyebrows in approval.

"She was still a teenager when I was born, but even though her parents pressured her, she wouldn't give me up. Irish Catholic, they wanted her to marry a nice boy from church. She wouldn't be forced to marry any boy and it got so bad that she ended up cutting off contact with them. She moved to Toronto, finished high school and raised me practically by herself. She always said I was the finest mistake she ever made."

"What a story. Your mom must have been something." Erin leaned closer.

"Yeah," she said. "I used to skip beside her when she walked me to school, and sometimes she would skip too. She was so pretty with her strawberry hair and green eyes. I loved her freckles." Allie let out a protracted sigh. "She was a good mom."

"I like the name she gave you. Alyssa." Erin let the delectable word roll slowly off the end of her tongue.

"I prefer Allie. My mom called me Allie." She let silence hang between them and Erin wasn't sure she would bring herself to continue. Finally, she spoke. "She was like me, or I am like her." She bit back, but the words had already left her lips.

"She knew things?" Erin prompted, and waited. A half minute ticked by before Allie filled the silence.

"Yes. She was totally unfazed when the babysitter would make a big deal about me knowing things. She'd just say 'mmm hmm' and pay the sitter. My mom would pick up the phone right before it rang and we'd both run to answer the door before we heard the doorbell. It was like a game and great fun to play with her."

"She knew about people too. She tried to teach me how to tell who was good and who was not, by noticing how it felt when I was near them. That sounds silly, doesn't it?"

"No, go on." Erin shivered and surreptitiously reached up to scratch the nape of her neck.

"She said something about the air being messed up around the bad people and we could feel it in our skin and our minds if we paid attention." She glanced self-consciously at Erin. "I was six, remember, and I didn't have a very sophisticated vocabulary."

Erin nodded.

"We used to practice at the bus stop. We'd stand by someone and she'd whisper to me, messy or not messy? I'd be very quiet until I could tell, and then I'd smile or frown my answer back to her. She looked so happy when I guessed it right and I really wanted to make her happy."

"My mom finally had enough money to buy a car when I was in first grade. She said it made her feel rich. It was a little red car, I don't remember what kind, but she drove it fast. She always buckled me up in the back seat and I watched her eyes in the rear view mirror. She felt so far away up there. Then everything went wrong." Allie's body tensed and Erin softly squeezed her hand.

"You don't have to tell me if you don't want to."

"I need to tell someone. I've never told this to anyone. It's killing me." She looked Allie square in the eye. "And I trust you."

"When you're ready."

Fiona's tail thumped on the floor and Allie shielded her face with both hands, like a little girl. "It's my fault," she said in tiny sobs. "I'm the reason my mom died."

Erin's heart lurched. "You were a child! What could you possibly have done? You must be mistaken."

Wrong-Way Rachel chose that moment to leap onto Allie's shoulder and she grasped at her desperately, pinning the squirming feline to her chest. She relaxed a little and the cat purred.

"It is my fault," she choked out. "I know I was being a precocious little monster that day. I don't remember where we were going. I do remember that I wanted so badly to go to McDonald's, but my mom said I should eat the lunch she'd packed. I kicked the back of her seat with my pink winter boots and yelled that I wanted a Happy Meal. She told me to stop kicking so I yelled louder. I saw her eyes frown at me in the mirror and that's the last thing I remember before the accident."

"It was an accident," Erin protested. "You didn't cause it!"

"If she didn't have me kicking her seat and yelling, my mom would have seen that truck coming off the side road. She would never have hit it."

Depleted, Allie collapsed into herself, sobbing wetly into the cat's fur. "This gift has been a horrible weight on me ever since she died. It is a constant reminder of my mother and what I did to her!"

Erin wrapped her arms around Allie and the cat, rocking both.

* * *

"Whatcha doin' honey?" Pajama clad, Erin stretched her spine and wandered into the kitchen in search of the morning coffee she craved. Allie bolted upright from her chair and clunked down the lid on her laptop. Wrong-Way Rachel, who had been viewing the screen from her spot on the table, leapt down in the commotion, landing softly on three kitty feet. She stalked out of the room.

"I forgot to make c-coffee," Allie stammered. Her face flushed right to her ears. "I'm sorry. I was going to make you toast too." At her feet, the dog thumped her tail hollowly on the floor, remaining silently loyal to her master.

"Since when are you my personal servant?" Erin leaned over to ruffle the hair between Fuzzy Fiona's soft ears. Her interest was piqued by that computer and by Allie's distracting behavior. When Allie opened the cupboard to find coffee, she lifted the screen and a knowing smile spread across her lips. "You don't have to take a silly test to tell you what you already know."

Allie turned around and her blush intensified from pink to

crimson when she saw Erin looking at the screen. "You're right, it's stupid, but every single time I've taken that online test, it says I have zero psychic ability."

"You've taken it more than once?" Erin's amusement faded with Allie's obvious distress. "You can't believe that stuff. It's created by someone who doesn't have a clue and there is absolutely no veracity in the results."

"I know, it's probably a basement programmer trying to harvest user information. But I need to understand if all this is real, or if I am losing my mind."

"You are real," Erin said. "That is not." She hugged her girlfriend and gently stroked her hair with her fingers. "You don't ever have to go out of your way to make me breakfast, baby. I'm a big girl. I will make myself a coffee and grab a sandwich from the Stop 'N—" She hesitated, realizing that her frequent visits to the store would be no more. It was a strange sensation, an unanticipated sense of loss. The Sportsman's Stop 'N Go, with its silly fish sign, had been a fixture in this town for as long as she could remember. "I'll pick something up for lunch somewhere."

Allie smiled at her, more relaxed now. "I, of all people, know what a load of crap there is on the internet."

"Why don't you tell me when you get these thoughts? Kind of like how your foster parents did it. They worked as a team with you, although you didn't realize it at the time."

She nodded reluctantly. "I guess I could. But they don't always make sense right away, or ever."

"Deal," Erin said. "You can call me whenever." She considered the inquisitive minds at work. "Or text me. That works better."

CHAPTER THIRTEEN

It's another day, like all the rest. Nothing is going to happen, nothing is going to change, until I make it. I take the path through the brush so I can't be spotted, and ease through the back porch window because the door's locked. When was the house ever locked? Where did the keys go? I grab a few things from the fridge and put them in my pack. Some granola bars, beef jerky, a package of cookies and a bag of Cheetos go in as well. The Cheetos bag is too large so I rip the top open, eat a few and squish the air out so it packs down.

In the master bedroom, I slide the old coffee can from the shelf and dump the money on the bed. There are at least six twenties in the pile but I can't bother to count all the lesser bills. I wad them up and cram them into my pack. The brown handled lock blade knife from the bedside table fits nicely in my pocket.

I am tired of waiting. Today's the day this panther needs to pounce. I will rid myself of this place, these people, this life. I scoot down the path to the shed and quietly slip inside. Today, I have a special treat. I use the bottle opener in the workbench drawer to pop the cap on a beer I brought in my pack and take a long swallow. It's almost warm, but I don't mind. It's the taste of power. The taste of freedom. No longer will I bow down to a lesser being.

The storage cabinet has my surprise and I retrieve the unlabeled bottle from the top shelf. The remainder of its contents replace the beer I drank, and I flip the it upside down to drain every last drop. The angry mix fizzes so I mop it up with a rag and snap the cap on, bending it back into shape with a pair of needle nose pliers. I hold it up to the light to examine my genius. It ain't perfect, but it will do. Someone is in for a big surprise, and someone is going to have a very good day. That second someone is me.

I rap twice on the wood floor hatch and hide behind the workbench. There is a dull thunk below and the hatch pops up a crack. I see his slitted eyes through the sliver of an opening, and they focus on the beer bottle I've placed there, like a baited rodent trap. The hatch door creaks up a few more inches.

"Ah, it's you," he says to the air, and smiles. "Danke." His hand reaches out for the bottle and returns a moment later for the opener.

You're welcome. I grimace through clenched teeth. I wait until he's gone back down the ladder and head for the trail. This panther is deadly. Goodbye forever, old man.

* * *

Erin was dressed and at work fifteen minutes before her shift began, with an acceptable looking submarine sandwich in a plastic bag.

"Hey stranger." Officer Ryan Striker slid into a chair in the briefing room and adjusted the radio on his belt. He reached over to pointedly pluck a wisp of cat hair from Erin's uniform collar and then directed his gaze to a larger clump adhered to the hem of her trousers.

"Your wife lets you go out like that?" He smirked mischievously.

"I can't keep up." She shrugged. "I'm a love magnet."

Striker's smirk widened to an amused smile and then his expression darkened. He laid two fingers on the newly healed pink skin above her knuckles, where the gauze bandages ended. His bristly eyebrows puckered in genuine concern.

"I'm all good. Just need to keep my forearms wrapped for another day to avoid infection."

"Hey pint-sized partner, are you sure you should be here?" Hired at the same time and now virtually inseparable, Officer Mark Jenssen plopped down beside Striker. He tucked his compact frame into the wheeled office chair and rocked backward, pointing his boots tippy toes to the ground. His smooth face settled into its customarily satisfied grin.

Erin nodded at him and he smiled back. Constantly moving,

Jenssen had the energy of a teenager after an espresso. He drummed his ballpoint pen on the faux wood finish of the conference table and tapped one heel simultaneously. The two men always reminded her of the Muppets Ernie and Bert, but Erin would never say that out loud. Striker cemented the look with his overly animated eyebrows. They were good, honest workers. It would take a great deal of effort not to like them.

"I got the green light from my doctor yesterday," she said smugly, although she had nearly bullied him into clearing her for duty. In return, she'd promised to keep unhealed skin covered, and not to do anything stupid at work. She became aware that she was also tapping her foot under the table. It sounded like she and Jenssen were the percussionists in a badly composed song. She made a conscious effort to stop, and instead oriented her ballpoint pen horizontally on the table in front of her. She tilted it and oriented it vertically with the edge.

It had been two agonizingly long days since she and Allie had taken their night time excursion to Gunther's property and she was so glad to be back at work. She had been wasting crucial time. Skipping the part about Allie's dream, Erin had kept Zimmerman in the loop about her search, and he had also dutifully kept her apprised of his efforts to locate Lily. Erin was disheartened that they had, so far, both come up empty.

A faint blip alerted Erin to a new text message and she nearly tore the button from her shirt pocket in her haste to check it.

Allie: U THERE?

Erin: Yup

She tilted the screen away from the Muppets to respond.

Allie: U SAID TO TELL YOU EVERYTHING. HERE GOES.

Erin: Why r u yelling? Something bad happening?

She held her phone close to her chest.

Allie: SORRY, ANDROID GLITCH. CAPS STUCK ON :-)

Erin: Get an iPhone.

She smirked indulgently. It was not often she could tease Allie about technology.

Allie: HA. THAT WOULD BE A STEP DOWN ;-)

Erin: Ok. What's up?

Allie: CAN'T GET THE OLD MAN OUT OF MY HEAD TODAY. FEELS LIKE SOMETHING BAD IS HAPPENING.

Erin: Like what?

Allie: I KEEP SEEING HIM HIDING IN THE JUNGLE. HIDING FROM MEN WITH GUNS. HE HEARS A LOT OF GUNS.

Erin: Did you say Jungle or was that another glitch?

Allie: JUNGLE. AS IN TARZAN. I KNOW IT'S WEIRD. YOU SAID TO TELL YOU, SO I'M TELLING YOU.

Erin: Ok. sorry. Anything else?

Allie: HE'S IN A CAVE OR SOMETHING. MIGHT BE HURT

Erin: hurt? how?

Allie: NOT SURE. FELT HIS ENERGY GO AWAY AND THEN NOTHING. HALF HOUR AGO.

Erin: Ok.

Allie: Got to go. Bad headache. Might have to call in sick.

Erin: Try ice first. Text me later ok? <3 TTYL

Erin reviewed the text, imagining Allie at that very moment, curled into herself, massaging temples with fingertips. Could her messages be any more cryptic? No wonder she had a hard time sorting her thoughts out if they made this much sense. There was a pang of guilt for encouraging her to embrace the one thing that gave her such pain.

Zimmerman walked in, carrying the clipboard with the Sergeant's Log, and she quickly slipped the iPhone back into her pocket. If he was conducting briefing, that meant Acting-Sergeant Derek Peterson was not. She sat straight up and paid attention, working to catch Zimmerman's eye while he shuffled through pages to familiarize himself before beginning.

"Derek called in sick again today," Zimmerman began, by way of explanation. Beside her, Ernie and Bert exchanged concerned glances. "Thank God Erin is back, but we are still short-handed. Yesterday was such a clusterf—" Deeply ingrained manners overrode his obvious frustration. "Uh, we received a high volume of calls that we were unable to properly attend to yesterday. This resulted in complaints about service from the public. The administration has authorized me to call in two additional officers to help us clear the backlog of calls that we are experiencing. Dan Whitby and Natalie Listerman will be reporting for duty shortly."

Ernie and Bert grinned in unison, but Zimmerman glared at them. "Dan and Natalie are here for one day only," he said. "They are dedicated to clearing the backlog. Please remember that we are professionals, people. Let's not abuse the situation by making this the class of 2010 reunion coffee break." The grins vanished, and Zimmerman continued briefing the three officers on relevant All-Points Bulletins, Missing Persons and Stolen Vehicles from related counties. After he had finished, he shot Erin a meaningful glance and she stayed behind until The Muppets had exited the room.

"I've put out feelers to my sources about Gunther Schmidt and his granddaughter Lily, and I need to talk to you about the information I received last night." Zimmerman told her when the other two officers were out of earshot. His grave manner stifled any smart-ass comment she might have been tempted to make. "This information is between you and me. I don't know how to say this so I'll repeat what my informant said." He stalled for a moment, until Erin closed her notebook and tucked her pen back into her pocket.

"My informant says that our Acting-Sergeant Derek Peterson has earned himself a bit of a negative reputation with the criminal element. He has a few drug addicts who provide him regular information on the local scene. They say he has special relationships with some female snitches and, this is rumor only, they perform certain favors in exchange for him looking the other way with regard to their drug involvement."

"Sexual favors, I assume?" Erin asked the obvious. So Derek's lecherous behavior was not an act.

Zimmerman nodded solemnly. There was nothing amusing about a police officer abusing his position.

"How could that be related to the disappearance of Gunther or Lily?"

"Unfortunately, it gets worse. There are also rumors about Derek Peterson's obsession with a little girl. Word on the street is that he had a stalker photo of this girl and showed it to a snitch who thought it was weird. A few months ago one of the parent supervisors at the elementary school phoned in a complaint about a man with an old red Mustang watching a grade six girl in the school yard. She said the man was creepy."

"Lily." Erin blanched. There was no question that Derek's Mustang was uniquely identifiable in a town this size.

"You guessed it. The grade six girl was Lily, but here's the disturbing part. Derek was the investigating officer when that call came in, but he didn't file a report. He had dispatch code it as an unfounded complaint."

She stared at him, open-mouthed. Of all the deplorable personality traits she'd attributed to Derek Peterson, she'd never imagined this.

"I don't want to go jumping to conclusions here, but there is something I remembered that looks like it might figure into this equation." Zimmerman looked down at his clipboard and rapped his knuckles on the first page, as if reconsidering the words he would say. "When we went to check Gunther's place for Lily, I saw Derek's car parked on a little turnout off the access road. I didn't think anything of it at the time because it's not far from the public boat launch and everyone parks in there. Now I realize its proximity. It wouldn't take more than a few minutes to walk through the woods from one location to the other."

"We can't ignore the fact that no one has seen Gunther or Lily since the fire at the Stop 'N Go." Erin continued to connect the dots. "It also sounds like Derek's been paying unusual attention to Lily. At the same time she's missing, he's coincidentally not showing up for work." She exhaled through clenched jaw. "I feel sick to my stomach hearing about what he's doing with vulnerable women."

"Might be," he emphasized. Drug addicts don't always give the most accurate information. The steely look in his eye told Erin that, although he was trying to keep an open mind, he believed Derek capable.

"I agree that we don't want to draw any vicious conclusions," she said evenly, "but it's pretty clear that we don't have time to waste. We need to talk to Derek and we need to properly search Gunther's property."

"It was the middle of the night when you last went out there," Zimmerman said.

"It was dark, but—" Again, she neglected to tell him about Allie's part. "I'm quite certain that there were no cars parked in that roadside turnout when we drove by. I would have seen the reflective taillights. So, why is Derek coming and going out there?"

"I think it's fair to assume that Striker and Jenssen, along with our two relief officers can hold the fort while we follow this up." He grabbed his duty duffel bag to head out.

"I'll meet you in the back parking lot." Erin snatched her own bag and hauled it out to her cruiser, quickly tossing it into the truck. As she drove, she radioed dispatch with their intended location.

Soon, the two cars rattled nose-to-tail over ruts on the rough gravel road at the city's periphery. Leading the way, Erin slowed when they neared the roadside turnout, and her heart thudded in her chest. Those were the dust covered taillights of Derek's prized red Mustang! The car was nosed into the bushes, squeezed as far off the road as possible. Prickly branches scratched the hood's custom cherry red paint job. A quick check revealed that it was empty, the leather interior as pristine as if it were still displayed in an auto showroom.

She paused with her hand near the door. There was a thrumming vibration from within and she instinctively stilled to locate the source. The sound halted abruptly and began again. With her nose almost pressed to the driver's window, she spotted a cell phone jammed into the ashtray of the center console. In addition to the insistent buzzing, its screen emitted a bluish glow with each missed ring. She turned to see Zimmerman standing at the rear of the car with his cellular to his hear.

"Derek's not picking up—"

"Because he ditched his phone in his car." Erin pointed.

Zimmerman tapped in a second number. "Hello? Karen? It's Chris Zimmerman from the station." A short pause. "Yes, I'm fine thank you. I'm working on our upcoming shift schedule and I'm wondering if Derek is feeling any better, or—" Another pause, this one caused him to raise an eyebrow but his voice remained neutral when he spoke again. "Yes, you're right. I'm sure it must be a clerical error. I'm sorry to have bothered you. Can you have him call me later?" He disconnected the call and turned to Erin. With a subtle shrug, he merely cocked his head.

"Let me guess." Erin squeezed her eyes into little slits. "He's sick in bed and can't answer the phone."

"His wife said he left a little while ago."

Erin reached onto the hood and flattened her palm against the warm metal. That part was true. Derek had parked here recently.

"She also said that his mother had a car accident and he was driving to St Paul to see her in the hospital." He pensively ran a finger along the thin layer of dust on the car's rear spoiler. "This Mustang is definitely not on the way to the hospital in St Paul, but I'm not going to be the one to tell Karen that!"

"His mom must be one crappy driver! He used that same excuse last summer." Erin blurted. "He came back to work with a sunburn and we figured he was probably on a three day drunk at Highland Fest."

"Lucy, he's got some 'splaining to do," Zimmerman quipped, his accent nowhere close to Ricky Ricardo's in the 1950s TV series I Love Lucy. "Let's get over to Gunther's. There has to be something we've missed." He was first back to his car and left Erin coughing in a cloud of gravel dust before she'd even opened her door. Despite the head start, he did not speed and she easily caught up so that they both puttered down the road one after the other. She kept a vigilant eye leading up to the house and outbuilding, and guessed that her fellow officer was doing the same.

When they arrived, Gunther's old Ford truck was parked right out front as she'd last seen it. It did not appear to have been moved and, as expected, the keys still dangled from the ignition. Erin jerked open the driver's door and extracted them, stopping only when she noticed Zimmerman gaping.

"All your training go out the window, Officer Ericsson?" Both hands jammed into his pockets, he drawled his words like a Texan. "You had better not be thinking of using that house key without a warrant."

"Of course not." She slid the key slowly back into the ignition. He was right. This had become way too personal and suddenly the rules were flexible. She didn't even notice when it had happened. Was it the night she came out here with Allie?

"Did you call Kathy yet? Maybe there is a hit on those fingerprints."

"No time this morning," she said defensively. "Besides, if she had a match, she would be singing it from the rooftops, not relaying a message through my trusty sidekick. I will get a hold of her after we're done."

He bared his teeth in mock annoyance but waited until she backed away from the truck. When she turned her attention to the shed, the first thing she noticed was that the door was now padlocked tight, no longer hanging open on rusted hinges. She opened her mouth to comment but Zimmerman had left. He slowly circled the shed and then and sighted toward the river, like a bush guide. Erin saw it too: a clearly defined trail of bent grass marking the passage of one dragged canoe and two pairs of feet. One size large and one small.

Blades of grass were still springing upright. Adrenaline surged. No words needed to be spoken. Instantaneously, they understood the significance. As fast as she was, Zimmerman was faster. She could not catch the long legged policeman who bounded down the trail to the weather bleached dock. He stopped to peer down the river.

"Just left," he panted. "Just now." He shot off into the brush in a hopeless attempt to follow the canoe from the riverbank. There was no conveniently beaten trail here and the riverbank was clogged by tall conifers, weedy thickets of young poplars and dense low growing prickly ash. He heaved his lanky torso through, dragging monstrous heavy boots behind him. Chickweed and thistles tangled his legs and wild buckwheat entwined his boot laces until he ground to a halt minutes later, Erin lapping at his heels.

She panted with exertion, one hand up over her forehead to ward away whipping branches. He lunged sideways like a trapped bear until he was ankle deep near a cluster of cattails. Aquatic weeds and dark organic matter sucked at his legs. This was no way to catch a canoe paddling downstream. He leaned over and gripped both thighs in defeat.

"I saw her," he panted. "Just before the bend. In the boat." He waited until he'd caught his breath and when he turned to Erin, his dark eyes burned. "I'm goddamn sure Derek was at the stern." Now sunk in mud to his knees, he morosely folded backwards until the seat of his uniform trousers slogged into the soggy weeds. His sidearm submerged. "Aw, now I'm in the loon shit."

Equally cheerless, she found a large stick and extended it to him from a safe distance where she kept her boots securely planted on a flat rock. Miserably, he grasped the other end of the stick and wrenched himself upright from the peaty muck. It released him with an angry sucking noise and he scraped a handful of goo from his sidearm. Anchored by Erin, he inched himself out on his belly until he was lying beside her.

"Lost my boot," he wiggled bare toes on one mud-caked foot, "and my sock." He lurched up like a harbor seal, bare elbows scraping against rock, and eyed the evil sinkhole for his stolen boot. Spotting the dark shape, he extended Erin's rescue stick and hooked the knobby end through bootlaces, prying it loose from the intense suction. He examined the mud-filled boot dubiously, peeled out a gooey brown layer and slapped it against his knee. "There's no hope for that sock," he said. He tore off his other boot and tied the laces of both together for easier carrying. Then he set off in his bare feet.

Erin followed him back the way they'd come. At the dock, he unfastened his duty belt and it landed on the wood with a dishearteningly wet slop.

"We could take the aluminum fishing boat by the shed," she offered half-heartedly. Even if they could find paddles, without an outboard motor it would be like trying to paddle a tuna can down the narrow stream. There was no hoping of catching the more agile canoe.

He didn't answer, just waded to his waist near the dock, being overly careful to keep his feet on stable ground. After much splashing and swearing, he emerged cleaner and picked up his duty belt to slosh off the worst of the mud. He left the sidearm fastened in its holster. It would require a thorough cleaning later.

"Well, don't you look like Miss Perfect." He scrunched his face at Erin.

She self-consciously brushed dirt and lichen from the knees of her trousers and ran a hand through short blonde hair. He grinned at her and she breathed in relief. He was being sarcastic. Z-man was back. Re-energized, he strode past her and she followed in the wake of his dripping uniform and the slap of his wet trouser legs until they reached their cars.

"We need to find out what the hell Derek is up to, and where Gunther is." Erin's eyes drifted toward the house and he shook his head imperceptibly. "First, let's go get that damn warrant." He slid behind the wheel of his cruiser and was gone.

Erin knew it would take him a couple of hours to clean up and do the paperwork. That gave her time for a little digging of her own.

CHAPTER FOURTEEN

Two miles from city limits, down a hard packed road, Erin parked her cruiser beside a newly built covered patio attached to a thirty-year-old farmhouse. When she stepped from her car, two red squirrels stopped their noisy arguing long enough to gawk at her and then ran off chattering into the trees. On the deck, potted plants hung in macramé baskets from every overhead beam, each design different, each plant thriving. Vibrantly colored flowers exploded from planter boxes surrounding the deck, and flowering vines crept up lattice borders. She shuffled dirt from her boots at the bottom of the steps and tromped her way up to the entrance. A half sanded wooden chair sat propped between two sawhorses in the middle of the deck, a work in progress.

Gina opened the door before she had a chance to knock and beamed in delight when Erin stepped inside. Her facial swelling had gone down and the transformation was striking. She'd trimmed her chopped hair short and the new look was surprisingly refreshing, younger somehow, less intimidating. Most of her scrapes were covered by an open necked denim shirt with long sleeves casually rolled to forearms. It was hard to imagine that the trauma she had suffered was so recent.

"I wasn't sure you'd be up and around yet," Erin began. "But they said you checked yourself out of hospital yesterday."

"What do doctors know? I feel fine. Look at you. You're back at work already." Gina glanced at Erin's rumpled uniform and waved her through to the kitchen. "About time you came to visit me. I've only been waiting since grade what? Five?" Erin's face flushed and Gina laughed again. "Don't worry, you know I'm all talk. I'm not going to eat you."

Erin plunked herself down onto a wooden chair and put on her best grin. She leaned forward, elbows on the table. All around her was evidence of Gina's dedication to, and obvious skill with, woodwork and handicrafts. Gleaming hardwood floors, custom cabinetry, and even the macramé on the brand new deck. She was good with plants too. Her indoor plants bloomed as cheerfully as those on the deck. It took a special person to breathe such life and happiness into her surroundings and Erin felt remiss. Gina was right. In the twenty-odd years she'd known her, she had never been out here. With her tough chick public persona, she hadn't imagined her living in such cottage chic.

"Coffee?" Gina rummaged through a hand-painted cupboard. "You love your coffee. I got some funky Eco-friendly beans in a Get Well basket."

Erin nodded and watched Gina make coffee.

"I know this isn't really a social call, but I'm going to pretend that it is." She smiled, sad little lines crinkling out from the corners of her eyes. "Sugar? Cream?" She sounded like a fifties housewife and Erin could find no words of response, so she shook her head. Black was how she had always liked her coffee. Gina slid a steaming mug over and sat across from her at the table.

She took a tentative sip, pleasantly surprised by the robust brew. She took another sip but, single-minded in her purpose, the niceties of the language still escaped her.

Gina directed her best come hither look at Erin and tried to flip non-existent long hair over her shoulder. Disconcerted, she stopped midway and tucked the new shorter locks behind her ear. She laid her chin on the back of her hand and sighed. "Fine. Ask your questions."

"Have you seen or heard from Gunther Schmidt since the fire?"

"No, and no," Gina said patiently. "Do you still think he's the one—?"

Erin ignored her question and posed another. "Do you have any idea where he could be?"

"He's hiding is he?" Gina eyed her with lifted eyebrow. "That old bugger is good at that, for sure." Excusing herself for a moment, she returned with a time worn photo album. She flipped pages until she settled on one black and white image and turned it around to face Erin. Two smiling men stood in front of a vintage milk truck, arms around each others' shoulders. Both wore ill-fitting deliveryman uniforms and tattered boots. She pointed to the baby-faced teenager. "That's Gunther Schmidt's father Heinrich." Erin could see the resemblance in the features of the proud boy. Gina's finger moved to the taller man, in his early twenties. "That is my great grandfather Albert."

"Your families go back that far?" Gina had told her that the families were intertwined but this was history. "That photo looks like it was taken in the dirty thirties."

"Sure was," Gina said, with an amused snort. "But those two rascals weren't delivering milk in that old Garford Truck! My great granddad used to ride with Gunther's dad all over the county hauling homemade whiskey. You ever hear of Minnesota 13?"

Erin nodded, a half smile on her lips. Like most kids around here, she'd grown up hearing all about the families who earned more money making whiskey than growing crops in the dirt poor Prohibition days of the 20s and 30s. Families almost seemed to take pride in their own ancestors' bootlegging stories, and even kids in the schoolyard bragged about great grandmas so tough they took the rap and served jail time so their husbands could quietly keep making whiskey.

"That whiskey recipe was passed around and for a number of years before the end of Prohibition, Minnesota 13 was made right here in Morley Falls," Gina told her. "My great granddad's neighbors were making it and needed someone with a truck to deliver it. Great granddad conveniently drove a milk delivery truck. He enlisted the help of Gunther's father who was the kid down the road with a strong back. Those boys knew how to keep a secret. Voilà, they were all making money. After a while, they did so well that great granddad quit his job."

Erin became aware that Gina's flirtatious pretensions had vanished. Was this the real Gina behind the tough façade? She leaned forward to listen while the enthusiastic family historian spoke. Erin had always suspected that there was more to Gina than she liked to show.

"The solid rubber tires on the truck made the ride bumpy and they were losing too much whiskey anyway." Gina put down her coffee mug, a wistful sparkle in her eye. "Great granddad bought a 1930 Ford Model A that he bragged could outrun the cops, but I doubt it was as exciting as all that. They spent most of their time picking up supplies and delivering it to the hidden stills. Those two were a perfect pair. They regularly hauled seventy-five pound bags of sugar on wooden skids through the bush to wherever it was needed. They grew muscular and they learned to be sneaky." Gina winked at Erin.

"How does this help me find Gunther now?" Erin queried. The stories fascinated her but she had limited time to hear them all.

"I'm getting to that, girl." Gina frowned at Erin, a schoolteacher chastening an impatient student. "When Prohibition ended, the stills were abandoned and they turned to trapping. By then, Gunther's grandfather had learned a great deal about backwoods stealth and concealment and he, of course, passed this on to Gunther who became a pretty renowned trapper and fishing guide before he turned twenty. He had shelters built all through the woods that he would use when he needed to overnight out there. Sometimes he didn't return to town for weeks. Gunther also helped his dad with things that might not have been totally legal at the time."

"It's a small world and Gunther became friends with my Grandpa Jack before they both got called up for service in the seventies. All I know is that granddad came home from Vietnam a changed man, and he made sure we all knew that Gunther was the man who brought him back alive. Those two used to go out fishing for days and they must have stayed in some old shack because they never took any camping gear. Grandpa Jack is dead now and it feels like Gunther sort of stepped into his role. I can't believe—" Erin suddenly leaned forward and Gina stopped talking. "Sorry, I guess I went off on a tangent there about the war. You had a question."

"Vietnam? Did you say Gunther was in the Vietnam war?" She flashed back to Allie's texts this morning.

"Yeah, I think he did more than one tour. He was special ops or something. That's what they said."

"You said that he was good at hiding. Can you be more specific?"

"Right. That's what I was getting to before you distracted me." She winked at Erin again but her wink had lost its lascivious undertone. "All those guys became experts at hiding stuff and at hiding themselves. They kept stockpiles of emergency rations in little hidey holes near the still. Even after Prohibition ended, old habits died hard. When cops came out searching for somebody, the homeowner calmly sat out front, whittling and looking as innocent as a newborn cub. All the while, there might be a few of his wanted buddies hunkered down in an underground bunker nearby, sipping whiskey and dining on his wife's homemade blueberry preserves until the heat passed. Nearly every one of those old homes or shacks had a false wall hiding another room, or a secret basement dug out nearby."

Erin nodded her head, considering all the possibilities. "That same property has been in Gunther's family for generations."

"Most of the old hidey holes were converted to basements or root cellars, or demolished over the years, but some might still be in use." Gina stood up and took Erin's coffee mug.

"Gunther seems like a man with a few secrets and there must be a hidey hole out there somewhere." She rose to leave.

Gina pulled a small plastic Tupperware container from the fridge and handed it to Erin, who tentatively accepted it. It looked a lot like the mystery containers in the fridge at the police station. She thumbed the edge of the lid but Gina stopped her.

"That's not for you, Sugar," Gina told her, a familiar sly crook sliding into the corner of her mouth. "That is for your handsome friend Chris. Tell him they're fresh and there's more where that came from." She laughed out loud at Erin's expression. "Keep them cool, and give them to him as soon as you can."

Intrigued, but too hesitant to ask any more questions, Erin headed out to the deck. She remembered her manners before she slammed the screen door. "Thank you for the coffee, Gina, and for the visit. I'm glad you're feeling better."

"Come again sometime." Gina the fifties housewife waved goodbye to Erin when she backed the cruiser down the driveway. The radio crackled her name as soon as she arrived at the main road. It was Zimmerman.

"You are fast." Erin thumbed the mike in response.

"Meet me back out there in ten." The radio hissed when he released the button on his mike. He was not often a man of so few words. She stepped a little harder on the gas pedal.

By the time she pulled up at Gunther's house, Zimmerman had the trunk of his car open and pulled out a set of bolt cutters. Officer Mark Striker popped out the passenger's door like an eager puppy and took the cutters.

"Gina sent you this. She said to keep it cool and she has more." Erin paraphrased, and handed Zimmerman the Tupperware container. His eyebrows shot up and he flushed a mottled pattern from Adam's apple to earlobe. He peeled the lid and Erin turned away when he examined the contents. Whatever Gina had sent, she bore no responsibility. He laughed and trotted over to gently place the container in his car.

Erin followed Striker to the shed where he gleefully attacked the lock, and she gave the door a shove the second the shackle released. It opened with a screech and the two of them squeezed through, shoulder to shoulder.

Except for the empty space where two paddles had been, it looked virtually the same as before. While Striker rifled through drawers, Erin walked to the little fridge and yanked open the door. Gone were the half dozen cans of beer, the bread and the cheese. An empty plastic wrapper lay discarded on the bottom. Erin shut the fridge and turned to the cabinet. The last time she'd been here, the door had been closed. Someone had been in there recently and had left the door ajar. She opened it and compared the contents to her memory. Something was missing. One of the unlabeled dark bottles from the top shelf. She looked around and found it lying in a metal garbage can near the door, empty. She picked it up, held it to the light and then placed it into a plastic evidence bag.

"Might be something. Might not," she told Striker, who asked the question with his eyes.

"That cabinet looks like it's full of taxidermy stuff but those bottles are old. Now everything is bottled in plastic." He included the bottle in his photographs before she marked the bag and set it by the door.

She left Striker to finish up in the shed and joined Zimmerman at the house. She found him kneeling by the rear door of the house, happily whistling a little tune while he raked a set of lock picks in the keyhole. One thumb deftly kept pressure on the tension bar while light fingers on a pick in his other hand gently manipulated the lock.

"Z-man, you are full of surprises. I didn't know you could pick locks," she said. "You sound positively cheerful."

"Been doing it for years. I am a multi-talented man." He did not rise to her bait about his cheerfulness. As he worked, his whistling became more morose. He screeched to a halt a few minutes later when, moisture dripping from his temples, he wiped palms on thighs. "Darn it. It's too hot out here. You wanna try?"

She took the picks and emulated his technique, Zimmerman verbally firing instructions at her. "Cookies?" she queried. "She sent cookies." He didn't so much as twitch. "Cinnamon buns?" Her stomach grumbled with the sweet buttery possibility. A wily eyebrow raised and he began to whistle again, his devious manner beginning to grate on her. "Frigging butter tarts?" His whistling skipped a few beats and he chuckled. "Are you gonna hog them all for yourself?" This made him chortle loudly and she wrinkled her nose at him, working on the lock until Striker's amused face appeared beside them.

"Can I have my picks back?" He tilted his head in silent criticism of Erin's dubious technique. Finished a walk through the surrounding grounds, prickly thistles still clung to Striker's pant legs and he brushed a dried leaf from his sleeve. "I should have known better than to leave them in Z-man's car."

Erin shot an accusatory look at her smugly annoying whistler and backed away from the door. She handed over the picks. Striker bent, inserted the pick, and opened the door with a flourish a moment later.

"Bert's dad is a locksmith," Zimmerman said defensively. "I would have—"

"You did NOT just call me Bert!" Striker jabbed him in the ribs, feigning anger. Erin snorted through her nose trying to stifle a laugh. How could she have imagined that she was the only one who thought that Striker and Jenssen looked like Bert and Ernie?

"I could have done it if my hands didn't sweat." Zimmerman shoved them into his pockets with a facetious pout.

"Don't think so, Zee." Striker said confidently, furry dark brows crowding down over his eyes in amusement. It occurred to Erin that he actually liked the nickname. He was hamming it up.

"Does that make you Kermit, Frog-man?" Erin directed this last at Zimmerman, who replaced his pout with open-mouthed faux outrage.

"Oh, Miss Piggy, you're so cheeky," he quipped back. He looked through the open door and his playfulness vanished. "Are we going to stand around here all afternoon or are we going to do this?"

She marched past them and began with the kitchen. There was

always something in the kitchen. Zimmerman deposited a copy of the search warrant onto the counter and made for the bedroom. That was also likely to yield results. Striker busied himself taking photos and making notes while Erin sat at the table and rifled through Gunther's mail. The old man led a simple life with not many bills to pay: Power, electric, water. She opened each, and stacked them to the side.

The cable company was canceling service if the bill wasn't paid, the school wanted money for outstanding fees but offered to reduce the amount if Gunther filled out another form requesting financial assistance. Dated two months ago, the form was still blank. She was temporarily blinded by the brilliant flash from Striker's DSLR camera aimed in her direction.

"Whoa! I don't want to be in the picture." She bolted out of the chair. He shrugged and continued shooting. "Give a girl a little warning would you?" She took the last handful of mail and ducked out of camera range to finish.

There were three unopened envelopes from the First Minnesota Bank and she slid her pen down the flaps to tear them open. The monthly statements were what she expected: A pension deposit at the beginning of each month, followed by withdrawals for bills, gasoline and groceries. As she perused the itemized list, she noticed one oddity. Near the middle of the month, there was an extra deposit. Gunther was getting supplemental income. Income to the tune of $650 a month. She made sure that Striker photographed the documents before sliding them into an evidence bag and marking the label.

When she finished, she joined Zimmerman and watched him from the master bedroom doorway before she entered. He neatly stacked piles of clothing back into dresser drawers, and was he still whistling? An opened and empty coffee can lay on the quilted bedcover.

"You are not obligated to tidy up," she reminded him, rapping her knuckles on the inside wall. "We don't work for Molly Maid."

"It's a habit," he confessed. "My mom taught me to clean up after myself." He stopped stacking as she moved from wall to floor, tapping her knuckles against wood. "What are you doing?"

"Looking for false walls, hidden floor hatches," she said. The skeptical expression never left his face so she explained. "This house was built a long time ago, there is a lot of history here and people who did not always obey the law needed places to hide stuff." He gave a pessimistic shrug and continued searching and repacking drawers. She finished her knocking and proceeded to the other rooms. Striker ignored her, as if her actions were completely normal.

She had just finished Lily's room, the only one in the house that looked like it was inhabited by a young girl, when Zimmerman loomed in the doorway, Striker right behind him.

"There are clothes all over the floor," Erin told them. "It looks like she packed in a hurry but I can't find anything to suggest where they've gone."

Zimmerman waved an opened envelope at her, and she crowded close to view the contents with him. There was no address or mailing label on it, indicating that it had been hand delivered. "We've been wondering why Derek has been hanging around out here," he said, his voice tense. "How is he going to explain this check he wrote to Gunther?" He pulled out a personal check, showed it to them, and Striker photographed it.

"Perhaps he bought something from the old man?" Striker didn't sound like he would even buy this story himself. "Maybe it's a loan, or..." His voice trailed off and he lowered his eyes. "You're right, I like the guy, but this looks bad."

"Is the check for $650?" Erin asked. Striker's head popped up from behind the camera's viewfinder and she didn't need to see it to know that it was. Zimmerman nodded warily and she held up the evidence bag with the bank statements.

"Derek paid the same amount to Gunther on the same date for the last four months, and probably longer. These are all the statements I could find." She waved the plastic bag like a flag. Her phone chirped and she handed the bag to Zimmerman, who stowed it with the check. She turned away from both men to check her text message. It was her girlfriend again.

Allie: R u there?
Erin: Got your caps lock fixed?
Allie: Just did an update. Did you find Gunther yet?
Erin: Not at house. Finishing search now.
Allie: No, he's there.
Erin: House empty. Shed empty.
Allie: Check again. I feel he's there. Pls.
Erin: OK. Will keep looking. Headache better?

Allie: Ice helped. Called in sick anyways. Going to watch old movies today.

Erin: LOL. Such luxury. Take it easy.

Ignoring inquisitive stares from the men, Erin turned the volume off and tucked the iPhone back into her pocket. It was unheard of for Allie to take a day off work, and if she was skipping her daily workout, she must really be having a bad day.

"Something doesn't sit right," she announced, as if it were her idea. "I think we should take another look around the property before we call this done." She headed out the back door, leaving Zimmerman and Striker to exchange a look.

Striker lifted a shoulder noncommittally. "Chicks," he said, and followed her. "I'll take the bush side by the dock. I think there might be a few thistles down there I haven't got on my pants yet."

"Okay," replied Zimmerman. "I hate to say it but look for old wells, root cellars, you know what I'm talking about. Erin is headed past the driveway to the north end so I'll take this area by the house." Striker tromped off through the brush and Zimmerman pulled a broom from the back porch, using the handle to probe through the shrubbery growing wild against the house. He walked all the way around but there was no hidden access to the foundation. Erin did the same with a stick over by the shed.

She flattened the grass near the side of the wooden structure, knelt down and directed her flashlight into the dark spaces underneath. As far as she could see, it appeared to be sitting on a collection of cinderblocks. The moist dark earth had been home to many small critters over the years but none were in residence now and grass had grown thickly all around the building. She could not see through to the other side and poked her stick at gaps in the cinderblocks. At the side furthest the door, she found no gaps at all. The foundation was continuously solid. Why had the builder expended more effort here? To take more weight? To conceal something?

She laid on her belly in the grass but weeds obscured her view. She poked into the darkness with the stick. A spirited grasshopper whizzed into her shirt collar and she jumped to her feet, trying to dislodge it with body contortions. It scrabbled down her back and lodged somewhere above her belt line, twitching its legs. Untucking her shirt, she vigorously flapped the fabric until the hopper escaped out the bottom and turned to see Zimmerman regarding her with interest.

"Rain dance?" he asked, poker-faced.

"Grasshopper dance," she deadpanned in response.

"Did you save it for me?" Zimmerman looked genuinely interested. "Merlin would be highly appreciative."

"Yes, I have a whole pocketful of grasshoppers," she retorted sarcastically. "Right alongside the half dozen mice I caught for my cat." Did she say *my cat?* Now she was taking ownership of that ornery feline!

"You seem fascinated by this end of the shed," he said. "Let's have another look inside." This time, he did the wall thumping and Erin stomped her way across the floor. It reverberated with a dull thud until she reached the far side, when the sound became hollow.

Erin's iPhone silently vibrated in her pocket and she covertly viewed the text message on her screen.

Allie: Old man thinks enemy is here. Afraid to die.

Erin texted back: Maybe he hears me.

She quickly stuffed the phone into her pocket when Zimmerman joined her. He stomped one heavy boot onto the floorboards and a fine plume of dust escaped the cracks of a loose one. Then he leaned over and tugged a couple of soft cotton threads trapped in the wedge.

"These aren't even dirty yet," he stated. "They're fresh." He handed them to Erin who looked more closely. She twisted the light blue threads between her fingers.

"Lily was wearing a light blue cotton nightgown," Erin blurted. "Get something to pry this up."

"How do you know what she was wearing?"

Allie told me. She dreamt it. My girlfriend is psychic. Or something. The words sounded ridiculous in her head and would sound more implausible if Erin said them out loud, even to someone she knew as well as Z-man. She kept her mouth shut and grabbed the largest flat screwdriver from the tool bench, jamming it between the cracks in the boards. A two-foot square hatch opened upward and Zimmerman wrenched it backward on its hinges to reveal a narrow ladder leading downward to a dank underground cellar. In the scant beam of her flashlight, she strained to see the hard-packed dirt floor in the cinderblock-lined room. Plastic wrappers and crushed beer cans littered the floor.

Erin placed one boot on the top rung of the ladder. "I'm smaller," she explained. "I'll go." He held the trap door up and she shinnied down. The first two ladder rungs squeaked angrily with her weight. The hidey hole, as Gina called it, was about six feet deep, and six rungs to the bottom but Erin only took the first three. Halfway down, she leapt to the ground and shone her light into the face of Gunther Schmidt, lying supine on an old army-style cot.

The smell below ground was foul, a mixture of vomit and urine. She spotted a bare incandescent bulb affixed to the ceiling and yellow light illuminated the room when she yanked the chain. The scene before her was awash in a sickly twenty-five watt glow. The additional light revealed blankets tossed carelessly aside on a second cot in the hidey hole. A small TV, now switched off, perched on the edge of an overturned plastic milk crate, its electrical wire snaking upward through floorboards.

"He's here!" Erin shouted. There was scuffling above and she hoped Zimmerman was not going to try to get through that hole. It would be truly claustrophobic down here with him and a corpse. Erin peered down at Gunther, partly covered with a moth eaten blanket, his face a waxy pallor. She detected no obvious signs of life but reflexively placed two fingers against the carotid artery at the old man's throat. She sprang back, startled by the presence of a faint pulse.

"Call an ambulance!" she shouted. Lying on the floor with head and shoulders squeezed down through the hatch, Zimmerman let go of his flashlight. It swung crazily on its wrist strap, creating deranged shadows around her as he hiked himself back up through the hole.

"Is he alive?" His muffled voice came through the ceiling.

"Unconscious!" she called out. "Heart rate around thirty beats per minute!" She listened while he repeated the information over his radio.

"How's his breathing?" Zimmerman called back.

"I don't know," she yelled. At first, she hadn't thought he was breathing at all. She leaned closer and recoiled at the scent on his breath, like he'd polished off a pound of Ukrainian sausage. "Quick and shallow, like a baby bird. Do they want me to actually count?" There were no remnants of any meals down here, aside from a few beer cans and candy wrappers. She wondered where the garlicky food had come from.

"That's okay," he called down. "Ambulance is on the way!"

131

Heavy boots stomped above her and Striker's raised voice. "I found a police radio down by the river. Stuffed under the planks on the dock."

So that's why they had so narrowly missed Derek. He had known they were coming. How had they overlooked the radio? Aside from Zimmerman's foray into the boot sucking mud, she hadn't been thinking much beyond the abducted girl and the canoe disappearing down the river, had she?

"Nicht schießen." Gunther's lips moved ever so slightly to let the words pass. Erin leaned closer but he did not repeat it.

"He's saying something in German!" she yelled to the men upstairs. "Do you know German?"

"A little," Striker's face appeared at the open hatch. "What did he say?"

"Something like nick sheesen."

"Are you saying Nicht schießen? I think that means 'Don't shoot'."

Erin stared at the old man. Was he having flashbacks to his time in the Vietnam war? Had Allie been tapping into his hallucinations? Her texts made a lot more sense.

"Mr. Schmidt," Erin urged tersely, taking him by the shoulder. She knelt beside the cot, careful to avoid a soggy puddle of what smelled like vomit. "Can you hear me? An ambulance is on the way. Help is coming."

Gunther's bloodshot eyes flickered open for a second and focused on Erin. "Helfen meine Enkelin," he mumbled faintly, "Achten." Then the old man's eyes clamped shut once more. Above her, Striker squeezed his head and shoulders through the hatch, much as Zimmerman had before, and watched the interaction.

"He said to help his granddaughter. And then he said to be careful," Striker translated. "Peew, it stinks down there," he added, as if Erin hadn't noticed.

She shook Gunther's shoulder firmly again. "Do you know where Derek Peterson took Lily?" Gunther Schmidt lay motionless, but his eyes moved erratically under their heavy lids. Was he once again dreaming of hiding from enemy soldiers in the jungles of Vietnam? Erin tucked the blanket closer around his shoulders and waited the twelve minutes until the medics arrived.

"Hi Andy. Michelle." She nodded at each medic when they

descended the ladder after handing their equipment bags down to her.

"Long time no see, Erin," Andy, the first medic down the ladder greeted her with a sarcastic smile. It had certainly not been a long time. Andy was one of the medics who had taken Erin to the hospital after the fire but she didn't want to have to rehash that all over again. Not today. She left his comment alone and the two of them got down to business, squeezing into the nauseatingly cramped hidey hole beside Erin.

"Sir, Sir!" Andy firmly squeezed the sensitive trapezius muscle between Gunther's shoulder and the base of his neck. There was no response.

"Gunther Schmidt," Erin prompted. "His name."

"Mr. Schmidt," Andy amended. "Can you hear me?" As he spoke, he motioned to his partner and Michelle handed him an oxygen mask which he snapped over Gunther's mouth and nose. She adjusted the flow on the tank's dial until she was satisfied.

"It could sure use an air freshener down here, couldn't it?" Michelle wrinkled her nose then easily flipped the empty cot onto its side and shoved it against the cinderblock wall so she could arrange equipment bags. Kicking two beer cans aside, she clucked her tongue sanctimoniously and began extracting required equipment. "You think he had enough to drink? Seriously."

Michelle, a tall slender brunette, curved herself as gracefully as a dancer around her partner to take vital signs, verbalizing each in turn. "BP sixty over forty-two. Heart rate thirty-eight BPM, Respirations thirty-six, O2 Sats seventy-eight, patient is cyanotic," she said into her radio. She quickly affixed electrodes for the heart monitor, watching the output. It appeared as a series of tiny blips on the screen, a foreign language. She noticed Erin's perplexed expression and explained what this meant in layman's terms. "His blood pressure is low, his heart rate is slow, but respirations are quick, indicating distress, and he is cyanotic so he is not getting enough oxygen in his system."

That much made sense to Erin. She shone her flashlight onto Gunther's face and noted that behind the transparent oxygen mask, his lips were a definite bluish color. Giving the medics more room to work, she wormed her way back to the ladder. Andy squatted beside Gunther and started an intravenous line, his dark features a study in concentration. Skilled fingers finessed the needle to insert a catheter into the vein like the conductor of a tiny orchestra.

Andy noticed Erin's poised notebook and pen. "You should write down that he has wicked garlic breath, which can be fatal—" he paused and Erin narrowed her eyes in disbelief, "—to relationships! Yuk. Yuk."

"That was beyond bad," she retorted.

"Just kiddin' Puddin' Face." He slapped a beefy thigh like a comedian in a comedy sketch.

"Seriously." She frowned her disapproval, more of the nickname than the initial bad joke. "Will he make it?" She had a lot of questions for this man and she wanted answers as quickly as possible.

Michelle shrugged. "Hard to tell. With these vitals, he is at risk of seizure and cardiac arrest." She removed the pulse oximeter she'd earlier placed on the tip of Gunther's index finger and pressed the bezel of her flashlight firmly against the discolored nail bed.

"Mr. Schmidt," she said in a commanding voice. Can you hear me?

Gunther's fingernails were ringed with light colored lines, almost the same hue as his pale skin and Erin couldn't help but cringe a little. That level of pressure on a tender fingernail woke most people with a cry, but the unconscious man merely emitted a faint moan.

"He's GCS4. What if he goes down?" Andy asked her. "Should we intubate before we transport?"

"We are close to hospital," Michelle answered confidently. "Let's see if he'll take an OPA and we can load and go." Andy gave a quick nod and, within seconds, had inserted the oral airway. When he finished, he glanced at Michelle who motioned lifting. The two medics had worked together long enough that the rest did not need to be said aloud.

Michelle called up to the officers above, who leaned over the hatch. "Can you grab the stretcher for us so we can load him up as soon as we haul him out?" Zimmerman's face stayed put but Striker's disappeared and boots quickly tromped across the floor above. The boots returned a moment later, along with a loud dragging noise, and there were choice expletives uttered by Striker, followed by Zimmerman's rumbling laughter.

"You don't have to drag it," Zimmerman told him. "Let me show you. Here's the release catch." More expletives from Striker, and then

Zimmerman called that they were all ready.

Andy grasped Gunther Schmidt from behind, wrestler style under both shoulders, and lifted him backwards up the ladder like an oversize sack of corn. Michelle pointed a finger at the oxygen tank and IV bag, and nodded once to Erin. Then she hefted the bags and followed Andy up the stairs, working with him as a single unit to transfer the patient and ensure all attached equipment was unencumbered.

Erin grabbed the indicated equipment and scrambled to keep up, feeling like the cockeyed caboose of a long, awkward train. Hands reached down when she ascended and relieved her of the tank and IV bag, so that when she surfaced in the shed, Gunther was already securely loaded on the stretcher and on his way out the door.

The air outside the shed was sweet like springtime after a rain and Erin filled her lungs to replace the foul stench from below. She craved a shower, badly, and she had probably been in the hole not much more than a half hour. She retrieved a bottle of antibacterial hand sanitizer from her car's glove compartment and liberally applied it to her palms. When it had dried, she repeated the process, this time ensuring she had cleansed front, back and fingernails. She remembered Gunther's nails. She had never seen such discoloration. Was that the result of years of alcoholism and the continual neglect of one's body? How long had Gunther been in the hidey hole? And Lily? Had they been hiding from the police, or from Derek?

CHAPTER FIFTEEN

At home, Allie poured boiling water into a mug and dangled an herbal sachet into it, dunking the bag absent-mindedly. She carried her mug to the living room and seated herself on the sofa in front of the oversize flat screen TV. She searched through the online channel menu until she found what she knew she needed to see. There it was on channel 128, a classic favorite of hers since she'd first seen it in her teens with her foster mom. The two of them had stayed up many nights watching movies together and now Allie found it was still a wonderful stress reliever. She sat back and sipped her tea, feeling relaxation wash over her. The movie reel started in her head when she closed her eyes.

In this version, Erin played the part of Cary Grant as Mortimer Brewster, the recently married newspaperman who must now go home and deliver the news to his sweet old aunts. When Erin gets there, she discovers that they're both insane and have been murdering men. She runs around in the slapstick comedy trying to keep her new bride while preventing her aunts from murdering anyone else. She snatches away a glass of poisoned wine from Gunther Schmidt, whom the aunts were attempting to murder, and saves his life.

By the time Erin, as Cary Grant, happily exclaimed 'I'm the son of a sea-cook', Allie jolted upright on the sofa. The onscreen credits were rolling. She had missed the entire second half of the movie. She puzzled over the fact that Erin had been a continuous thread in her dream and that Gunther had been saved. That certainly fulfilled the

136

'tell me everything weird' criteria. She must text her.

Allie: You found him. He's sick.

Erin: Yes. Any idea where the kid is?

Allie: Need to tell you about this movie.

Erin: ? random, but I did ask you to tell me everything...

Allie: B&W Cary Grant movie. Two dotty old ladies killing lonely men, crazy guy blowing bugle, weirdo Dr Einstein, and Cary Grant trying to fix it all.

Erin: Are you drinking or something? LOL

Allie: Not funny.

Erin: Sorry.

Allie: Don't know what it means. Hope you can figure it out. Now go find the girl.

Allie put down her phone and knitted her brows together. It did not seem at all odd that the knowledge of Gunther being sick had come to her while she typed the words. Relaxing during the movie had made it easier for the thoughts to flow, and there was no headache or nausea with the dream. It seemed that the more she allowed herself to consider the possibility that they were only bits of information, the easier it became. Still, it was confusing, with seemingly random thoughts coming in fits and spurts. She was uncomfortable about omitting the part where Erin had played Cary Grant, with Allie as her new bride in the strange dream movie. That was too outlandish.

* * *

Striker rode back to police headquarters with Erin. In the trunk, gently cradled in a cardboard box, were a few items from Lily's room, most of the trash from the hidey hole, and the bottle she'd seized from the shed. Zimmerman carried an envelope containing the damning bank statements and other papers he'd seized. Of all the items they'd taken into evidence today, she was most interested in the mysterious bottle, but then she'd sometimes been accused of having an overactive imagination. It was probably nothing. Old cleaning supplies finally disposed of or something? She would turn it all over to Forensics as soon as she could.

"Do you like old movies?" Erin feigned innocuous conversation.

"Not enough shooting and killing," Striker grunted. Like her, he was tired and in need of a shower. "I like action films." He watched the road for a moment and then reciprocated by attempting to continue the conversation. "But my aunt has seen every movie ever made since the beginning of time."

Erin perked up and eyed him with more interest.

"You like old movies too." He sighed as if this was somehow a character flaw, and she was disappointing him on some level.

"Yeah, I really do," she lied. "I can't remember the name of one of my favorites. It's about two crazy old ladies who murder guys and there is a crazy guy who blows a bugle and a nephew—"

"Aw, that one's easy," he interrupted. "I watched it with my aunt when I stayed with her on summer holidays as a kid. She absolutely loved that movie, but it made me nervous. I was afraid to drink any juice for the rest of my visit!"

"Why?"

"I didn't want to die! The movie was called *Arsenic and Old Lace*." He laughed at the memory. "The crazy old ladies kept killing men with poisoned wine!"

A lightning bolt connected with Erin's brain. Arsenic! Allie's cryptic texts unraveled themselves into one coherent message. Gunther Schmidt had been poisoned.

At the station, she hastily scribbled a note for Kathy Banks and stuffed it into the evidence locker beside the items she'd seized from Gunther's shed. She'd been careful to seal the top of the bottle to preserve whatever droplets might be left. She had barely finished when Zimmerman thundered down the hall toward her, his size 14 boots bearing down like army tanks.

"Those bastards won't authorize overtime for this, but I'm going to search for the girl on my own," he said breathlessly. "Striker is coming too. He's changing into his civvies and calling around to borrow a boat right now. No luck so far, but someone will lend us one."

"Does a missing kid not matter to the brass?" Indignation, like fire in her gut, burned toward the stubbornly tightfisted police administration.

"That's the thing," Zimmerman said. "Old man Gunther, the prime suspect in Gina's arson and attempted murder is in the hospital, under police watch. They say the kid is safe and sound with one of our fine officers and she can't possibly be in danger! They want us to wait until they can speak to Derek and clear it up, or at least until tomorrow."

"Are you serious?" Erin's indignation ratcheted up another notch. "They can't trust Derek! He poisoned Gunther! The girl is at risk every moment she is with him!"

"Poison? I thought he drank himself into a coma. Did the paramedics say he was poisoned?"

"Well, it's pretty obvious." Erin back pedaled, stalling for time to think. She recovered and began to count points off on her fingers. "First, Gunther is unconscious, pretty much in a coma. Second, he had been hiding out for days but there were not enough beer cans down there to drink anyone but a six-year-old into a coma. He hadn't been into town to buy more because his truck hadn't moved." Puzzle pieces whizzed into place in Erin's mind, pieces unconnected before this moment.

"Third, we saw the beer cans in the fridge the last time we were there, but the bottle was different. Where did that come from? What was in it? Fourth, there are plenty of chemicals around, and taxidermy chemicals, especially the old ones like the empty bottle I seized, often had toxic substances in it. Even poisons like arsenic." She had Zimmerman's rapt attention and he leaned forward, waiting for her to finish. She raised the pinky finger on her right hand. "Fifth is that Gunther had garlic breath."

"Are you yanking my chain?" Zimmerman had been nodding during this tirade but his expression turned to utter disbelief. Like a child who has begun to suspect that the Easter Bunny might be a fabrication, Zimmerman drew back. "You think he had, what, poison pizza?"

"No," Erin clarified patiently. "Arsenic can smell like garlic on a victim's breath. I smelled it and the paramedics smelled it."

"Arsenic," Zimmerman repeated quietly. He gave her a frown that she mistook for suspicion.

"I watch a lot of documentaries," she explained awkwardly, leaving out the part about Allie's text tip. "I like true crime stuff." He didn't look at all mollified. "Think about it. It would explain a lot of things. Like Mr. Schmidt's sudden mental and physical decline. His alarming appearance and personality change. People thought he was destroying his liver with alcohol or he had cancer or something."

"Okay then, arsenic." He reluctantly repeated the name of the poison again, nodding slightly as if trying to wrap his head around the idea. "Since this is your theory, I want you to be the one to call the hospital and give them a heads up. It will save a lot of diagnostic time and maybe Gunther's life if you're right." He leveled his gaze at her. "But it's your ass if you're wrong. Now, excuse me, but Striker and I have a girl to find." He made as if to move around her but Erin blocked him.

"Count me in too. I don't give a crap about overtime either. You drive and I'll call the hospital on the way to my parents' place. We'll borrow their boat."

Before Erin called the hospital, she texted her girlfriend and shielded the screen from Striker's prying eyes in the cramped back seat of Zimmerman's Chevy Crew Cab.

Erin: Ur info was right. Now going to find girl. Don't wait up. Will text when back in cell range.

Then she phoned the hospital and wheedled a skeptical nurse into connecting her with the physician in charge.

"This is Doctor Holloway." A gravelly male voice came on the line and Erin hoped he would take her seriously. He listened quietly while she carefully explained her theory until she thought she'd lost the signal. Finally he responded, but he was not speaking to her. The background noise changed subtly as if he walked down a hallway, and she understood that he was on a cordless phone.

"Would you wash that patient's hands for me," he ordered.

"You want me to—?" Erin was confused.

"Sorry, Officer. I was speaking to the nurse." She shut her mouth and listened. The minutes ticked by and there was a great deal of rustling noise, or was that static? She grew anxious that they would be out of cellular range before the doctor spoke to her again. "Mee's lines," he finally said.

Erin shook her head. She had no idea what he was talking about, or even if he was talking to her.

"I said, he has Mee's lines, Officer Ericsson." The doctor's voice boomed through the earpiece.

Erin shrugged.

He answered as if he'd seen the gesture. "Horizontal banding of the fingernails is an indicator of poisoning."

She flashed back to the hidey hole where she had dismissed Gunther's strangely discolored fingernails as being dirty.

"You might be on to something," Doctor Holloway said. "The preliminary toxicology report noted lactic acidosis but that also appears in a number of other conditions, such as alcohol poisoning, which was the initial diagnosis. Since he's been cleaned up, I'm noting hyperkeratosis and hyperpigmentosis, specifically on the soles of his hands and feet. Now that we have a specific toxin to look for, I will review the blood cell counts and serum electrolytes. If I see evidence of hemolysis, we'll screen him for possible blood transfusion." Erin rapidly thumped her foot on the floor. Why didn't he give her the short and sweet layman's version like Michelle had earlier?

The doctor's voice rose and his postulation gathered steam. This was likely the most unique case he would have all year. "I'll have blood and urine samples sent for analysis, but my preliminary hypothesis based on the Mee's Lines and anecdotal reports of breath odor, is strongly indicative of repetitive nonlethal exposure culminating in a final toxic dose. I'll request an EMG but that might have to wait until he can be transported to a larger facility with more advanced neurological investigation technology." Erin, unfamiliar with much of the medical terminology, zoned out when he recited something about micrograms per liter. It sounded like he was referencing a textbook. She said a few apologetically placating words to end the conversation and get the doctor off the phone. Assured that Gunther Schmidt was in expert hands, she hoped he would be in good enough shape to answer a few questions when she returned.

She tucked the phone into her shoulder bag and left it in her father's garage when they arrived. Electronics were useless in the bush with little to no service. Her off duty pistol would be safe there too, locked away from tiny curious hands.

It took only fifteen minutes for Erin's mom to pack food for all three of them, and get the fishing boat ready down by the dock. The 15 horsepower Mercury motor that Erin and her dad had repaired was securely bolted to the stern. Erin's dad tossed two lifejackets onboard for her fellow officers already assuming their positions, Zimmerman on lookout up front and the more experienced Striker manning the stern. He followed the lifejackets with a couple of pairs of rain gear, two paddles and a bailing can. Zimmerman looked at the rain gear and then at the sky, which had begun to darken considerably.

"Looks like maybe a little rain this evening," Erin's dad told him.

"I hope this is not a bad omen, Mr. Ericsson." Zimmerman laughed as he caught the bailing can but his Adam's apple nervously tightened at his throat.

"Nah, she's fine," Erin's dad reassured him. "Leaks a bit sometimes but nothing serious." Zimmerman pulled on his lifejacket and fastened it all the way to the top. Striker was less concerned, nonchalantly stowing gear and familiarizing himself with the vessel. Unlike many others raised in this area, Zimmerman had little exposure to boating and would have to rely on his partner.

Mrs. Ericsson handed over two large thermal bags and both men politely bobbed their heads in unison. They knew that each bag was packed to the brim with goodies and Erin remembered the ample lunches her mom had packed her for school. Her friends had teased her, dubbing them truck driver lunches, but they always eagerly circled her like sharks to help devour every last bit. Her mom must have suspected that she was feeding half of Erin's elementary class.

"We just fixed the motor. Take care of her, boys." Erin's dad untied the fourteen-foot aluminum fishing boat from the dock and gave it a solid push toward the middle of the river channel.

Striker squeezed the primer bulb on the fuel line a couple of times and pulled out the choke knob before he gave a quick yank on the starter rope. The outboard motor hacked out a cloud of blue smoke. Undeterred, he shoved the choke in, pulled it out, and tried again. This time the motor coughed raggedly, and after a minor adjustment, settled into a smooth idle. He adjusted the throttle and switched to reverse until the bow swept around to point downriver. He cranked it into forward and they puttered off without ceremony. Zimmerman gripped the edge of his seat with one hand and held the other up in a tense salute like a soldier going off to the battlefield. Nestled alongside him was the .303 hunting rifle Erin's dad had insisted he borrow. Just in case.

Before they were out of sight, Erin loaded her gear into the lightweight aluminum canoe. They'd all made the decision during the drive that the men would take the motorboat and search the main channel all the way out to the big lake. They could cover more territory and would have room for passengers if they were successful. Confident paddling solo in a canoe since she was eight, Erin had agreed to serve more of a reconnaissance role. With no propeller to worry about, she could poke around all the narrow weed-choked tributaries off the main river. The lightweight craft could also be easily portaged across otherwise inaccessible terrain between waterways.

Stowed at the bow, and serving as counterweight, was Erin's own truck driver lunch and her dad's Mossfield 12 gauge. Before she pushed the canoe off, Erin's mom nervously tucked in an extra paddle and a set of bright yellow rain gear, wrapped around a box of shotgun shells. Her worry lines said she hoped it didn't come to that. Erin raised a hand in a silent wave and turned the bow downstream. She set off with long powerful paddle strokes.

There were almost four hours of daylight left before nightfall when they would all meet back here. She was confident she could easily make it to Blue Water Campground, and if she had calculated her distance correctly, she would arrive at the base of the big lake before the rangers closed up for the night. She could ride back with them and return for the canoe later.

CHAPTER SIXTEEN

Paddle in. Pull back. Paddle out. I watch the droplets of water catch the sunlight when they run off the end of the blade. I've spent a lot of time in small boats but this might be the longest stretch of hard paddling I've ever done. Sweat drips off my nose and right now I am so thirsty I can't work up enough saliva to spit even if I wanted to. Seriously, I could use a beer, but I gave the old bastard the last one I stole. I've always believed that stolen beer tastes better. I wonder if he agreed. I snicker, imagining his stinking corpse rotting in the hole in the ground. He should have known better than to try to tell me what to do. Ten years from now, when they tear down that shed, he'll finally see daylight.

I scoop a handful of water but most of it drains between my fingers before it ever reaches my mouth. It's been hours since my feet have touched dry land and, besides my thirst, the one overwhelming thought in my mind is that I need to pee.

I see the Minion dip a paddle in and then turn it upright like a friggin' flag to guzzle water running down the blade. How did such a stupid idiot figure that out when it hadn't occurred to me? Minion is proving to be useful. I make my face curve into what I hope is a pleasant smile and copy the maneuver. The water running into my mouth is like nectar of the gods. Better than beer. But now I really gotta pee.

There's a small clearing and I point it out. We turn and the bow grinds through the weeds. I push hard on the mucky river bottom until the keel rasps on the sandy shoreline. I poke my paddle one last time at a pair of circling water bugs before I toss it into the middle of the boat and step over the side. I don't give a crap if water fills my shoes. This panther's gotta pee so bad I can almost taste it.

I take my pack with me and head off on my own into the brush to relieve myself on a scrabbly plant with white berries. Doll's Eyes? That's what they are: Poisonous, like me. I make sure I aim for the berries and finish with a sigh. When I'm done, I find a flat rock down by the shore and stretch out for a rest. I search around in my pack and pull out a granola bar, ripping the package off in my haste to eat it. The Cheetos are long gone and so are the things I took from the fridge. I tossed the empty bags overboard an hour ago.

Minion is splashing around by the canoe, probably looking for me, but I'm not moving from this spot until I goddamn well feel like it. Dragonflies buzz me like crop dusters and I half-heartedly swat at them. The sun slips behind a cloud and in the shadow a cooling breeze sweeps over me. About time. I don't know how much more of this heat I can stand. I breathe deep and want to purr. Do panthers purr? This one does when it smells freedom.

* * *

Allie emptied her computer case on the queen size quilt that Erin's mom had made for them when they'd moved into the house. Shaking it upside down, she dumped out every last ballpoint pen and pocket pack of Kleenex. There would be no need for any of that today. She changed into a T-shirt and a pair of urban hiking shorts, the ones she loved to wear when she walked Fiona. On her feet were her favorite leather walking shoes, and she'd tied her hair into its usual tight ponytail.

The first thing she stuffed into the empty bag was her red Columbia windbreaker and pants, followed by Erin's MiniMag flashlight from the bedside stand. It was kept close for those times when they blew an electrical fuse and she needed to traipse to the basement to tinker with the ancient fusebox in the middle of the night. Erin hadn't yet gotten around to the electrical work, so using the hairdryer made that happen with more frequency than she liked.

Attuned to the fact that something different was happening, Fiona trailed inquisitively behind her when she made her way downstairs to finish packing. Wrong-Way Rachel was holed up somewhere sleeping off the catnip she had enjoyed earlier. The exhausted cat would not be interested in poking around the kitchen counters for another couple of hours.

Allie retrieved a small hatchet, the first aid kit, a bottle of insect repellant, and a coil of yellow polypropylene rope from the storage bin in the front closet. A pack of matches, zipped into a plastic bag, went in after that. She hesitated and leaned, staring into the bag. Fiona whined, wetly nosing the back of her knee and she startled upright. She reoriented herself and searched the hallway closet until she found the red Swiss Army knife her ever practical foster mom had given her. It was an immeasurably handy tool and she slid it into the front pocket of the computer bag. In the kitchen, she added what seemed like random items. Fiona wagged her tail when Allie reached into the bottom cupboard for the bag of dog treats.

Leaving her wallet and cell phone behind, she locked the door and loaded the dog into her sadly abused car. She tossed her bag onto the front passenger seat and started the engine. Fiona's tongue dangled out the side of her mouth and her fabulous tail swished energetically. She snuggled into her assigned spot in the back. Allie took a deep breath and backed out the driveway.

She drove on autopilot, absent of conscious decision making. The car navigated across paved streets to the outskirts of town where she turned off and bounced down an unmarked road. Potholes and ruts were deep, scraping the vulnerably low undercarriage of the tiny car. Allie paid no mind and continued until the narrow road became a single lane. It dwindled to twin rows of tire marks through a field of weeds. She drove aggressively, slamming the gears between first and second, forcing the four cylinder engine to its limit. Mud sucked at the tires, rendering them virtually useless. They spun on the unforgiving terrain. She slammed the shifter back into first gear, made her way past a stretch of spongy ground and built up speed, shooting down a narrow tree-lined path.

Fiona's nose twitched in excitement when she sensed their proximity to the river, her tail whipping faster than ever. Allie gunned the engine one last time. The Mini Cooper pitched forward down the bank to the thick aquatic grasses at the river's edge. Water spurted over the hood when it lurched to a stop and then sank ungraciously to its axles in muck.

Stunned, Fiona flattened herself on the floor. The dog shot into

146

the front seat and pawed at Allie's shoulder when brown water seeped in. As if sleepwalking, Allie calmly unclipped her seatbelt and shoved at her door but it was blocked and would not budge. Unruffled, she unrolled her window, retrieved her bag and exited into the knee deep mud. Fiona followed and instinctively headed back up the bank for drier ground, all four paws thrashing through the weeds.

"You're a retriever," Allie said. "You're supposed to like water." The mundane words surprised her when they escaped her mouth and she suddenly looked around, as if this was the first time she'd noticed her surroundings. She grimaced at her favorite shoes sunk under two feet of sludge. Pulling them free, she crawled onto the hood of her car, wrenching off a windshield wiper in the process. She sighed at it and tossed it through the open window. Fiona watched her, barking nervously from the top of the riverbank. Allie swung the computer bag over one shoulder and stood up on the bubbled paint of the car's hood. She held a hand over her brows to shield the sun and watched the river.

A solitary figure in a canoe appeared upstream and Allie waited. Erin's posture stiffened when she recognized her girlfriend and the sunken Mini Cooper. Her paddle strokes quickened. Fiona's barking grew feverish when Erin's canoe pulled closer.

"Baby!" she called out. "What are you doing here?"

"I am coming with you!" Fiona chimed into the conversation with a worried bark of her own.

"You can't. Your car!" Erin nosed the canoe into the grasses and out of the river's current.

"You have to take us! You can't leave us stranded out here!" Allie pointed at the dog pacing onshore as if that would be the deciding factor.

* * *

She was right. The closest house was miles from here, if she could even find it in the woods. Erin knew she could not leave her out here alone. She pointed to a rocky outcropping fifty feet downstream and backed the canoe out of the weeds. "Meet me there!"

Allie bounded onto the roof of the car and then, like an Olympic long jumper, made one giant leap toward the riverbank. Fiona ran to greet her when she landed ankle deep in mud and dragged her sodden shoes up the bank. The dog circled as if they had been separated for days and trotted contentedly behind her to the prearranged meeting spot. They arrived as the canoe's bow eased onto shore and Erin disembarked, hands reproachfully on hips. She faced Allie, who beamed triumphantly.

"What were you thinking?" Erin said, more tersely than she had intended, and Allie's smile drooped.

"I-I'm not a hundred percent sure." Allie's lip almost quivered before she recovered. "I know I needed to get here, to this very spot, as fast as I could. I didn't understand until I drowned my car and saw you coming down the river." Erin's expression softened. "You can't leave me here. You have to take me with you."

"And the dog?" Erin massaged Fiona's soft ear. "What do we do with the dog?"

Allie lifted a foot into the canoe and began to board before Erin quickly grabbed the teetering gunwale and motioned her back. She took a deep breath. They would have to start from square one. She slid the boat back off the rock until it was buoyant in the water and waded to her thighs beside it. She relocated the gear and rotated the canoe until the bow was facing out. Directing Allie to enter from the stern, with her weight centered, she reminded her to hold fast to the gunwales. Allie did as instructed and slid her hands along her way to the bow. As if it might leap out and snap at her, she studiously avoided the shotgun lying across Erin's pack.

She had a great sense of balance and there was a minimum of wobble during the procedure. She slid gracefully into her seat, bag at her feet. When she was settled, Erin gently picked up Fiona, hoisting the nervously compliant seventy pound canine into the middle of the boat. The dog's body tensed and she stiffly settled into a spot dead center. She stepped one sneaker over the side and pushed the canoe away from shore with her other foot. It destabilized momentarily as everyone on board adjusted their position and then settled low in the water. Fiona whined softly and Erin reached forward to pat the dog's back.

"It's okay, buddy," she crooned. "You're a good girl." Fiona's tail thumped against the aluminum keel and she sniffed a spot under the thwart. Sufficiently distracted, she shifted her weight a little more and hunkered lower in the boat. Erin slid her paddle out slowly so as not to alarm the dog and made strong strokes to get the craft back into the river's downstream current. Paddling solo, she tilted the blade at the end of each stroke to correct the yaw.

Allie took up the extra paddle in front and wholeheartedly tugged it through the water, thrashing the wooden handle against the metal gunwale. After a couple of noisy strokes, she peered around at Erin, who thrust her paddle deeply into the water, drawing it back until it was even with her hip. Erin pointedly withdrew the paddle and repeated. Allie watched the demonstration and then dutifully replicated it at the bow, forcefully propelling the canoe forward. Taken off guard by Allie's unexpectedly strong stroke, Erin was forced to dig in to correct their direction.

"I'm so glad you are not a lily dipper," she quipped, and Allie shot her a baffled look. The view from the stern lifted Erin's spirits and she marveled at how easily her city girl had transformed herself once she'd committed to being in the great outdoors. Allie's strong arms pumped rhythmically when she paddled, ponytail swishing back and forth like a metronome across muscular shoulders. It was hard not to want to reach out and stroke the soft caramel colored skin at her neck.

Erin steered them downstream once more, and the two women settled into an easy rhythm. Fiona heaved a great sigh and settled her head on Erin's pack. The sky grew darker and rain clouds gathered in the distance. A half hour passed before either of them spoke.

"Do I need to ask how you knew where to find me?"

"I don't know," Allie told her. "I just came." She pulled her paddle from the water and twisted around in her seat. "I don't remember actually thinking about what I was doing. I just did it. I packed stuff, loaded the dog and drove. I didn't understand why I had driven my car in the river until I saw you come paddling around the corner. I couldn't risk missing you."

"Hmmm." Erin had no response to that. They paddled on for a few more minutes.

"I don't have a headache!" Allie exclaimed. Fiona's ears twitched upright, settling back down when no apparent danger emerged.

"You better not have candles and wine in that bag, because I have no time for romance." Allie kept paddling, but Erin could imagine the impish grin on her face. In other circumstances, it would be an immensely enjoyable canoe excursion. She turned her mind to the urgent purpose of this particular trip.

"Two other officers went downstream in my dad's fishing boat," she said. If Allie wanted to help, she might as well know what they were looking for. "They are checking the main channel but they can't get into any narrower streams, or places with too many weeds. This canoe rides higher in the water and doesn't have a motor to get tangled. We will be able to check all of those areas." Up front, Allie nodded. She did not miss a stroke.

"Look up ahead," Erin whispered and Allie's ponytail bobbed to attention.

"A moose!" she said, a little too loudly, causing Fiona to let out a tiny yip. The wary moose raised its head and, with unusual grace for such a large ungainly creature, stepped up over the riverbank. It disappeared silently into the trees. The only evidence of its passing was a narrow divide in the cattails where it had crossed the river.

As they passed the spot, Erin pointed to the separation in floating lilypads and the trail of bent grasses. "That is what we are looking for. A canoe recently passing will make a path like that if it heads to shore. If we see any others, we need to investigate what caused them."

"What else are we looking for?" Allie was an eager partner.

"Campfire smoke, disturbed wildlife, anything that might have been discarded—"

"A note carved into a tree by Lily that says exactly where they've gone?" Allie quipped, finishing her sentence.

"With a map." Erin loved that girl.

CHAPTER SEVENTEEN

"You have food!" Minion says. I slowly slide the plastic package from my beef jerky over the edge of the canoe and into the water. I manage a grimace in response. It's not my fault Minion was too stupid to bring anything.

Minion stops paddling altogether and gawks at me. *Let's go. Paddle.* I can't tell if that look is angry or sad. Minion's stare is still frozen on me, paddle not moving. The canoe turns sideways in the river and we drift. We are headed for a tangle of branches from a fallen poplar and will be stuck there in a minute. *Fine.* I dig in my bag and throw the package of cookies over. Minion fumbles and has to scrabble around to grab them before they are soaked in the mucky soup at the bottom of the canoe. I hide my smile. *Now keep paddling.*

The sky is dark as mud and the air is cooler, enough to make me shiver, by the time I spot the dead tree ahead. Birch bark peels like sheets of white paper off the trunk and one naked branch signals me to the little creek I've been looking for. I point it out to The Minion who gives me a dumbass look and shrugs like a moron. I have been here before, many times, and what usually takes me twenty minutes in the motorboat, took friggin' forever to paddle.

My arms are welted with mosquito bites and I splash a little water onto them but it doesn't take the itch. The one thing I forgot was the thing I could use most right now. Everyone knows you don't go into the woods without your bug dope. We hop out at the shore and Minion helps me tug the canoe over a fallen tree blocking our way. We drag the boat through the guck and the fiberglass hull screeches against a rock, startling a flock of sparrows. The commotion in the trees makes me jump.

"Sheisse!" I yell and duck my head, just in case. "I hate birds." The Minion stares at me again. *Would you stop eyeballing me?*

We leave the worst of the mosquitoes behind at the river and haul the canoe to the top of the bank, turning it upside down in the brush. The faded green hull blends into the ground and won't be noticed. I take the knife from my pocket and snap it open, sinking the blade into the bark of the tree above the canoe. It sticks out like a brown handled warning to anyone who might come this way. Caution, danger ahead. Stay out.

In the trees, the pesky mosquitoes of the river are replaced by swarms of blackflies and a dark cloud of insects hums above me, homing in. Always most hungry before a storm, they bite through the tender skin behind my ears and I swat uselessly. I pull the front of my shirt over my mouth and nose so I can breathe, but they still feast wherever they can. It's enough to make you insane. I see blood drizzling down Minion's neck and I hope his tastes sweeter than mine to the blackflies.

There is a narrow animal trail along the creek and I lead the way deeper into the bush, my panther feet coming back to me on dry land. The branches whipping by break up the bugs so I move fast to take advantage. Minion follows right behind me and I cinch up my backpack straps to keep it close. A five-minute walk from the main river, where the creek disappears underground, is my secret hideout. It's a one room wooden shack that I found two years ago and it's mine. The metal roof's rusty but it doesn't leak, far as I know. The old door's half busted but it still keeps out the critters. There is plastic covering the single window beside the door and I replace it from time to time with new stuff. I kind of hate letting Minion in on my secret place but today it can't be helped. I twist the latch on the door and we get inside, trying not to take too many flying vampires with us.

Minion examines the three legged stool, wiggles the little table and kicks at the frame of the wooden bed like a friggin' army inspector. Finally Minion sits. I shake the leaves from the chimney pipe and kneel to light a fire in the stove. It's nothing special, only a square metal box someone hauled out here long before the place was mine. It has a couple of hinges on the grated door in front and a pipe that goes back out the wall under the roof overhang. It works great and I've even come out here on a cool fall afternoon to get away.

I've barely got the fire going when the rain comes, gentle at first like whispering leaves, then harder, crashing on the metal roof. And the thunder, like all the bastards in hell are shouting at once. I sit on the dirt floor in front of the stove and watch the flames lick up every last bit of wood I stuff in. Just seeing the bright little fingers surround and devour the sticks of wood gives me a tickle in the base of my stomach. Fire is my friend. I could sit here all night but the heat is getting too intense. Sweat beads my forehead and I remember that I am not alone. The invader is here. I close the grated door and back away.

Minion wants to talk. Talk about our day. Talk about our future. Talk about the fire. Talk about the old man. I can't even hear with the godawful racket of the rain, so I curl up like a big dangerous cat on the other side of the bed and try to keep myself to myself until morning.

* * *

"I see something!" Allie scooted forward in her seat to point into the weeds and the canoe teetered dangerously. Fiona whined and Erin calmed her after she stabilized the boat with her own weight.

"Baby! Don't flip us!" Now Erin spotted it too and dug in her paddle to turn the small craft. Hung up in the lilypads out of the main current was a bright red and orange plastic bag. Allie peered down at it in the water when Erin steered them past. "We missed the junk food party!" The bag had not had a chance to make it further into the weeds, or to be submerged by the current, and had likely been tossed earlier in the day.

"Cheetos!" Erin plucked it out of the water and examined it, crushing it in one angry fist. Fiona sniffed the air with interest and she tucked the empty package under her pack on the floor. "I know Striker and Z-man did not have Cheetos. Derek, the lunch thief, must be the junk food litterbug." She clenched her jaw and put more energy into each paddle stroke. If they hurried, they might be able to catch up. Sensing her urgency, Allie matched her stroke for stroke and the canoe skimmed across the water's surface, a sharp V rippling in its wake.

A half hour later, Allie called out again, this time remaining steadfastly glued to her seat. She balanced her paddle on thighs and pointed a gracefully long finger into the trees. "We need to look there."

"Do you see something?" Erin squinted. Allie did have better eyesight. She tilted her paddle and steered them toward a flat rock on a sandy stretch of riverbank. As they approached, Erin noted a sharp indentation from a canoe's scraping keel that she had totally missed. There were two sets of footprints in the sand, disappearing into the grass and then returning. In addition to her surprisingly strong paddling, Allie proved to be an observant scout. Like she had been born in a canoe, she vaulted over the bow and pulled the boat onto shore by the painter line. She lifted the relieved dog out over the side and Fiona daintily stepped to dry land, lapping water on her way.

The women followed Fiona's nose on a quick excursion ashore. The dog led them to a couple of plastic granola bar wrappers and a circle of footprints digging into the sand by the canoe's landing spot. Someone had been waiting here. Were they waiting for something or was this only a resting place? With no questions to their answers, they launched the canoe back onto the river.

Erin was glad she had taken a moment to zip into her rain gear while they were onshore and she was sure Allie felt the same when the first couple of soft raindrops pattered onto their hoods. It was still a long ways to the Ranger Station at Blue Water campground and, judging from the darkening storm clouds, they could waste no more time here.

Scarcely back into their paddling rhythm, they spotted a smear of red around the next bend. This time Erin saw it too and was alarmed when they came upon her dad's aluminum fishing boat. Abandoned in the weeds at the river's edge, the motor's propellor was pivoted up on its mount revealing severely twisted blades. She immediately knew what had happened. She had seen damage like this before, and it signaled the kiss of death for the motor.

"This looks like your dad's boat," Allie said. She pointed to the double set of footprints exiting up the muddy bank. "Why did they leave it here?"

Erin nodded at the misshapen propeller. "They must have hit a dead head."

"A dead head?" She lifted her paddle abruptly from the water.

"It's what they call a partially submerged log that is hard to see. You want to be careful not to hit it with your motor prop, or this happens. You are dead in the water." Erin thrust her paddle into the river bottom to hold their position steady in the current, and leaned over the stern. She retrieved a piece of paper weighted onto the seat by a sizable rock. At least eight inches of river water sloshed in the bottom from a cracked hull. Zimmerman must have been bailing water like a madman before Striker was able to maneuver the boat safely to shore. She grinned when she read the note, obviously intended for her, and handed it up to Allie.

Z DID IT.

This was crossed out and underneath was scribbled in pen.

NO IT WAS THE MUPPET.

Allie looked at her quizzically, so Erin explained. "The guy driving the boat is supposed to be careful not to hit anything. The guy in the front is supposed to be keeping lookout and yell when he spots something. If the guy driving is going too fast, or if the guy in front is not watching carefully, bad things can happen."

"Okay. I get why they are blaming each other, but who is Muppet?"

Erin laughed. "You haven't met Striker yet but, if you've ever watched Sesame Street, you'll get it."

"Sounds like they are both behaving like juveniles with your dad's boat."

"Believe me, my dad will probably be ecstatic to hear that they not only destroyed the motor, but the boat too. He's been trying to convince my mom that he needs a new one for ages. She always says, Oh Tom, yer boat's bin workin' just fine now. You don't need ta waste yer money on a new boughten one. Now come here once and help me peel dem pah-day-duhs while I go checksie the roast in the oven."

"Your mom does not sound like that!" Allie stifled her laugh.

"Dern-tootin, she does when she's had too much blueberry wine, don't ya know that then?" Erin was having fun with this. "My pappy does too!"

"Maybe your dad does, a little." Allie had to admit that she had heard a few unusual colloquialisms here and there.

"Ya, fer sure. You betcha he does. Pret'near every time the inners come over!"

"Well, I wouldn't want to be the one to tell your dad, in any language, that I broke his boat!"

"Oh-fer-geez, right now Z-man and The Muppet are paying their dues. They are feeding the skeeters out in the swamp and they'll be lucky if they make it to the forestry road 'fore dark. Then they have to pray someone comes along to give them a ride." There was a sudden chill in the air and Erin zipped her rain jacket right to the top. When the thunderheads arrived, the mosquitoes would be intolerable here on the river too.

"I wish you would stop calling him Muppet. When I finally do meet Striker, I am afraid I will slip and insult him! Aren't you worried about them?"

"They're big boys. They have food, they have rain gear, and they have their guilt. They'll be fine." Erin had her doubts about Zimmerman, whose woodsman skills were questionable, but Striker should be able to find the road. "Those storm clouds are getting closer. We'd better hurry." She pushed her paddle in deep and leaned on it until the canoe was back out into the current.

Allie peered into the rippling river water. "What if we hit a dead head?" She kept her paddle balanced on both thighs and explored the bottom of her pack.

"Don't worry, babe. This sneaky little canoe doesn't ride as low and we will skin right over it with a little bump. Besides, your eagle eyes will spot it long before we get close."

"Are you trying to say I might be helpful?" Allie produced a bottle of insect repellant and applied it liberally. She pretended to put it back into her pack and then neatly tossed it back to Erin, who caught it mid-air.

"Best girlfriend ever," Erin said. "What other goodies do you have in there?"

"All kinds of junk I threw in." Allie shrugged. "I don't really remember." She opened the bag wide. "Apparently I have a hatchet and some rope and treats for Fuzzy Fiona, best dog ever." She cooed, flipping a Milk Bone into Fiona's waiting mouth. The dog chomped her biscuit loudly.

Stomach suddenly rumbling, Erin took the cue and unzipped her mom's truck driver lunch. She let the canoe drift downstream, occasionally correcting their trajectory with a well angled paddle stroke. There was a surprising variety of food in the cooler bag, enough to last two people a couple of days. Apparently, her mom was still intent on feeding the entire neighborhood. Fiona nosed her knee and Erin covertly snuck a piece of ham into her drooling mouth. They quickly munched on sandwiches, yogurt and strawberries before digging in their paddles once again in a much more satisfied state.

Thunder sounded in the distance, angry black clouds blotted out the sunset, but despite uncomfortable blisters, Erin and Allie kept paddling. They needed to reach Blue Water campground before the sky fell.

CHAPTER EIGHTEEN

Erin looked at the clouds. "Tell me how it feels when you get one of your premonitions." Talking seemed more productive than worrying about the approaching storm.

"You want to talk about feelings?" Allie laughed while she paddled. "That's what, twice in one week? What's happened to my ever-practical lover?"

"I'm only making conversation."

"I don't know what to tell you. I'm new at this. All my life I have worked so hard to suppress all the weird feelings I get. Now I try to relax when I sense thoughts coming and let it happen," she said thoughtfully. "I guess I need to find a way to pay attention to what I'm doing too because I have no idea what I packed in my bag, and I didn't intend to destroy my car."

"I don't mean to sound like a shrink but you're telling me what you do, not how you feel. How does it feel?"

Allie thought for a moment. "I'm not sure how to describe it. When stuff like that happens, I'm not aware that I'm actually using my brain. It's purely sensory. Depending on the circumstances, it can be a draft in the room, the hair on the back of my scalp prickling, or an aversion to a certain person. I often get persistent thoughts and I know that if I don't go do whatever is bothering me, it will never leave me alone. I can't ignore it or they will get stronger until it gets so uncomfortable that I can't concentrate on anything else."

"Kind of like the night you felt we needed to go to Gunther's place to look for Lily? She was there, you know. We just couldn't find her."

"I know. She was hiding and I couldn't help because I let myself get too upset."

"It's not your fault," Erin said. "What do you feel when you think about finding Derek?"

"It's funny, but when I try to imagine where Derek took the girl, I get confused. It's like there is a whole other part of him that is a separate entity. We need to find Derek, but not Derek. It makes no sense. Like he is not himself, more like a part of his essence. Wow, that sounds strange."

"And confusing."

"What's also confusing is that I sometimes see a dark animal prowling. Like a cat. A dangerous wild one."

"All that confusion must have been hard for you, especially in your teens when everything is so dramatic to begin with," Erin said. Allie breathed more deeply talking about it and Erin recognized it as a relaxation technique she often used. She was reluctant to push Allie to talk about this if it made her so uncomfortable, but could not resist the one burning question she had left. "Is it scary for you?"

"Most of the time it's an ethereal sensation, like hmmm, would you look at that? That's interesting. If I do this, then that will happen, or I must do this right now. It's like I'm a spectator in a drama movie and it doesn't involve me, but there have been a few times when I've been terrified."

"You don't have to—"

"Who else can I tell about this stuff? At least I can't see your face so I can pretend you're not laughing—"

"I would never laugh at you," Erin answered before Allie finished her sentence. "Trust me that I love and care about you."

"I do trust you," Allie said. "Yes, there have been some disturbing times, and I'll tell you about one really bad experience. I was at the airport with my foster mom one time. I was around twenty-three, and we were on our way to Vancouver for a little holiday because I had recently graduated from U of T. We hadn't gone through to the gate for our flight yet and it was quite busy in the main terminal. It was a regular day and I was looking forward to the trip when my world suddenly tilted sideways."

"My entire field of vision narrowed to a single person, a man who was walking through the airport with a suitcase. Everything else distorted until all I saw was him. He was such a strong figure, like a black mark on white paper, and I could not tear my eyes away." Allie stopped paddling when the memories came rushing out. Simultaneously, Fiona began to whine. The dog stood up and tried to circle but the canoe rocked so she quickly sat down again. She nosed forward until her muzzle touched the back of Allie's shirt.

"I knew, I just knew, that at that moment he was doing something bad, so unbelievably evil that I could not imagine the depths. I was terrified. I couldn't breathe. I couldn't speak. All the air was virtually sucked from my lungs when he passed by me. I remember sheer horror and the overwhelming feeling that someone needed to do something to stop him. I was utterly repulsed. I felt like passing out and running away and following him all at once but, in the midst of all my panic, there was an overwhelming knowledge that it was not safe for me to follow him. I knew I needed to get as far away as possible. I rushed out the furthest doors and gulped air for at least ten minutes before I was able to tell my foster mom what was going on."

"That must have been awful." She almost regretted making Allie dredge up this memory. The dog's whine intensified and she tried to stand up again. Erin reached out to stroke her fur until she laid down.

"What was more terrifying was what else I saw." Allie forced herself to fill her lungs before she spoke again. "I'm aware that this sounds totally insane but he was not alone. He was a strong malevolent force making his way through the airport, but there were others, like wispy half-formed non-corporeal creatures, traveling with him. They surrounded and followed in his dark oily slipstream. They were very excited by what he was doing and were goading him on with more power." Fiona's high-pitched whine became a pathetic whimper.

"Omigod!" Erin exclaimed. If this story had come from anyone else, she would have walked away in disbelief. Instead, she wanted to wrap her arms around Allie and give her comfort. "What a horrible memory! I'm sorry I asked you this. It was truly insensitive of me."

Allie's words rushed out. "When he was near me, every particle in my body vibrated so wildly that I feared flesh would separate from my bones. I needed to get away before I would suffer mortal damage." She heaved a deep sigh and finished. "I did not go after him because I knew I was powerless to stop him."

My foster mom helped me to calm down. She was always so warm and accepting of my quirks, but it ruined our trip because it took me days to overcome the awful experience. I never did figure out what the man did but I'm convinced my feeling about him was right. It still practically gives me chest pain to remember."

"Are you okay?"

"I have only told that story once before. It was easier this time. It's messed up, isn't it?"

"I can't disagree," Erin said gently. "Is this stuff in your head all the time?"

"No," A hint of uncharacteristic sarcasm crept into Allie's voice. "Usually it's all sunshine, rainbows and puppy dogs." She paused until the sarcasm evaporated. "I think I've learned to block it out so well that, unless it's really serious, I have to make a deliberate effort to let that stuff in. Having a dog helps. My sweet Fiona is like an emotional barometer." The dog's tail whipped back and forth at the mention of her name. "Somehow she senses how I feel and lets me know when I should calm down. She's telling me to relax right now. It's okay, sweetie." The dog whined softly, and she scratched her under the chin. "I haven't had any trouble controlling it until recently. I'm not sure what changed."

"Maybe it's because you're more open," Erin offered, "because of me."

"You do make me crazy, honey."

"I believe you. I believe you feel things, you see things others can't. I hope you understand that this does not mean anything is wrong with you."

"I'm okay," Allie said. She sliced the paddle roughly through the water and Erin scrambled to keep up in the stern. "We need to paddle harder because the storm is coming!"

The long anticipated thunder grumbled above and accompanying rain spattered from the sky. In the distance, lightning zigzagged down from blackened clouds unleashing their fury.

"We need to get off the river now!" Erin called out.

"No!" Allie insisted. "This is not a good place. We have to go further." The heavens lit up and a flash blinded them, followed by an ear splitting crack of thunder that shook them to their spines. Panicked, Fiona was on her feet in an instant, ready to leap into the water.

"The lightning is close!" Erin yelled. "It's too dangerous to be on the water. We need to get shelter now!"

Despite Allie's continuing resistance, Erin steered the boat to the closest reasonable landing spot on the river and Fiona fled over the side, swimming like a muskrat to shore and disappearing into the trees before they'd landed. Allie slung her pack over her shoulder and leapt out after the dog, leaving Erin alone.

Erin secured the canoe upside down under the trees and was on hands and knees clearing out prickly ground cover when Allie returned with the dog. She flattened an area under an overhang in the rock face and positioned the canoe as a partial windbreak.

"Fiona wouldn't listen to me," Allie's brows pinched together. "I don't know what's wrong with her." The dog strained at her leash, nose to the ground, and Allie tugged at one end.

"This is the first time I've ever seen you chase after her." Erin crouched and held the dog's head in her hands. "What's the big deal, Fuzzy Fiona? Are you sick of being in the boat? Or is it the thunder?" She stroked the soft hair between Fiona's ears. "Lots of dogs are really afraid of thunderstorms." Fiona growled, a low sound deep in her throat.

"I've never seen her like this." Allie pulled Fiona closer and put her arms around the dog. "You're not a tough girl, pumpkin. You're more of a lover, not a fighter, aren't you girl?" Fiona growled again, hair rising sharply along her spine. This time her nose pointed directly toward the forest. "I think the dog might be reacting to me."

"Maybe. You really did not want to stop here," Erin reluctantly agreed. "But we had to get off the river fast. It was too dangerous."

"It felt wrong. I don't know why. Perhaps I am being weird after telling you all that stuff that scared me. I must have short-circuited my brain." She twisted her mouth in a wry grin.

"I'm prepared to cut you some slack because you've had a rough day," Erin quipped and Allie gave her a pained smile.

"I smell smoke," Allie faced upriver, "from that direction."

Erin crashed through the undergrowth to the river's edge and climbed onto a rock with the best view of the river. "They had to get off the river too!" she exclaimed. "I smell it now. Derek, that bastard, has a fire somewhere close, no more than a mile or two!"

"I don't see smoke, but I smell it. Fiona must too."

"If we go at first light, we might be able to catch him before he leaves his camp!"

"And we can still save the girl," Erin said.

Allie followed her back to the clearing by the rock. "Are you going to make a shelter? Can I help?" Without waiting for a response, she looped the dog's leash around a stump and foraged for wood.

Erin stomped down the rest of the weeds and collected branches under the trees. By the time she returned with an armful, Allie had used her yellow polypropylene rope to lash a beam and two support poles between tree trunks. A thick stack of coniferous branches was already piled beside her. Erin quietly added her meager armful to the stack and stood open-mouthed.

Allie arranged more branches to complete the support for the structure, all without using the hatchet she'd brought. Rain pelted down and they stacked layer upon layer against the support poles until it was capable of keeping out the worst of the weather. They shook water out of their gear and crawled into the shelter. Allie kept her bag close and pulled the watchful dog in after her. She unfolded her red Swiss Army knife and whittled a notch into the end of a stick.

"You bring marshmallows or something in that bottomless mystery pack of yours?" Erin's humor was half-hearted. She was decidedly feeling outdone by her city-raised girlfriend. She rubbed both palms on her thighs in an attempt to scrape off tree sap, but it tore open her blisters. Maybe Allie had Band-Aids in her magic pack.

"I'm going to make a little rack so we can dry out these soaking wet shoes."

"Where did you—?" Erin caught the words in her throat. It would be rude to imply that she had believed her girlfriend incapable when it came to the outdoors.

"I read about it on the internet." She winked, amusement flickering in her dark eyes. "WikiHow."

"Ohhhh. Okay." As implausible as it seemed, Erin was not willing to argue the point.

Allie waited an interminably long time before she confessed. "I used to go to YMCA camp every summer as a kid in Toronto. They never let us leave the paved campground paths but we did learn how to tie knots and make shelters. I also earned the distinction of being the undisputed Kangaroo Wrestling champ for three years in a row." Erin couldn't tell if she was pulling her leg. Allie rooted around beneath the overturned canoe and extracted a wad of dry birch bark, along with an armful of kindling. A package of matches appeared from her pack and she quickly arranged the bark under a teepee of kindling and struck a match.

"And you learned to make fires at camp too." Erin said, incredulous at how fast she breathed tiny sparks to life under her hands.

"Haven't you heard that every foster kid can light a fire?" she quipped. Erin blanched at the awful stereotype and Allie laughed. "Just kidding. Yes, I learned fire starting at summer camp." Within moments flames licked the sides of the kindling and she added a few larger sticks of dry wood from her cache to the fire.

They propped their shoes on Allie's ingeniously useful drying rack in front of the fire and settled back into the radiating warmth to shed wet clothing. Unwilling to allow herself to be useless, Erin unzipped her cooler bag and pulled out what was left of her mom's truck driver lunch. If they had to wait out the storm here, they might as well sleep with full bellies.

Showing no interest in the food, the dog pricked up her ears and stayed on her feet, growling restlessly. Erin patted her head and uttered soothing words but Fiona paced nervously between them. When they had finished eating, she took a length of Allie's yellow rope and tossed it over a tree branch a safe distance from their sleeping area. She hoisted the cooler bag eight feet off the ground and tied the rope off, leaving the remainder of the food dangling mid-air.

"Why are you bear proofing our food?" Allie asked suspiciously. "You said there were no grizzly bears around here. You said the story about your Auntie Vicky was only for fun."

"I said there were no grizzly bears," Erin qualified. "There are plenty of black bears that would love a ham sandwich and the rest of my mom's peanut butter cookies. I don't want them to come looking for them in our shelter."

"Fiona's behavior concerns me," Allie said. The dog's whining had become background noise for the storm. She nonchalantly nudged her computer case, reassured by the bulky shape of the hatchet. "It can't be the thunder she's worried about now. We haven't heard any for at least a half hour. Something is out there and it's bothering her. I feel it too. Something is coming. Something bad that I can't change."

"That sounds ominous!" Erin pulled her dad's Mossberg shotgun from under the canoe, checked that it was loaded and slid it back. "What do you sense?"

"I'm not a gypsy fortune teller," Allie snapped. She gripped the dog's collar and directed her to lie down but Fiona pulled away. "I can't tell the future whenever you want." She poked a stick into the fire until the end glowed orange. "I'm sorry for being testy. I'm trying to make the best of it but there's this persistent sensation in the back of my mind that something bad is coming."

Goosebumps prickled across Erin's skin and she crowded closer to her girlfriend, pulling the dog onto their joint laps. Fiona resisted, panting with anxiety and reluctantly sank to her belly. "I bet you were also the undisputed camp champion of scary bedtime stories."

"I learned to shut my mouth after the first year. Seriously, have you ever seen an entire teepee full of freaked out little girls? It doesn't take much. It's crazy mass hysteria."

"What did you tell them?" Erin's curiosity was worse than a cat's.

"I told them what happened at the lake."

"Which was..."

"I felt that a boy had drowned there. His friends laughed at him because they thought he was messing around. The boy struggled for a long time but he wasn't a good swimmer and he panicked. After a while, he went under the water and never came up. I told the kids that his ghost stayed to haunt the lake and tried to drown other kids. Okay, I made that last part up so it would be it a scary story for them, and I embellished the drowning part so it was more dramatic." She grimaced uncomfortably. "After the mass hysteria incident, not a single kid would go near the water for the rest of camp and I got in trouble with the counselors. They packed up the canoes for the season and nobody could try them."

"I guess that would cure you." Erin knew that Allie had toned down tonight's version of her story and imagined the hullabaloo it would have caused for a group of prepubescent girls sleeping outdoors at summer camp.

"I also didn't like being called Spooky Indian Girl. Luckily there was a whole different crop of kids the next year and the nasty nickname faded away. The sad part was that they didn't have a canoe instructor either, so I was never able to try it." She sat up abruptly. "Do you hear that?"

"What is it?" Erin strained her ears and wasn't sure if she'd actually heard a high-pitched keening wail, or if Allie's ghost story was giving her the heebie-jeebies. She was instantly in a crouch, one hand reacquainting itself with the location of the shotgun.

"I thought—No, it's only my imagination. Listen, the rain is stopping."

"Oh." Erin settled back, calmly adjusting her position as if her heart was not crashing in her chest like the cymbals in a Chinese Opera. "We should try to sleep so we can leave at first light. If Derek reaches the big lake before we catch him, he can get his hands on a motorboat and who knows how far he'll go. He might make it to Canada."

Allie reached into her bag and withdrew Erin's MiniMag flashlight, handing it over. "You might need this."

"Best girlfriend ever." Erin smiled and kissed her at the corner of her mouth, her favorite spot.

* * *

Allie laid her head on Erin's shoulder and unsnapped the dog's leash. Surely Fiona would settle if her people were also able to relax. She closed her eyes. Sinister shapes intruded and she tried to clear her mind. With menacing shadows approaching from every angle, she had never felt so unsafe since she had reached adulthood. Eventually, she drifted into a fitful rest, somewhere between sleep and consciousness, somewhere between the safety of Erin's shoulder and the danger of the shadows pacing out of sight.

Frenetic barking woke her and she jolted from her dark dream, struggling to reorient herself in the tiny space. The fire had died to embers and she was alone. Fiona was gone, and so was Erin. *Bears!*

Allie wrenched her shoes off the drying rack and jammed her feet in, hatchet in hand. She was out of the shelter and moving at a gallop in an instant. "Erin! Fiona!" she screamed. She circled the lean to, unsure which direction to take. More barking. Her dog had never sounded so fierce. "Fiona!" Allie charged toward the sound, beating frantically at the brush with her hatchet. "Erin!"

She froze when wailing howls reverberated through the night and her brain transformed into a billion electrified neurons. Adrenaline shot through her veins and she vaulted a jumble of rocks in her way.

She ran blindly in the darkness toward feral voices strained in their savage chorus. Closer now, a small splash of light spun randomly through the trees. One sound differentiated itself from all the others and Allie's heart lurched. Fiona's frantic barking was overtaken by ferocious growls. She gripped the hatchet like a baseball bat and searched for the flashlight, a tiny candle of hope.

She found them in a small clearing illuminated faintly by the half moon, which had serendipitously chosen to peep through the clouds. Holding the shotgun at her shoulder, Erin circled warily. At her knee was Fiona, standing stiffly with hackles raised and teeth bared in a display of primitive ferocity. Fiona relied on Erin's body position to compensate for her lack of vision.

The dog charged forward, backed up and then altered her direction to charge again. Erin's shotgun trajectory followed but the shadows moved too quickly for a shot that would not endanger the dog. When Fiona stumbled on her hind leg, Allie involuntarily called out.

"Fiona! Erin!"

A growl nearby startled her and she leapt forward into the pale circle of moonlight with Erin and the dog. In the tiny flashlight beam, Allie could see their aggressors. It was not a bear after all. She had read enough bedtime stories to recognize that in this darkness was truly the big bad wolf of her childhood nightmares. Sharp teeth and yellow eyes glared back at her and two other sets of yellow eyes joined the first, weaving menacingly in and out of the flashlight beam. Erin shielded Allie's body with her own, pushing her back toward the trees, but Allie resisted and stood beside her, brandishing the hatchet.

"Allie!" Erin shouted. "Stay behind me!"

"No! I want to help!" Allie shook her head defiantly. "What's happening?"

"I heard a bark and ran out to find Fiona here. She's been bitten, I think. She was trying to chase them away."

Despite the injury she concealed, Fiona stood her ground in front of Allie, every hair on her spine bristling with protective instinct. Just beyond the light projected by the MiniMag, there were threatening growls and the savage gnashing of razor sharp teeth. Wary of the light, the wolves kept to the shadows. With the dog between her and the wild animals, Erin had no clear shot. In frustration, she pointed the shotgun to the sky and pulled the trigger. Fire spewed from the end of the barrel and the explosion split the night like a thunderclap. The animals panicked and bolted. Fiona flattened herself onto the ground like a well-trained soldier.

"Are they gone?" Allie's dark eyes shone with all the fervor of a warrior. She reached down to touch her dog's head and Fiona whimpered quietly in response. "It's okay sweetheart. We're going home now. It's okay—"

"Maybe not." A searing flash of anger replaced Erin's initial relief when her flashlight's beam illuminated a set of yellow eyes. They were back.

Fiona rose painfully to her feet and gave a low warning growl but the wolves smelled blood and they knew their quarry was weakened. The first wolf Allie had seen, the natural leader, rushed forward and snapped at them, lips bared from wickedly pointed teeth. Fiona summoned all her instinctive canine strength and snapped back with equal ferocity, her bark high pitched in contrast with her adversary's feral baying.

Two pack members circled stealthily behind Allie and Fiona pivoted her stiff legged stance to snap a warning to the newcomers. They attacked as one, charging at Fiona but Allie stepped into their path at the last moment. One black beast's canine teeth struck her skin, below the knee, and came away bloodied. Hearing Allie's sharp cry, Fiona lunged and bit deeply into the wolf's muzzle. It yipped like a wounded puppy and retreated with its pack mate to the tree line. Fiona faced the retreating cowards and barked menacingly.

Attention diverted, the leader struck without warning from behind, clamping sharp teeth around Fiona's injured leg. Erin slammed the butt of her shotgun down on the wolf's spine and then aimed a vicious kick at its throat. With a snarl, it clenched powerful jaws and flinched away from her foot before impact. Instead of releasing its grip, it gave its head a cruel twist, tearing flesh from sinew. The dog yelped in shock and agony, hind end awkwardly collapsing. Stunned, Fiona staggered upright on forelegs and frantically dragged herself toward Allie. The attacking wolf charged again and Allie wildly swung her hatchet, the blunt end glancing off its skull. It yowled in pain, backing off to shake its massive head, but there was only a moment's reprieve before it rushed in again from the side, directly toward Allie.

With a ferocious scream of her own, Erin stepped directly into the wolf's path and stomped toward it like a madwoman. She fired once, twice, three times, racking the shotgun hard between trigger pulls. The multiple cracks of the 12-gauge stunned the wolves into flight, all but one. Lead shot ripped open the leader's throat and laid bare a patch of skin on its chest. Halfway into its powerful strike, the wolf's body struggled mid-air, twisting like a frenzied black demon before it plowed a furrow into the grass at Allie's feet.

She dodged sideways when it struggled, twisting and lurching as if it would rise to attack again. Finally, it lay motionless on its side. Blood spilled dark and wet from ragged wounds, soaking into the forest floor. With shotgun still held tight to her shoulder, Erin cautiously approached and nudged the carcass with the toe of her running shoe before lowering the gun.

"Will they be back?" Allie fell to her knees and held Fiona's trembling head in her lap. "Oh! Fiona!" Anguish made her voice thick and she ran a calming hand across her dog's matted fur. The dog panted in distress but there was trust still gleaming in her moonlit eyes.

"I doubt it, not without their leader." With a watchful glance at the trees, Erin laid the shotgun against a rock and knelt down beside Allie. Fiona's hind leg extended stiffly at an odd angle. Flesh hung in ribbons and Allie gently checked for other injuries along the length of her body. Blood gushed from deep puncture wounds in the dog's chest. She pressed her hand tight to stem the flow but it seeped around her fingers. She used both hands but still the blood spilled. In her gut, she knew. She knew, but she could not make herself voice the words to Erin. She gave her a meaningful stare and hoped her eyes would tell her what her mouth could not.

"Oh! Oh, Fiona…" Erin said in a strangled whisper. She bent her head to the dog's ear. "You are such a good girl."

"You have been so strong and so brave." Allie's voice faltered and a sob escaped her lips. A helpless lump wedged tight in her throat and she buried her face in the dog's neck, mixing tears with Fiona's blood.

Erin laid one hand on her girlfriend's shoulder and the other on the dog's heaving ribcage. There was nothing anyone could do. Minutes later, Fiona lay still and for a moment, the earth too became devoid of sound and motion. Allie looked up when the moon's muted glow brightened and was mesmerized by the intensity of millions of tiny stars blazing back at her. It was disorienting, as if the night sky had fallen to earth and was right here with her now.

"I'm so sorry, Fiona!" Allie cried. Her dog was dead. Beautiful, loyal, frightened, glorious Fuzzy Fiona was gone.

CHAPTER NINETEEN

What the hell was that? I jump straight up from the little wooden bed frame and land on my feet, like a cat. The rain ended and the thunder died out hours ago, so what was that? I swear to God it sounded like gunshots. Three in a row, like somebody means business. I shake the Minion's shoulder.

"Did you hear that?"

Minion sits up and looks at me with groggy eyes. "What? No. Must be thunder," then lays back down.

Nothing? How can you say you didn't hear anything? Didn't you just jerk out of your sleep like I did? Only thunder? I don't think so. Someone is close. They are coming for us. "Get up! We need to go!"

"No, it's too dark. Wait until morning. I'll paddle all the way to the Great Lakes if you want me to. Let's sleep some more, please."

I am so frustrated I can't think! I pace for a while, listening to the Minion sleep. I'm angry and something else. Fear? Nah. When I calm down, I crawl back in and close my eyes. *Fine. I will wait, but at the first light of day, we are out of here.*

* * *

Erin held Allie while she cried, both soaked through from tears and the night's rain. The stars were fading but the sun did not yet hint at daylight. Erin had been right, the wolves hadn't returned, but now they needed to get moving. They stretched stiff limbs and Allie insisted on carrying her dog back to the lean to. She tenderly laid Fiona on the ground and Erin wrapped her in her raincoat. Eyes puffy, Allie sat beside the mound on the earth. A trickle of blood ran down her leg.

"Oh! You're hurt!" Erin exclaimed. When had that happened? Allie hadn't complained for one second.

"It's not serious." She bent her knee to reveal three puncture wounds. Two on the inside of her calf looked deep and ugly, dark blood still oozing down her ankle. The third on her shin was more of a scrape of teeth against bone. Although shallow, they looked painful. "See? It's nothing."

Erin ignored her protests. She ripped a strip off the bottom of her T-shirt, soaked it in water and cleansed the wound.

"I have a first aid kit in my pack," Allie said in a monotone.

"Of course you do. Did your intuition also tell you to bring disinfectant?"

"I don't remember." She hugged her legs to her chest and sank her forehead onto her knees.

Erin located and searched through the kit until she found a small bottle of isopropyl alcohol. Allie really had thought of everything. She sat obediently while Erin tended to her wounds and dressed her leg with a sterile bandage. "You need a tetanus shot. Rabies too."

Allie turned her head away. "As soon as we get back. I promise."

"What do you want to—?" Erin looked over at the distressing shape bundled in her raincoat. Her voice struggled against the aching lump in her throat.

"It doesn't feel right to take her in the boat," Allie said slowly. She avoided looking at the bright yellow mound. "Fiona so loved the woods. She was my city dog, but her heart was happiest in the trees."

Erin bit her lip.

"I think she would rather be in the woods." Allie picked up the little hatchet and stalked to the shelter. "Why did it have to be Fiona?" she said through her teeth. She swung in an arc, the blow slicing through rope and separating the beam from its upright support. Gripping the hatchet in both hands, she smashed it again and again. Her hatchet cracked through wood as ferociously as the attack they had survived. After it had been reduced to splinters, she slumped to the ground, curled around the raincoat shroud and sobbed.

Erin's heart twisted in her chest for her girlfriend and she stroked her hair until her tears dried. Then she took the hatchet from Allie's bleeding fingers and scraped the debris away from the spot where they had last all rested together. She plunged the blade into the earth, hacking dirt out in a deep oval. She slashed through tree roots, dislodged rocks and finally both women dug with blistered hands until they had made a sizable hole. A hole suitable for a burial.

Allie wiped muddy hands on her thighs. "This is a good spot." The slightest splash of pink was growing in the east and rosy light washed sluggishly across the sky. A few chickadees had awakened and their carefree notes lilted through the air while they flitted in search of breakfast. It would be sunrise soon.

A young Gray Jay landed on the branch of a spruce tree overlooking them. Its inquisitive warble caught their attention. The bird ruffled slate gray feathers and settled them against the softness of its chest, seeming to preside over their private moment.

Erin tossed a pine cone in its direction. "Go away whiskey jack." The bird startled up and perched on another branch, closer than the first.

Allie put her hand over Erin's. "I don't think Fiona would mind." The charcoal capped bird tittered in response and swooped down to rest on the handle of the hatchet, still embedded in the ground. Erin shot it a dirty look but let it be. The intrusive little camp robber was looking for food they might have left behind.

Ignoring the bird, Allie cradled Fiona but could not bring herself to place her in the grave. She gently rocked the dog in her lap and tucked the raincoat as a mother would. Moist eyes peered helplessly up at Erin. "I can't. Please help me." Erin guided her hands and they both settled the carefully wrapped package into the hole. Allie caught her breath. "Goodbye, my sweet friend," she murmured.

"Sleep well, Fuzzy Fiona." With bare hands, Erin helped scoop moist black earth into the hole until the yellow raincoat was buried. They foraged until they had a mound of rocks constructed as a cairn over the grave. It would serve to mark the spot and deter predators.

When they finished, Allie squatted at the river's edge and let cool water run over her hands. Blood and dirt swirled through trembling fingers and a sob escaped her lips. Erin bent to help her.

"Should we go home?" Was this worth it? What if guys at the station were right? What if Lily was fine? What if they were wrong? She looked to Allie for the answer. Allie, who had given so much more than she had anticipated. Erin was prepared to turn back now, leaving all of this behind, if her girlfriend uttered only one word.

Allie straightened. "We need to finish this." Intense fire flashed in her dark brown eyes. "Fiona didn't give her life for us to run home with our tails between our legs. I will be fine. I keep seeing an evil predator capable of making the wolves last night seem like children's toys. It's been growing more dangerous but right now it's running and we need to catch it." She pushed the canoe upright and mercilessly dragged it on its keel through the trees.

"What is Derek going to do?"

"What I see in my head is a dark predator, like a raging wild cat. We need to hurry."

Erin retrieved their belongings and scrambled to follow. In the trees, the whiskey jack hopped overhead from branch to branch, never losing sight of them. When had her soft-skinned, latté-sipping girlfriend become this fearless warrior?

Allie was in the boat, paddle in hand, before Erin could even load their packs. She pushed them off and lightly stepped over the gunwale to assume her stern position. Digging her paddle in, she took off with feverish energy and Erin splashed awkwardly to keep up. The canoe yawed sideways in the river, forcing her to thrust her paddle out to correct it.

"That was at least an eighty pound male gray wolf," Erin volunteered inanely, once Allie's frenetic rhythm had slowed to merely a quickened pace. "They're also called Timber Wolves. Before a teenager was attacked last year, I hadn't heard about wolves attacking anyone in Minnesota, ever. It's quite unusual—"

"I don't want to talk about it." Allie clipped her words. "Can we be quiet for a while?"

The Gray Jay flew above them, circling once before landing on the bow deck. The bird chirped, a sweet silvery note that contrasted with all the awful emotions. Erin narrowed her eyes. It was tempting to want to swat the pesky critter away with her paddle.

Oblivious to their feelings, the bird cheerfully hopped over and pecked at the cooler bag. Allie stopped, rested her paddle and sighed. Reaching in, she tore a piece of crust from the last ham sandwich. The bird skipped and expertly caught it mid air when she tossed a morsel. She tossed another and the Gray Jay did it again. It flitted off toward the trees to stash its prize and was back in a minute, begging for more. When the bread crust was gone, the bird sat on the gunwale and made a pleased warbling sound deep in its tiny throat.

Allie took in a breath, stretched her neck from side to side and relaxed her shoulder muscles. She took up her paddle and dug it firmly into the water, this time at a more reasonable pace. The bird stayed with them for half an hour before careening off the end of the canoe and disappearing into the bush. Dark gray wings flashed through leaves from time to time, and the chirping continued to follow them downriver.

"I feel so stupid." Erin's brain snapped to attention when Allie finally spoke.

"What?"

"I knew something bad was coming. Why couldn't I tell what it was? If I had known—I could have—Fiona wouldn't—" Allie's voice cracked and she nearly released her grip on her paddle. She struggled to reclaim it and pulled it across her knees. "I hate this fucking so-called gift! What is wrong with me?"

Erin could not remember Allie ever using the F-word. She wanted to hold her, to soothe her, but she knew her girlfriend was far too angry right now. "Maybe it's a way to protect yourself. Maybe there was nothing you could have done to change what happened. Maybe there is such a thing as fate."

"It's my fault she's dead."

"It is not your fault." Erin knew where Allie's guilt was leading her now. Six-year-old Allie was reliving the loss of her mother. "And it wasn't your fault then either."

"Do you really believe in fate?" Allie said through her tears.

"I can't rule it out. I met you, didn't I?" Erin meant it. Meeting Allie was like a force of nature. It had to be.

"Perhaps I can't control everything that happens." Allie picked up her paddle again and took a few strokes. "Fiona was the best dog I ever met."

"Absolutely," Erin agreed without hesitation. "Best dog ever."

* * *

"Get up! Get up, I said! It's time to go." I've been awake for half an hour, pacing around the shack and watching the sky lighten until finally I can see down the trail to the river. The last of the glowing embers has died in the stove when I kick the side of the bed frame.

175

"Get up!"

Minion's eyes open slowly, like it's freakin' Sunday morning in the suburbs and then rolls a lazy ass over to look out the window. "Storm's gone."

No shit, Sherlock! "It's morning. Let's go!" Minion puts two feet on the floor and I lead the way out the door. Trotting down the little path to my warning tree, I narrow my eyes at the chip in the bark where I'd stuck in my knife. Did it fall out in the storm? I pull the canoe aside and check the ground. *Where the hell is my knife?* Minion avoids looking at me and I figure I've got a pretty good idea where it went. I'll get even when the time is right. I drop my backpack in the canoe and shove it down the bank to the water.

Minion loads up first but dives a hand into my pack on the way by. It is so fast, I have no time to stop it, and suddenly Minion is crouched there in the middle of the boat with my granola bar. I angrily give the canoe a shake. Minion jumps over the seat and sits down before it capsizes, looking at me with big cow eyes.

"Hey!" I yell. *That's mine.*

The granola bar goes into Minion's slimy mouth before I'm in the boat and there's no chance to get it back. I reach for the pack instead and stuff it under my feet, away from prying fingers. "Stay out of my stuff!" I'll keep it closer from now on. Minion looks at me like I've taken away Christmas and I point to the river. "Let's go."

CHAPTER TWENTY

Allie's sharp eyes located a division in weeds, footprints and drag marks on the sandy bank where a tiny creek spilled into the main river. "It's them!" The tracks were recent, unspoiled by the night's storm.

"They must have camped there last night!" Erin loaded four shotgun shells into the Mossberg's magazine tube and cradled it upright between her knees and shoulder. "He can't be far. Let's catch that evil bastard."

Allie paddled with renewed energy, creating deep whirlpools that swirled back to Erin who vigorously split them when she dug in with her own paddle. Four quacking ducks careened overhead, glistening water droplets spattering off frantically flapping wings. Above the treetops, where the river disappeared around the next bend, a flock of redwing blackbirds startled upright in frenzied flight. Allie hurried her stroke and Erin adjusted the weight of the shotgun on her shoulder. Did Derek know they were coming for him?

Sweat glistened on Erin's brow and her blistered hands were bleeding when they caught their first sight of the green fiberglass canoe. Just a fleeting glimpse of Derek in the stern before they disappeared around another bend. He was not looking back and, if luck was in their favor, he would not look back until it was too late. They were closing the gap.

"I don't think they saw us," Allie said, and Erin hissed a shushing noise through her teeth.

"Quiet," she whispered. "Be so quiet."

Like she'd done it all her life, Allie dipped her paddle into the water without a sound, without a splash. The muscles down Erin's spine tensed and the heady rush of adrenaline hit her system. She focused on the trailing ripple of water in the river ahead and a moment later the green canoe was back in their sights. Just a mere one hundred feet behind, the shotgun slipped from Erin's shoulder and she scrambled to recover it before the steel barrel clanged against the aluminum gunwale. In her haste she fumbled, and her paddle struck the canoe's center thwart, the dull thump resonating across the water. The two women held their breath, waiting for the inevitable reaction.

Slowly, from the bow seat, Lily stopped paddling and her pale hooded face turned toward them. Her mouth opened in an O shape and she emitted a high-pitched cry. Behind her, Derek whipped his head around and shock registered. He yelled something to Lily, who put her paddle into the water, but didn't take a stroke. Derek struggled to paddle on his own but he was no match for the women, who closed the gap and their bow cut into their quarry's rippling wake.

"Give it up, Derek!" Erin shouted, a hint of adrenaline infused anxiety making its way into her voice. "I'm taking you in." This was a fellow police officer, and arresting him conflicted with everything she had come to honor.

Derek wrenched his paddle from the water and let the canoe drift sideways in the current. Sweat ran down his flushed face and he fixed Erin with a cold stare.

"Are you okay Lily?" Erin called. The girl put down her head.

"You still pissed at me for stealing your lunch?" Derek taunted.

"You know this isn't about that," she said through clenched jaw.

His eyes dropped to the shotgun. "You gonna shoot me? For what? I ain't done nothin'."

"Tell me what happened to Dolores," she spat. Lily hunkered down in the front seat with her chin bent to her chest.

"You are talking through your deluded arse, girl. I told you the case is closed. That batty old broad blew herself up." He sneered dismissively, before shooting a hard look at Allie who visibly flinched. "Why don't you two bugger off and have your little romantic picnic somewhere else?"

Erin's blood began a slow boil. Allie massaged her temple, fighting a headache.

"Gina was almost killed!"

"Gina? What are you saying?"

"You nearly burned her alive!" Their canoes had drifted closer, almost close enough to touch.

Panic flickered in his eyes. "You're insane!" Without warning, he struck out with his paddle and slammed it into the side of the aluminum canoe, rocking it violently. "Back off!" One hand reached to his waistband and he withdrew a pistol. By the time Erin had recovered the boat's stability, the gun was leveled at her. Lily tucked her legs into her chest and watched cautiously from beneath her hood, her colorless face frozen.

"It's over," Erin said evenly, one palm facing outward. "We found Gunther Schmidt." Lily's head snapped up and two startled green eyes peered directly at Derek, who gave a slow shake. He glared back in a thinly veiled warning. Then like two angry laser beams, his gaze swung to Erin. His beefy hand was rock solid, finger tensed on the trigger of his Glock semiautomatic. "You found Gunther, did you?"

"I always knew you were a bastard, but Old Man Gunther? Were you tired of paying him off?"

"Oh, don't give me the song and dance about Gunther being a war hero. He's no choir boy. Besides, he and I have—" he searched for the right word, "—a gentleman's agreement. It's none of your business." Lily swung her legs around in the bow seat and faced Derek. Her features distorted in exaggerated suffering.

"A gentleman's agreement? Is that what attempted murder is called in your twisted world?" How long had Gunther Schmidt lain in that hole, sick and dying? Erin regretted ever thinking he was capable of this madness. The pistol wavered in Derek's hand and his eyes flitted to Lily's. The girl looked away.

With his attention diverted, Erin slowly raised the shotgun's barrel until it pointed at Derek. "You're done," she said calmly. "Just lay the gun down, nice and slow. You are not going to shoot me with your service pistol." He hesitated, looking at her under hooded eyes. Finally he lowered the Glock.

"What happened to us, Erin?" We could have been something." His expression darkened when he scowled at Allie who stared back this time. "Now look what you've become."

"What are you talking about?" Erin's throat ran dry. What kind of trickery was he attempting? "There has never been an us."

"There could have been. There almost was." He sounded miserable, like a sad little boy. "We were so good together in high school. If only you hadn't set your guard dog on me. We could have really been something."

"My guard dog?" Erin was confused. Derek transformed from an angry dangerous man into a wounded little boy and his behavior scared her. A fragment of memory unwound like a thread. Grade ten, Derek standing all cocky with his football buddies, asking her to the spring dance. He had been so arrogant. She had known she was a lesbian long before then. Everyone at school knew. Why had he even asked? She remembered his friends laughing when she continued to avoid him in the hallways.

"I tried to talk to you afterward, but your dog was always there in my face. She never let me close to you." Anger crept back into his voice and the little boy was gone. "I think Gina got what she deserved."

"No!" Erin's long forgotten memories flashed by in quick succession. Realization struck her like a kick to the chest. Gina had always been there for her, behind the scenes, acting as a shield between young lesbian Erin and a high school world not often kind to girls who were different. Like a big sister, Gina had deflected the taunts, as well as the brunt of Derek's obsession, allowing her to reach adulthood relatively unscathed. Erin understood that she owed her ability to find happiness now in part to Gina. "She did not deserve—"

"Bitch!" Derek spewed the words like a slap in the face. "I should shoot you." He brought his pistol back up and instantaneously Allie hurled her paddle, blade first like a javelin. It struck his forearm and ricocheted off the side of the boat into the water. The Glock skittered to the bottom of the canoe. The little green boat rocked dangerously and Lily's feet hit the floor. She grabbed frantically onto the gunwales, knuckles blanched with effort, and Derek balanced it with his body weight. Man and child both eyed the pistol, awash in an inch of water.

"Stop!" Erin thundered. "Derek, don't make me." His shoulders sagged and he slowly raised both hands.

"What are you gonna do? Tie me to a tree? Run for help?" He lifted his chin toward the river, where Allie's paddle had drifted out of reach. Soon it would be gone. "Except your girlie friend threw away her paddle."

The pistol was a problem. If she could just get it out of this equation. "Lily," Erin called gently. "Can you do one thing for me?" The girl's blank eyes veered to Erin's. "Just carefully pick up that gun and throw it into the water."

"I'm not sure you should—" Allie blurted.

"Don't—" Derek grunted but in a flash the pistol was in Lily's shaking hands.

"That's good," Erin said. "Now throw it over the side." Lily looked at Erin and then at Derek. The barrel of the Glock swept up to point directly at Derek's face.

"No, sweetie." Light jade eyes widened and his skin paled. "Don't do this."

"Just throw it over the side," Erin repeated. "We don't want anybody to get hurt." Tears spilled down the girl's cheeks. Her hands shook so hard Erin feared the gun might go off accidentally.

"He did it." Lily whispered. "He put the gas on at that old lady's house. He hit the other lady at the store and burned it down. He gave my grandfather that stuff. He killed him."

"Your grandfather is not dead," Erin reassured her. "He's going to be okay. He's in the hospital."

Lily shook her head. "Don't lie, he's dead."

"Really, he's okay."

Lily's foot jangled anxiously and she adjusted her small hands around the gun's grip. Her index finger tightened against the trigger.

"Has this man hurt you?" Erin's voice was calm and soothing. Lily nodded her head vigorously and her gaze on Derek intensified.

"Aw, honey," he crooned. "Don't do this. I'll make it all okay. You know I'd do anything for you, sweetheart."

"Shut up," Erin barked. His oozing platitudes toward the young girl made her queasy. He sat back in silence, keeping his hands in the air.

"He hurt me," Lily said. "He—" she paused and looked from Erin to Allie. A fat teardrop welled in her pained eyes. "He did bad things to me."

"No," Derek said.

"We will help you," Erin told her, ignoring him. The girl held her gaze for a long moment before dropping the pistol over the side. It sank like a stone into the river, and Lily looked back at her like a child who has pleased a parent. Derek grunted, crumpled over and placed his head in his hands.

When the canoes drifted side by side, Allie motioned for Lily to hand over both of their paddles. Erin looped the painter rope from Derek's canoe around her own stern thwart and tied it on. She passed the last ham sandwich from her mom's truck driver lunch over to the girl. With an appreciative smile, she devoured it.

"Where's your scaredy dog?"

Allie's spine straightened but she didn't reply.

"She's not here," Erin answered for her. How did the kid know they had a dog? Perhaps she had simply seen them walking Fiona in town. Erin straightened out the canoes and the two women paddled, the second boat following on its tow line. Derek sat miserably in the stern. Unarmed, he wasn't much of a threat and would be taken into custody when they reached the Blue Water Ranger Station. He couldn't possibly be stupid enough to try to escape, could he?

She had no sooner thought the words when there was a commotion behind her and she whirled around. Derek was already in the water, splashing furiously for shore. The fiberglass canoe lurched to its side. Half over on its keel, Lily frantically rocked as hard as she could until the little boat drunkenly stabilized. Perched uncomfortably in the partly submerged canoe, water surged around her skinny knees. The swamped boat stayed afloat.

Erin exchanged a quick glance with Allie, who placed one hand on each gunwale so she could barrel roll over the side. Swimming with a determined head-up front crawl, like a lifeguard, Erin was in fast pursuit. She'd grown up with the river in her backyard and was a strong swimmer. Mentally calculating her trajectory, she aimed to use the current to intercept her fleeing captive. Derek swam with sloppily panicked strokes and was nearing shore when Erin caught up to him.

She seized the collar of his shirt and he gulped a mouthful of water in surprise. He coughed it out and swung around, shoving two palms into her face. She dodged and came up under his elbow to wrap one arm tightly around his neck. Kicking with all her strength, she towed him toward shore but he twisted in her grip.

"Who do you think you are?" The corner of his lip drew upward in contempt. Sunlight shimmered off metal when he drove his right fist toward her. Red streaks muddied the water and he brought it up again. Erin recognized the outline of a four-inch lock blade, blood trailing off the gleaming end of the knife. Realization hit her along with the stabbing pain. He'd cut her. Yelping, she released him and kicked away.

"You," he said. "Why did it have to be you?" He glared at her and then eyed the shore.

"Derek, don't do this—"

"Duck!" Allie exclaimed.

Erin plunged underwater. His round house with the knife merely sliced through air. He dog-paddled in a circle, peering into the water. She burst through the surface behind him and again wrapped her arm around his neck like a vice. Her blood spilled a wet trail onto his skin and she took two deep breaths. Face reddened in his struggle, he pushed at her with meaty hands. The innate drive to breathe was more important than the urge to hurt her and he released the knife.

Tenaciously hanging on, she squeezed his throat and submerged, taking him down. *One Mississippi, Two Mississippi, Three*—she counted. She calmed her mind in the surety that she could outlast this panicked, oxygen starved man. Her lungs burned and her head throbbed but she kept him anchored to the riverbed. Finally his chest expanded to take in a lungful of water. When the tension in his body slackened, she kicked to the surface.

He burbled, spewing aspirated water while she towed him to shore. In her peripheral vision, Allie paddled feverishly to keep pace with them. Lacking experience, she struggled to maneuver the tethered canoes from the wrong end.

Erin set her feet on land first. She dragged Derek through the weeds and onto a patch of coarse sand. He coughed, water spurting from his nostrils, and Erin turned him on his side in the Universal Recovery Position.

"Bitch," he sputtered hoarsely, the bloodshot whites giving his pale eyes an eerie cast. He wearily laid his cheek on the sand.

Erin squatted beside him, chest heaving. She lifted the sleeve of her soaked T-shirt to examine her left bicep. Derek's knife had sunk deep into the muscle and she applied firm pressure to stop the bleeding.

A loud crack echoed inside her skull and the ground suddenly warped into blue sky. Dazed, her vision narrowed to ragged treetops and she pitched forward. Coarse hands pushed her onto her back and

Derek straddled her, pinning her with powerful thighs. A sour taste filled her mouth and she swallowed against it. Beside her on the ground lay the stick of weather scoured wood he'd used to nearly brain her.

Growling with rage, he pulled his fist back and smashed it into her cheekbone. There was a flare of light across her retina. The fist crashed into her face a second time and pain seared behind her eye.

"Stop it!" Allie's voice bellowed above the ringing in Erin's ears. "Get off!" The slide on the shotgun slammed forward and back in metallic warning and there was a stunned silence before the pressure on Erin's chest was gone. Allie stood over them, shotgun pointed directly at Derek's face. Dark fury blackened her eyes and her lips pressed together in a tight line.

He rolled away from Erin with a grunt and held his hands up, palms forward. His eyes locked on Allie, whose body language betrayed no weakness.

"Are you okay, honey?" Allie asked without taking her eyes from Derek's.

Erin's fingers explored her blazing cheekbone, where there was soft mush under the skin below the orbital ridge. "I think so." Adrenaline had served to temporarily numb the pain but it would hurt like a son-of-a-gun later. The slash on her upper arm was a more immediate issue and she pressed her palm to stem the flow of blood.

"Your arm!" Allie's eyes widened in alarm when she saw it.

"Okay, okay, you got me." Derek slowly lowered his hands and furtively searched for his stick.

Not about to be taken off guard again, Erin's attention snapped to his change in position. She leapt on him as soon as his fingers closed around the weapon. Wrenching it away, she pushed him to the ground. With one hand on either end, she forced the stick against the soft skin of his throat. His eyes bulged when she bore down with all the weight of her upper body. He gasped for air.

"Stop!" Erin snarled and Derek's face turned purple beneath the pressure threatening to break his windpipe.

"Do it! Do it!" Lily's voice hissed excitedly from somewhere behind her. "Do it!"

Erin's arm throbbed and the pain in her cheekbone hammered, but one clear voice broke through her berserk anger.

"Enough!" Allie shouted.

She shook her head, and took in the motionless man on the ground beneath her. She had almost killed him. Almost. If Allie had not stopped her—. She released the pressure on his throat and Lily withdrew to a spot in the trees. The girl crawled up onto the safety of a rock to watch.

"Rope," Erin barked. "We tie him up." She glared at the stick she still held in her hand. As if it had suddenly become radioactive, she flung it into the river. Then she bent and retched into the purple blossoms of a patch of Pickerel Weed.

Allie fetched the remainder of her yellow rope and together they made sure Derek's limbs were securely tied. He lay on his side, coughing weakly. Lily eyed them with interest from her vantage point, rocking slowly back and forth. Her face was an unreadable mask, blank like a porcelain doll's.

Almost. Erin had almost killed Derek out of what? Anger? Revenge? She avoided eye contact, shame rising in her throat like acid. When Allie bandaged her wound, she tentatively stole a glance and was surprised to see her brow puckered in worry. Why? They had him. It was all over, wasn't it?

* * *

It was nearly ten o'clock in the morning, by Erin's watch, when the steady grumbling of a motor approached. Soon, the shiny white hull of the Rangers' patrol boat came into view, one man standing at the controls and two others seated in front of the driver. Erin recognized Zimmerman and Striker, bodies angled forward like eager tracking dogs.

They had all set out in plain clothes but today the two were in full uniform, sidearms holstered on their duty belts. Zimmerman still carried Erin's dad's hunting rifle and he stood, gripping it like Rambo in both hands. The ranger driving the boat slowed their approach to a crawl, the bow sinking back into the water until it was level. It idled in the river's current beyond the beached canoes.

"Is everyone ok?" Zimmerman called out above the powerful rumbling of the twin Mercury motors. In a quick assessment of the scene, his eyes flicked from person to person, lingering on the injuries. Finally, they settled on the shotgun in Erin's tense fingers and his face tightened. To his credit, he did not press for immediate details. When Derek was in custody, there would be time enough to quiz her about what had happened and how it came to be that Erin's civilian girlfriend was here.

"He put up a fight, but we are all fine," Erin told him. She grimaced her apology to Allie. Now was not the time to detail their injuries nor their very personal loss. "We caught up to him an hour ago."

"Sorry we missed the party," Zimmerman said. He shot a meaningful glance to Striker who bent in hurried discussion with the ranger. The patrol boat eased forward and gracefully landed, bow brushing the shore. The moment it touched, Zimmerman and Striker launched themselves into ankle deep water and hefted Derek to his feet.

"You have brought a world of trouble onto yourself, my friend," Zimmerman growled. Derek stared straight ahead like a prisoner of war. The police officer withdrew handcuffs from the leather pouch on his belt and snapped them around Derek's thick wrists. He loosened off the temporary yellow ropes. "Might as well get on in there," he ordered, and prodded him roughly toward the boat.

With hands tied, Derek lifted one leg over the side and then landed like a sack of flour on the floor. He coughed repeatedly. Zimmerman boarded and assumed guard position. He caught Erin's eye with a wordless question and she gave a curt shake of her head in reply. No, the injured women did not need help into the boat.

With Derek securely restrained, Striker cautiously approached Lily like she was a wounded deer and encouragingly held out his hand. She skidded down off the rock and allowed him to assist her into the larger boat. He gently draped a wool blanket around her shoulders and seated her as far from the prisoner as possible.

"You're going to be okay," he murmured. She silently pulled up her knees and assumed her customary curled up position.

The ranger gestured and Erin threw him the painter line so he could reel in both canoes to secure them for towing. Allie was next into the boat and Striker fussed over her bandage but she stoically waved him off.

"It's nothing," she said and moved to make way for Erin, who was last to climb aboard.

The ranger introduced himself and shook her hand. Then he slowly turned the boat and they headed back downriver, canoes trailing behind them like an alligator's tail.

"Are you really okay?" Zimmerman whispered loudly into Erin's ear. "Your face is smashed up. Do you have a concussion? Can you even think?"

"He rung my bell, for sure," Erin admitted. "I think I'm okay for now. Might have broke my cheekbone, and the back of my head hurts."

Zimmerman raised an eyebrow at the bandage on Erin's arm.

"The evil bastard cut me," she whispered through clenched teeth.

His other eyebrow joined the first in a look of disbelief.

"And I'm worried about Allie."

"What is your girlfriend doing here?" He took in the bandage on Allie's leg. "You two are sure a sight."

"It's a long story," she replied evasively. Allie sat quietly beside her, staring at the floor. One hand absently fingered the dressing over puncture wounds on her calf and Erin knew what she was thinking. "The short version is that I found her stranded along the way."

Zimmerman's head nodded but his expression implied he did not have a clue how that could have happened. Mosquito bites covered both forearms as well as his neck, and Erin didn't doubt he'd had an adventure of his own getting through the swamp to the forestry road yesterday.

"I received a call from Doctor Holloway this morning," he told her when they picked up speed. He scratched a cluster of red welts on the back of his arm. The sound of the motors ensured their voices did not carry to Derek's position. "It seems the doctor had a conversation with Kathy Banks about poison. She sent the bottles you seized from Gunther Schmidt's shed to the Tox Lab. Since that was the only thing in the victim's belly, it's pretty likely that it was the source."

"Sure looks like someone had been poisoning Gunther for a long time."

"And Kathy still wants to talk to you about something else," Zimmerman reminded her. Erin would call when they returned.

Striker retrieved a bottle of spring water from the in-boat cooler and gave it to the girl. Lily guzzled half of it before stopping to catch her breath. She smiled shyly at him and he happily bobbed his head in pleasure. He closed the cooler with a solid thump and Derek eventually averted his thirsty eyes. "There's no more," Striker said to him without a flicker of pity. "You can talk to the guards after you are booked in."

Erin and Zimmerman watched this exchange and frowned. "I would at least have given him water."

She shrugged, undecided on the mercy for child molesters issue. "Is Gunther going to make it?" she asked.

"The doc said they've given him a blood transfusion and he's been awake and talking. The doc also says he's a tough old veteran and nothing short of an artillery shell was going to kill him."

"Gunther's actually talking?"

"Well, more like grunting, but the doc says Gunther insists that Derek is a nice guy. He brings him a six pack of beer every couple of weeks."

"I bet he's nice. He's nice to Gunther because he wants to be extra nice to his little granddaughter!" she hissed in his ear. "And he pays the old man off every month for what? For access to the girl?" Erin's blood throbbed in her ears, magnified by the drone of the boat's motor. Was the ringing from her anger or her busted cheekbone? She whispered when she noticed Lily looking at her. "The kid told me an hour ago that Derek does bad stuff to her. She also told me that he was responsible for the fire that killed Dolores Johnson, for what happened at the Stop 'N Go, and for what happened to Gunther."

"We need to find out everything she knows. Keep her away from Derek. I don't want her intimidated any more by him." Lily smiled at them and Zimmerman rested his hand on Erin's forearm. "Are you sure you're okay?"

Erin nodded a lie.

"If you're sure, you should interview her when we get back. You seem to have developed a bit of a trusting rapport." Lily inched closer to them on the bench seat and her eyebrows tilted in plaintive trust. "And she needs someplace to stay."

Erin gave the girl a small welcoming smile and Lily burst forward from her seat, burrowing into Erin's side. She put her good arm around the thin waif and wrapped the blanket tighter.

"It was scary. Now I feel safe," Lily said, her pale green eyes penetrating.

Erin tried to grin at Allie but was unnerved when her girlfriend's expression darkened. The knuckles of one fist pressed her temple and the other gripped her seat as if she were afraid to be flung into the river at any moment. She looked from Erin, to the girl, to Derek, confusion clouding her eyes.

"Don't worry, we are not taking her home with us." Erin leaned over and whispered in Allie's ear. "I'll call Child Services when we get back to Morley Falls."

Allie's breathing was unusually slow and deep. She closed her eyes and Erin knew it was a struggle for her to contain her emotions when she was in such proximity to the source of her nightmares. She hoped she would be able to get her away from Derek before she lost control.

Lily was asleep against Erin's shoulder when the ranger's patrol boat nosed into the dock at Blue Water Station. She nudged her gently and the girl woke with a start. She peeped around Erin's shoulder at Derek, who was disembarking with Zimmerman and Striker. Derek caught her eye and shook his head at her in a silent *no*. She crowded close to Erin, who tightened her arm around the girl.

Zimmerman read the prisoner his rights and loaded him into Striker's car. Unable to stop coughing, Derek bent double in the back seat while boats were secured and gear sorted out. Allie was last off the dock and she hurried to put distance between herself and the others. Near the beach, she sat on a driftwood log.

Erin found her when they were ready to leave. "Are you going to be okay, baby?" She sat down and squeezed her hand. Allie's face was ashen, like she had received horrible news from which she would never recover. "What can I do to make you feel better?"

"Everything is upside down," she whispered, though no one else was close enough to overhear. "Maybe I'm still so upset about losing Fiona that I can't think straight. All the thoughts in my head are twisted up somehow and I don't understand."

"You've been through a traumatic experience and this is perfectly normal." Erin knew how trite it would sound to Allie. She owed her more. "Let's get those puncture wounds on your leg taken care of and maybe the world will right itself. I'll get Z-man to drive you back directly and I'll be home as soon as I take care of Lily."

"You," Allie asked. "What about you?"

"The Steri Strips from your first aid kit are still holding. I can get proper stitches later if I need to. First I need to get Lily to tell me what happened."

Allie nodded reluctantly. "You won't be too long?" She followed

Erin back to the ranger station. Striker sat on a bench beside Lily, and the girl swung her legs like a carefree child. He smiled at her and she laughed as if he had told her a funny story.

"I think she might be okay," Erin whispered. Lily spotted them and came racing over, slipping her soft pale hand into Erin's. She turned her gaze to Allie, whose face was an indecipherable mask, and grasped her hand so the three of them were linked together.

Allie's entire body jolted as if electrocuted. Wide eyed, muscles rigid, she trembled violently. Blood drained from her face. It was as if the lights had gone out.

"Allie!" Erin dropped Lily's hand. She reached for her girlfriend, whose knees buckled before she collapsed to the ground.

"Is she having a seizure?" Lily asked with childish inquisitiveness. She squatted to look in Allie's face, but Erin held up an arm to allow distance.

"No, she'll be fine." She discreetly fingered Allie's wrist, pulse hammering rapidly beneath her fingertips. "Just take a deep breath, baby. You're okay."

Zimmerman saw them go down and sprinted over. "What happened? Did she fall?"

"She's not feeling well." There was no need to alarm the girl, who was already visibly agitated, so she lowered her voice. "I need you to get Allie to the clinic and get her leg examined." She was torn between her concern for Allie and her duty to the girl, both of whom had endured hellish ordeals. "She has an animal bite that might be getting infected. Make sure she gets a tetanus shot, and probably rabies too."

"She got bit? By what?" Zimmerman's eyebrows shot up and he grimaced when he lifted the edge of the bandage on Allie's calf. Erin's eyes flashed to the girl and back. He gave a curt nod. "Right. You get the kid somewhere safe and I've got this."

Erin stroked Allie's cheek when he carefully folded her into his arms. "Call me as soon as you can. I'll be at the station." Her mouth opened as if to speak but there were no words and she buried her face into Zimmerman's shoulder.

He carried the stricken woman like a rag doll to his car and helped her into the front. Fingers outstretched, she pressed her hand against the inside of the passenger window. The pressure blanched color from her fingertips before she withdrew it. Behind the ghostly halo of condensation that remained, a myriad of conflicting emotions flickered across Allie's face. She made intense eye contact with Erin before they drove off.

What is it? What is wrong baby?

CHAPTER TWENTY-ONE

"Would you like a soda?" Erin brushed aside the detritus left over from Lily's fast food meal and held out a can of 7Up.

After a quick phone call to ensure that Allie was okay, and another to have a Child Advocate attend, they took over an interview room at the police station. Erin activated the video equipment before they started. Through one-way glass, the Deputy Chief and probably a half dozen other curious spectators watched the proceedings.

"Can I have a Coke instead?" Lily smiled sweetly at Erin and then turned her face to the mirrored window. She puckered brows pathetically above sad eyes. There was a commotion behind the glass as someone sprinted downstairs to the vending machine. Erin offered the 7Up to the plump faced woman serving as Lily's Child Advocate. She looked underpaid, and thirsty.

Erin answered the light knock at the door and accepted a can of Coca Cola that had been quickly fetched for the girl. She handed it over and Lily cheerfully popped the tab.

"Did your arm bleed a lot? Did you know that one side of your face is all puffy and red? Did your girlfriend have a seizure? Is she gonna die?"

Erin self-consciously touched the bandage on her arm. It was a good thing Allie had brought her first aid kit. "Don't worry about that. We're fine."

"Can I come to your house?" The girl beamed and batted her eyelashes, the effect awkward on a child over five.

"I'm sorry Lily, but that's not possible. A nice social worker is coming and she will find you a safe place."

The smile vanished and she looked at her shoes.

"It's okay. You are going to be okay."

"Do I get my own TV and computer?" The smile was back.

"I'm sure every house has those." Puzzled, Erin studied Lily. She'd seen many traumatized kids in her career. Each child's reaction to stress was different, and there were all kinds of ways to compartmentalize emotional pain. Some kids went completely blank and non-communicative, or conversely broke into giggling fits when notified of a major trauma like the death of their parent. She had learned not to read too much into their initial reactions. "Let's talk about what happened first."

"I told you," the girl snapped. "He did it. He did it all." Lily narrowed her eyes, and her foot thrummed against dense industrial carpeting. "Don't you believe me?" Her advocate squirmed and made a quick notation on a legal pad.

"Let's take a nice deep breath, okay? Of course I believe you." Erin kept her face neutral. This interview had barely begun and already it threatened to derail. "I need you to tell me what happened."

The girl cycled through conflicting expressions before her mouth curved upward again. "All right." There was a slight edge to her cheerfulness when it returned.

"Good," Erin said soothingly. "Now can you tell me what happened?"

"We went down the river—" Lily began.

"Let's back up a little and why don't you tell me where you've been for the last week?"

She shifted uncomfortably in her seat and looked at her shoes again. There was a long pause before she looked directly into Erin's eyes. "I was under the shed with my grandpa. He made us do it. The bad man made us. We were hiding."

"Who is the bad man?"

"The bad man that came to get me and made me go in the canoe. You know. The bad policeman. He killed my grandpa and he hurt the lady and he burned the store."

"Did he say what happened to your grandpa?"

"No. He didn't tell me." Lily paused to think. "But I know he killed him by making him drink weird stuff."

"Your grandfather is not dead. Do you remember when I told

you? He's in the hospital and he's going to be okay."

"But I was so sure…"

"He really will be okay." What had this poor child gone through? "Would you like to visit him?"

Lily shook her head. "No, he'll be mad at me."

"I'm sure he'll be happy to see you." Erin placed her hand over the girl's but she flinched and jerked it away. *Okay, fine. Some people don't like to be touched.* "How long has the man been coming to your house?"

"After my mom died." The girl stopped, and her face blanched a lighter shade of pale. "I mean after she ran away." There was another pause while the girl picked at a fingernail. "I made a mistake. I want to start again."

Erin tilted her head.

"Actually, my mom ran away to California with a movie star and she's just fine. I don't want to talk about her any more."

"Okay." Erin frowned and the girl looked at her knees. "Why don't we go back to what happened with your grandpa's beer?"

"The man came every day and poured the stuff in my dear grandpa's beer." She plucked at a second fingernail. "But he wasn't dying. He only got sick so he had to pour the rest in."

Erin leaned forward until their knees were nearly touching. Lily inched backward and her chair bumped the wall.

"Tell me more about that.""

"I watched him from the window of the shed. I saw him every day."

"How do you know he was trying to kill him?" Erin scooted forward another couple of inches and the girl's eyes widened.

"I just know because of how sneaky he was. He always came when no one was home, and—"

"If no one was home, that means you weren't home. How did you see him if you weren't home?"

Lily glowered at the floor. "I just know because he was bad. I don't want to talk about it any more."

Perhaps it was too soon after the trauma for the child to make any sense at all. Nevertheless, Erin filed a mental note to check into the circumstances of her mother's disappearance. She also needed to delve into the nature of the girl's relationship with Derek.

"Tell me about the fire."

"The fire? The old lady in the blue car came home and opened the door and—or do you mean the fire at the store?"

"Why don't you tell me about the lady with the blue car?" Erin's pulse quickened. She was talking about Dolores Johnson! How had she known what car she drove?

"I don't remember any lady with a blue car. You are making me all mixed up." Lily dug her heels in and pushed back as far as she could.

"Okay, we'll come back to that." Sensing the kid was ready to shut down, she leaned away and gave the girl breathing room. She would back off that subject, for now. "Do you want to talk about the man?"

"He brings me a six pack of Budweiser. I mean, he puts it in the shed fridge for my dear grandpa. Sometimes he brings an envelope, and leaves it on the workbench."

"Is he your grandpa's friend?"

"No, not really. He just comes and wants to talk to me."

"What do you talk about?"

"I dunno. He wants to talk about stupid stuff. Like how am I doing in school, or do I have a boyfriend." She mimicked Derek's tone and lifted one corner of her lip in an imitation sneer. She certainly had spent a great deal of time around him and the similarity was unsettling. "Sometimes if I beg, I get a ride in his car." She tilted her eyebrows and made the sad face again.

"Where do you go in his car?" Erin asked.

"He gives me a ride home from school when he is not busy." The sad face reverted back to its practiced smile.

"And he picked you up at the Stop 'N Go the night it burned down," Erin prompted. The quick emotion changes were abnormal, no matter the situation.

"No, I wasn't even there that night." She dug clenched fists into hips. "The lady at the store lied. It wasn't me!"

"I was there too. I saw you."

"Oh yeah." She mulled it over. "But I went home and didn't go back at all. It wasn't me. I didn't even know where she kept the gas can!"

The alarm bell in Erin's head clanged. Did Derek tell Lily about that?

"What else can you tell me about the fire?"

The girl crossed skinny arms and let out an exaggerated sigh. "I don't know nothin' about no fire. I don't want to talk about it."

"Okay, let's talk about other things. You said the man does bad things to you." Erin needed to tread carefully with this sensitive topic. She avoided using incendiary terms like 'molest' or 'sexually abuse'. "What did you mean?"

"He's just bad. He did bad stuff to me." She picked up a stray paperclip from the floor and straightened it. "I don't remember."

"What did he do?"

"Everything. I don't remember." She pressed one end of the paperclip to the inside of her wrist and scraped it across pale skin. A red scratch appeared, and she smirked at Erin. "Does that scare you?"

"Please don't do that." Erin spoke softly. "You don't need to be afraid. Did he touch you?"

Lily raised her chin and peered down her nose. She subtly shook her head. "Yes, he touched me. All over."

Erin noted the conflict between verbal and nonverbal information. "Can you show me exactly where?"

"I don't remember. Maybe in his car." She used the paperclip to scratch her wrist again, and a tiny droplet of blood broke the surface. Pale green eyes stared directly into Erin's as she licked it. "You want some?"

The child advocate gasped and jumped to her feet. The girl grinned but her eyes were hard.

"That kind of behavior won't work on me, kiddo." Erin gently took it from her fingers and the girl lifted a corner of her lip. The advocate sat, but the tremor in her hands was not missed by Lily.

"Ha, I made you freak out."

"Let's get back on track, shall we?" Erin tucked the paperclip into her pocket.

Lily rolled her eyes and sighed again.

"I meant, can you show me where on your body." The disparity between the girl's words and body language confused Erin.

"Oh." She thought again. "Here and here." She squeezed an underdeveloped breast and then her crotch, smiling at the sharp intake of breath from her advocate.

"When did he do this?"

"Lots. I don't remember. This is boring."

The advocate cleared her throat and scribbled on her notepad. Lily's eyes flicked to her and back to Erin. "I just don't like him. I want you to make him go away."

The interview threatened to morph from a simple interview to a complex interrogation. "Did you ever tell anyone? A teacher at school? Your grandfather?"

The girl's mouth tightened. "I don't remem—"

Unexpectedly, the door to the interview room swung open and a dark suited man entered, followed closely by the Deputy Chief. In the entrance stood a stern looking social worker with a tight bun and ill-fitting navy pantsuit.

"This interrogation is over," the suited man said bluntly, moving between Erin and Lily. The Child Advocate abandoned the can of 7Up and rose abruptly to her feet. She opened her mouth to speak and then shut it. She stared down at her notes.

"This is not an interrogation," Erin countered, eyeing him sharply. "We are just gathering information. We need to—"

"I have been retained as Lily's lawyer and I'm telling you that she's done here." He spoke in a terse whisper to the child who left her seat to join the social worker at the door.

"Do I get my own TV?" Lily asked the woman in the pantsuit. The girl's face pivoted back to Erin and she shuffled out after the social worker.

The advocate looked from Erin to the lawyer, who deliberately ignored her. He directed his next remarks to the room in general. "In future, the child will not be spoken to by anyone in authority unless I am physically present." He met Erin's bemused gaze. "Are we clear?" He left as officiously as he had arrived.

The children's advocate cleared her throat, awkwardly gathered her papers and vacated the room right behind him. Erin was left alone with the Deputy Chief. He waved Striker in from just outside the door, and closed it.

"This has turned into a real cock-up." Deputy Chief Roger Williams was an old school cop, and had worked his way through the ranks to his current position. Graying at the temples, he was a bit paunchy but still solidly built for action. "One of our own behind bars and we can't even talk to the victim." He wiped stubby fingers across bristles on the back of his neck. "I understand you've all had a helluva time, so I'll make it short. Debrief. My office in ten. I saw Z-man coming in the back a minute ago. Bring him too."

If Zimmerman was back, Allie must be home by now. She needed to call her but instead she was shepherded into the Deputy Chief's office. Zimmerman looked at her furrowed brow and formed a covert circle with his thumb and index finger when they sat down. Allie was okay. She breathed but the worry at the back of her mind still nagged and she would not feel any better until she could actually look into her girlfriend's eyes. She fidgeted in her chair and tapped the armrest with her pen. There was not a day in recent memory that had seemed longer than this one.

True to his word, the Deputy Chief kept the debriefing short. Zimmerman and Striker talked about their boat catastrophe and their trek through the swamp. While they told their version of events, both men subconsciously scratched mosquito bites on legs and arms. They'd been picked up by a fisherman who had nearly run them over on the forestry road in his haste to get home before the storm. First thing this morning, they'd gone out in the ranger boat. Striker revisited his interrogation and the supposition that Derek was not entirely forthcoming.

Erin gave a condensed version of her events, minimizing some parts and leaving others out altogether. She didn't feel the need to expose Allie's gift, nor was she willing to detail their shared emotional anguish over Fiona's death. Their accounts were taken at face value, with written reports to be submitted within forty-eight hours.

When the debrief ended, Erin fled from a never-ending series of questions from coworkers. She finally bailed out the back door of the station and made her way to the parking lot. Her Toyota still sat right in front of the security camera. It seemed a lifetime since she'd ridden to her parent's place in Zimmerman's truck. In retrospect, the total destruction of her dad's fishing boat seemed a trivial matter.

"My God, girl! You are hard to get a hold of!" Kathy Banks caught her by the sleeve like a scolding parent. "I need to talk to you!"

"I'm sorry, Kathy." Exhausted, Erin blinked back salty tears. "It's been so crazy. I need to get home. I'm in a hurry. I can call you tomorrow after I've had some sleep. Promise."

"No. You can rest when you're dead," Kathy said with a smirk. "This is important."

Erin sighed.

"You need to know what I found."

"Did you get a hit?" Her interest piqued. Had there been a criminal fingerprint identification?

"I developed partial prints on the beer cans from the Dolores

Johnson case. The ones you gave me 'off the books'." Erin nodded and Kathy continued. "I also obtained prints from that beer bottle and the unlabeled dark glass bottle you seized with the warrant on Gunther Schmidt's property. They are all from the same suspect!"

"Who is it?" This would tie both crimes together with one culprit. Erin's heart leapt into her throat.

"The fingerprints were not identified," Kathy said and Erin's hope plummeted. As a police officer, Derek's prints would have been in the system. So, not Derek. Erin's head spun. "I need to tell you the rest. Those prints are small and have quite a fine ridge pattern."

"What does that mean?"

"The person who left those fingerprints does not have a criminal record, and they are most likely not from an adult male." Gunther did not leave the beer cans behind Dolores' house either. "You are looking for a child, or a small woman."

A child. A small woman. She remembered the window in Gunther Schmidt's shed. It must have been seven feet off the ground. Without a ladder, there was no way Lily had watched Derek through that window. The girl was not confused. She was lying.

Erin's disoriented brain snapped fast forward. But Derek had confessed. Why? Was he really a demented child molester, or was something else missing? She remembered Allie's reaction when she'd touched Lily, and the halo of her handprint on the window glass when she was driven away in Zimmerman's car. It wasn't an infection making Allie collapse. It was a powerful force overwhelming her with the truth.

"What about the duct tape?" Erin remembered the most damning evidence yet. Beer cans in the weeds behind Dolores' house were only circumstantial. The same went for the bottles at Gunther's. Lily had legitimate access to the property and those might all be explained away by a competent lawyer. The duct tape was used only by the assailant who bound and gagged Gina. That could clinch it. "Whose prints were on the duct tape from the Stop 'N Go?"

"Bad news there, I'm afraid." Kathy clenched her jaw. "Dave seized that evidence, remember? He should have used Gentian Violet, which does a good job of revealing prints on the sticky side of tape, but he apparently stuck the whole wad into the cyanoacrylate fume cabinet. After three days, when the C.A. had overdeveloped and obscured everything, he backtracked with another chemical process. By the time he did what he should have in the first place, any prints he might have found were obliterated."

"He fucking what? Fuck—"

"I'm so sorry, Erin," Kathy said. "I'm all swore out on that whole thing too. If it's any consolation, the brass is aware of his screwup and he's been suspended from lab duties. They're actually thinking of transferring him out of the unit but they don't have anyone ready to transfer in. His biggest mistake is when he hid the evidence and tried to cover it up. On a case like this, he should have reported it right away."

"He's drinking buddies with Derek, isn't he?" The picture became clearer. Had Dave suspected Derek's involvement and deliberately destroyed the evidence? Had Derek coerced him to do it to throw the scent off the real culprit? Could it be a vulnerable looking eleven-year-old girl? She did not have to say it out loud. Judging from the tight line of Kathy's mouth, it was a conclusion they had both reached.

"I need to get home."

CHAPTER TWENTY-TWO

Erin hurried to her truck and disregarded highway traffic laws in her haste to get home. Her truck's tires screeched around the last corner and into her driveway. She flung open the front door and called Allie's name.

"I'm in here."

Erin came to a standstill when she saw Allie hunched on the sofa. Wrong-Way Rachel sprawled across her lap, fluffy tail curled up around her neck. A veritable mound of crumpled Kleenexes littered the cushion beside them.

"Are you okay?"

"I was okay. Really, I was okay, until I saw Fiona's dish sitting on the kitchen floor." Her voice choked. "I'm sorry, I just lost it." She pulled another tissue from the box and dabbed at red puffy eyes.

"Oh, baby!" Erin swept the trash to the floor and sat beside her.

"I called Judy." She gripped her hand as if it tethered her to planet Earth. "I mean, I called my mom. She wanted to take the next plane down here but I told her we are fine and you would be home soon. I felt better after I talked to her and I'll call again later when I can keep it together."

"I'm glad she was there for you." Erin's guilt skyrocketed. "What did the doctor say about your leg?"

Allie gingerly touched freshly applied bandages. "It's basically a dog bite. It's not infected but he gave me a tetanus shot and antibiotic ointment anyway. He said rabies are rare around here so he'll wait a few days to see if I foam at the mouth."

201

"He did not."

"He said my physical injury should heal on its own." Allie tried to smile but it faded before it reached her eyes. "And he offered me a prescription for Ativan so I can sleep."

"You don't need a sedative or an anti anxiety drug, baby." If alcohol magnified Allie's abilities until they screeched out of control, Erin could just imagine what medication would do.

"I don't either. That's why I turned it down." She leaned into Erin's shoulder. "I only need you."

"I'm sorry I didn't give you a chance to tell me what was wrong at the ranger station," Erin began. "I thought we had it all figured out. I thought you were just overwhelmed by—by everything." She did not want to rip open the emotional wound that had not yet begun to heal.

Allie inhaled sharply. "I should have made myself talk to you. I was fighting a headache when we caught up to the other canoe but I was managing it. In my mind I kept seeing this big wild cat, the one we had been searching for. Suddenly it turned and came back to taunt us, to show us how invincible it was. When we all rode in the big boat, a flood of images poured into my mind. The pressure was unimaginable, like my head would explode into tiny pieces. It was spinning so fast that I had to get away from everyone as soon as I could. I was a little better when you came to get me, but when that kid grabbed my hand, I knew. The whole picture became clear." She searched Erin's face for any hint of doubt. There was none.

"I'm beginning to understand." Erin told her about the bizarre interview at the station, halted by the mysteriously appearing attorney. The girl had not called him, so how had he come to be there? Had Derek's phone call been not for himself, but for the girl? In retrospect, it seemed likely that it had. Something Allie had said about Derek slithered up Erin's spine and began to coalesce in her brain. "What did you mean when you talked about a part of Derek's essence?"

"Have you noticed that Lily's eyes are the lightest shade of green? Just like Derek's." Erin's bones shivered when Allie laid out the puzzle pieces. "They have the same hair and pale skin, don't they? She looks a lot like him, don't you think?" She waited for Erin to finish the puzzle.

"She's a part of him!" Erin shouted. Wrong-Way Rachel let out a perturbed squeak and with a peevish swish of her tail leapt off Allie's lap. The cat padded out the door to the kitchen and the last piece slammed into place. Erin gasped. "He knows what she's done and he's protecting her because he's her father!"

The mysterious deposits into Gunther's bank account. Child support? Gunther Schmidt had known too. For the price of a six pack of beer in the fridge and a monthly check, Derek fulfilled his fatherly duties and Gunther kept his mouth shut. Lily played the middle, one man against the other. For what? Her own amusement? Twisted revenge toward a father who deserted her at birth? What did she have to gain by poisoning her own grandfather? Macabre entertainment? Was she simply bored? And where had her mother gone? Nefarious scenarios filed through Erin's mind. She let her breath out, but tension stayed between her shoulder blades. Derek had confessed to it all and Lily was going to walk away, free to do as she pleased.

Erin sprang to her feet and paced across the room. She scrubbed an angry palm over her face until the skin reddened. "All this time, your thoughts were about her, not him. She's the one who watches and stalks." Erin remembered the night they nearly drove into the barricade on the road. "The rock in your back window. Was that her? Was she watching us at the bog too?"

"The energy felt the same. Like a dangerous wild cat. I think so."

"I feel like puking." Erin sat down hard beside Allie. "Oh my God, you should have seen her play everyone at the office, all smiles and batting eyelashes. Poor little victim!" Erin groaned. "She played me too."

Allie touched her knee, her hand warm through the fabric of her jeans. Confident, reassuring, sincere. "She thinks she has won. More people will get hurt. You must stop her."

"Derek confessed. He is taking the rap for everything she's done. I don't understand why. As far as they are concerned, she is a vulnerable little child with no direct evidence implicating her. I can't even talk to her now. How can I stop her?"

"I don't know. You—" Allie paused and amended, "—we need to find a way. I am in this now, as much as you are." She rested her head on Erin's shoulder and Erin hugged her tight.

* * *

"What did that bastard say?" Erin scratched a fingernail into a worn crease in the kitchen countertop. She switched the iPhone to her other ear.

"Not much." Zimmerman sounded distracted and she heard him get up to close the door. The background noise muted. "When I talked to Striker, he said Derek looked depressed. The interrogation lasted for three hours but he didn't say much, except that his wife is filing for divorce. He seemed more upset about Lily."

"I never guessed she was his kid. This town can sure keep a secret. In retrospect, how did we miss it? She looks just like him. What else did Derek say?"

"Striker said he confessed to everything. Everything but molesting the girl. That, he vehemently denied. Derek signed a skimpy confession, and refused to provide any more information. He simply crossed his arms, invoked his Fifth Amendment rights and asked to be taken to his cell. A disgraced police officer like him will do hard time for one murder and two attempts. The lawyer he phoned never arrived, so I wonder if that will be part of his defense."

"I'm sure the lawyer was for his kid," she said. "Who would have figured he'd be capable of such family loyalty?"

"You must have gone to school with Lily's mom, Tiffany Schmidt. Were you aware that she and Derek were an item?"

"I stayed away from Derek as best I could, but it seemed he always had a new cheerleader on his arm. I do remember Tiffany, but we didn't travel in the same circles. She hung out with the drug crowd by senior year and I avoided that bunch."

"You want this?" Zimmerman whispered. "Yeah, come and get it."

"What the heck are you talking about?" Erin shouted into the phone. "Are you doing weird kinky stuff?"

"I am feeding Picasso a cricket," he retorted. "Forgive me for multi-tasking, Ms. Perfect."

"You are one wacky guy. I was afraid I was intruding..."

He disregarded her insinuation. "Striker discovered that Derek couldn't possibly have burned down Dolores Johnson's house. He was with the Staff Sergeant, getting a lecture on deportment, when it happened. The call released him from the boss's office and he seemed genuinely perplexed about the origin of the explosion. He didn't have much to say about the fire at the convenience store either.

He said he drove Lily straight home and was with his wife by the time that happened. Unfortunately for him, he already confessed to it and his wife is so angry that she won't corroborate his belated alibi. She's been wanting to leave him for a while and this is the last straw. He'll rot in jail before she helps him."

"Derek hated Gina, but I doubt he tried to kill her. My money is on the kid. She blurted something about the gas can that was used to start the fire. She knew exactly how her grandfather was poisoned."

"Lily is a strange little creature," Zimmerman said. "The murder of Dolores Johnson. The arson of the store and attempted murder of Gina Braun. Do you really believe a kid is capable?"

"I wouldn't put much past her. Ice water runs in her veins."

"Even if Derek is her dad, why would he be willing to go to jail? Striker said he'd planned to take the kid north of the border to stay with a friend until he could sort out his life and come for her. I can see him ditching his job for a long-lost daughter, but going to jail? That's sheer lunacy."

Erin nodded. She focused on a spot in the distance. "It's possible that he was trying so hard to protect his kid that he impulsively confessed, figuring he'd get out of it later. He was the golden boy, remember? He always got what he wanted. Not this time."

Zimmerman continued her train of thought. "You might be right. By the time he realized what he'd done, he was looking at the inside of a jail cell. His wife had frozen their bank accounts, his lawyer refused to take on his appeal, and now he has to apply for a public defender."

"That makes more sense than the martyr theory. He's too arrogant and self-centered."

"So there he sits. You know what happens to cops in jail."

"I kinda feel sorry for him. He's an idiot, but---."

"Don't feel sorry for that jackass! Dude pulled his service weapon on you! Not to mention the souvenir he gave you on your arm. I'm glad he didn't go after your girlfriend."

"I don't think he regarded her as a threat." Erin's skin crawled at the thought of Derek harming Allie.

"Not until he was looking down the barrel of the shotgun in her hands. That girl you've got is no shrinking violet, that's for sure!" He snorted.

"She's definitely not."

"As far as I'm concerned, you don't owe Derek an ounce of pity."

"Still, I'd like to understand." Erin scrunched her shoulders forward in a semi-shrug.

"Gunther might have answers." She found a new crease in the edge of the countertop to trace with her fingernail.

He sighed loudly. "If you're so damn determined, Gina said she was going to the hospital to see him tonight. You could just happen to drop in..."

"Gina?" How did he run across her?

"Uh, she mentioned it..." A knock interrupted him. "I gotta go. My mom needs a hand. Give me a shout after you talk to Mr. Schmidt." He disconnected the call.

Erin jammed the iPhone into her pocket and found her keys. She left a note for Allie, who had gone to the gym. Fifteen minutes later, she parked her truck at the hospital and got Gunther's location from the information desk. She quietly opened the door to his room.

On the bed, Gunther Schmidt looked like a corpse. Skin on his ashen face had a strange mottled texture. His swollen jaundiced eyes took in the new visitor.

"I was in the neighborhood," Erin lied. "I decided to pop in for a minute."

"Hey stranger." Gina leaned back in a visitor's chair at the side of Gunther's bed, paperback in her hands.

"Louis L'Amour," Erin said, glancing at the cover. "My dad loves his old Westerns too."

"We are at the end of the chapter." She patted Gunther's hand. "Why don't we stop here and pick it up tomorrow?" He nodded and Erin noted a tremor in his movements.

"How is he?" She directed her question to Gina.

"I'm just ducky," he croaked. "I ain't dead yet."

Gina grinned at her apologetically.

"You're right, Mr. Schmidt. I'm sorry." Erin sat in the chair opposite Gina and he turned his puffy face to her. "I should have asked you."

"He's so much better than yesterday." Gina tucked his exposed arm under the blanket and pulled it around his shoulders. She brought a glass of ice water up and bent the straw to his mouth.

"Will ya quit yer fussin', girl? I ain't no infant!" His words were belligerent, but his tone was soft. "It's dang hot in here!" He shoved starchy bedcovers aside and pushed his arm back out. Against the stark sheets, dark-colored lesions speckled his temples and the palms of his hands. Had Doctor Holloway talked about it the day she told him about the arsenic? It had been hard to follow the technical specifics of that conversation. How had she not noticed the spots when she found him in his hidey hole?

He turned to Erin. "You fished me out, didn't you?"

She nodded.

"Well then, thank you for savin' an old fart like me. I appreciate bein' able to take a few more breaths in this lifetime. I wasn't sure if I dreamed that or not."

"Do you remember what happened to you?"

"'Course I do. Lily came and told me she'd made a mistake and the store caught on fire. I was worried she'd got herself in too deep this time so we were just bidin' our time until the coast was clear. I drank a bad beer, or two. That last one was a doozy. I remember upchuckin' and wakin' up in here. My angel has been fussin' over me pretty much ever since." He raised a corner of his mouth in a half smile and Gina wiped her eye. "I'm real sorry about sayin' mean stuff to ya, girl. I got no idea what came over me."

"It's okay. It wasn't your fault." Gina retrieved a tissue and daintily blew her nose.

"They said Derek Peterson confessed to givin' me the poison. I'm tryin' to wrap my noggin' around that," Gunther said. "I've known that boy since he was a teenager and he don't always make the best decisions, but I didn't figure him for tryin' to kill me."

"He confessed, but I don't think he did it." Erin sat forward in her seat.

"Well, you don't think I tried to off myself, do ya?"

"I think Lily poured the poison in your beer." Erin waited for his reaction. His body stiffened but he didn't immediately respond. He glanced at Gina, then back to Erin. He breathed a plaintive moan.

"Gottverdammt!" He whistled the curse through his teeth and sank his head onto the pillow. "She's been havin' a hard time but I didn't wanna believe she'd try somethin' like this." He looked over to Gina. "She's not the one who hurt you, is she?"

Gina couldn't meet his eyes.

His shoulders sagged. "Sie verloren ist."

"She is lost," Gina translated.

"Will you tell me what you know?" Erin's eyes flitted around the room, searching for pen and paper. She had not come prepared.

"She's my granddaughter! My blood. I can't speak out against her! She's only a girl, and so much like her mother, my sweet Tiffany. I miss her every day."

"Where is she?" With nothing to write on, Erin tapped notes into her iPhone. It was like having a mini computer in her pocket.

"Last time I seen her, she showed me a big ol' ring on her finger. Said she was goin' to marry Derek. Said he would leave his wife and be a father to Lily. She looked so happy." His gravelly voice wavered. "The next day she was gone and I never understood why. She didn't take a thing, 'cept her purse." Eyes closed in private agony, he bunched his hands into fists. "Maybe it was the drugs. She tried so hard..."

"Did Derek tell you what happened to her?"

"No, he was heartbroken. Said he searched every town within a thousand miles. Lily was eight by then and he tried to help out with her. She treated him more like a slave but he'd do pret'near anythin' for that child. Had so much guilt over leavin' Tiffany after he got her pregnant. They were just kids themselves." Gunther coughed and Gina sat up, alarmed. She rubbed his shoulder. "That boy used to hang around the house 'til I sent him home. It was no use sittin' around waitin' for her. She never called. I know how I felt when I lost my wife to the cancer so I felt bad for him."

"Will you give me an official statement?"

He closed his eyes and shook his head. "No. I can't. She's all I have left. I swore to help her." He coughed again, phlegm rattling in his throat. Gina leaned him forward and rubbed his back until he caught his breath. She focused pained eyes on Erin.

"Thank you for what you were able to tell me, Mr. Schmidt." She stood.

"Please, she's all I got. She's just havin' a bad time. She don't mean it. Ihr helfen."

Erin remembered that last word. She certainly wanted to help the girl. Help her face justice. She turned her back so he didn't see her anger. *You're wrong. Lily knows exactly what she's doing.* She quietly closed the door on her way out.

CHAPTER TWENTY-THREE

This house is like a sugar coated fairy tale for toddlers. The people are idiots, but aren't they all? It takes forever for the introductions and dopey questions, which I ignore of course. I'm too upset to talk about it, right? They buy it like stupid sheep, with their stupid sheep faces.

All through dinner I make my eyebrows do the sad thing but I really can't complain about the food. Pork chops and mashed potatoes. I even ate my carrots like a good little girl. I have to admit that it was way better than any dinner I've had since my mom left, well, since she went and drowned herself in the bog. It wasn't my fault. Her cooking is about the only thing I miss, and I can't remember the last time I ate a vegetable.

I don't miss the old man either but I realize now that I underestimated how tough he was. He taught me my favorite swear words, and tried to teach me about the woods but I outgrew him long ago. When he started interfering in my life, that was the end. 'Don't steal. Do your homework. Don't drink my beer. Sie verloren.'

I am not lost, I told him. *I know exactly what I want.* The nagging never ended. He was just like my mom and I didn't need him any more. Who knew he would be so damn hard to get rid of? I should have stuck around to make certain.

On the other hand, the man who called himself my father turned out to be a useful minion, but it pissed me off that he never gave me money when I asked. What was an extra ten or twenty dollars to him? He had lots, just look at that flashy car he drove. 'I already gave it to your grandfather,' he always said. 'Go ask him.'

He was apologetic about everything and when it came down to it, all I had to do was just point my finger at him. That pussy was on his way to jail and didn't even defend himself. I'm glad he's gone. Now I can find someone new.

At the dinner table there are two kids gawking at me. They don't dare come close because they know what's good for them. Badass panthers eat little kids. When their mom is not looking, I show my teeth and make monster faces until the youngest one cries. The older one, who is about kindergarten age, picks up her fork like she's gonna fight me if I come close. That cracks me up. She's no match for me. I make sure I'm smiling like a kind big sister when their mom looks over and she shushes the little one.

After dinner, the lady shows me to my room. I'm pissed that the cop lied to me. There is no TV, and definitely no computer. I was so sure I had her but she didn't buy my act and I don't understand where I went wrong. Did the old man say something? Did her zombie girlfriend figure it out? How?

Finally I'm alone and I sit on a little bed with a little kid comforter and stare at the little kid toys in the corner. I've checked the closet and all the drawers and there is not a damn thing in here that interests me. I'll get up after everyone goes to bed and see what I can find. Maybe I'll get lucky and there will be a Budweiser in the fridge. The picture of the guy with a beard that says Jesus is Lord makes me think my luck is not that good.

I poke my finger through a tiny flaw in the comforter and pull back until I've made a hole. I keep at it until it's big enough to put my fist in. From my pack I take out the wad of bills I stole from the old man's room and cram it deep inside. The lady here has already tried to take my pack, to clean it she said, but I know she's just gonna snoop. I can't let her take my money. I fold the edge of the comforter over so she can't see the hole and cover it with a pillow, just to make sure.

I had smiled a lot at the Child Services lady and acted like a freakin' five-year-old. She'd lapped it up like a starving dog. Tomorrow they are coming, she'd told me. Good, because I don't know how long I'll be able to keep up this game without that little kid stabbing me with her fork! I can't stop laughing. That kid doesn't know who she's dealing with. She doesn't know what I have in my pocket. Then I remember. My so-called dad took my knife. Minion took my knife!

If I had it all to do over, I wouldn't make the same mistakes. I'd do it better. There is a calendar on the wall and I suddenly realize that today was my birthday. Twelve years ago today, I was born. Well, happy birthday to me. I sleep like a baby because tomorrow they are coming. I'm going to be free.

* * *

A full night's sleep had worked its restorative powers on Erin and she awoke clear headed. The adhesive plastic stitches holding together the knife wound on her arm still held, a testament to Allie's first aid skills.

Allie was already eating toast when she sat at the table, phone in hand. She punched in the number and listened to the ring at the other end. Once, twice, would it simply go to voice mail? Erin leapt to her feet when the call was answered and patiently waited while she was transferred through to the supervisor. She calmly asked her first question and listened for a moment before her face turned crimson.

"Winnipeg?" Erin exploded, pounding a fist on the countertop. "That's all the way up in Canada! Do they even have a f— do they understand what they are doing?" She hit the disconnect button with such ferocity that the phone tumbled from her hand and crashed to the floor. Allie placed a calming hand on her shoulder and Erin sank to the kitchen chair. A sob escaped her throat and she wiped a frustrated tear before it had a chance to spill.

"What did they say?"

"They said I can't talk to Lily because she's gone. She's probably crossing the Canadian border right now." Erin's voice cracked and she sucked air through her teeth. "They contacted a relative up there, Gunther's nephew or something. He and his wife drove all night to get here. They left with Lily early this morning."

"So that's it, then. There's nothing you can do." Allie said the words but there was no finality in her tone.

"That kid probably lifted her middle finger to her dad in jail, and then waved cheerfully to everyone from her getaway car." Erin's acid tone was unfamiliar.

Worry worked its way into the creases at the corners of Allie's eyes.

"Children's Services is frigging expediting the paperwork because of the circumstances."

"They can't possibly believe that Derek is responsible for everything! Why aren't they keeping Lily until they are done investigating?"

"There wasn't any direct evidence to implicate her. It's all circumstantial. Even if a charge could be substantiated, it would be dealt with by the juvenile court system." Erin pinched the skin at the bridge of her nose. "Their emphasis is on rehabilitation and protection. She and her lawyer would chew them up and spit them out. At the very least, she would laugh in their faces. It was most likely an easy out to send her off with the first family that would claim her."

"It upsets me too, but you can't change this."

"I'm afraid of what she will do to Gunther's family. You know what she's capable of! You know what she is!"

"You need to leave this alone now," Allie said. "She is gone. It's not good for you to keep this kind of hate."

"I'll feel better when I fucking feel better," Erin retorted. "I'm going to put in a call to Winnipeg PD and they can at least keep an eye out."

"I'm not sure that will go over very well."

Erin pulled away from her, stalked across the room and wrenched open the coffee cupboard. Allie stared at the empty dog dish on the floor, and a wounded silence echoed in the room until the coffee machine hissed.

EPILOGUE: ONE YEAR LATER

Erin eased the throttle back and stood at the center console, navigating around a floating log. A powerful four-stroke Yamaha motor rumbled at the stern of her father's brand new fishing boat. The sleek black hull split the water, spraying out either side. Erin wore a tank top, not concerned about exposing the thin pink knife cut. Her bicep had healed but the scar would forever remain untanned.

Jimmy and the twins had begged to come with them on this important day and the serious-faced five year old shuffled his feet around the large cooler bag with which he had been entrusted. Grandma Ericsson had packed their picnic lunch and he was proud to be in charge. The girls sat right up front, eyes peeled for water hazards, and their mouths never stopped talking.

Erin detached the canopy so the wind could ruffle her hair. She knew Allie liked that windswept carefree look and she bent down to kiss her on the sweet spot behind her ear. They intertwined their fingers, making the girls giggle.

"Rock a-starboard!" Sophie called out.

"Rock a-starboard!" Erin confirmed and veered left to avoid it.

"Deadhead a-port!" Victoria and Sophie yelled in unison. That one was fun to say and neither girl wanted to miss out.

"Deadhead a-port!" Erin repeated. She lowered her speed and steered past the half sunk log and then cracked open the throttle. Zooming around the next bend in the river, the kids screamed with delight when water spattered high up onto the bank. She grinned at her girlfriend, who gave her a small smile in return, clutching a package tighter to her chest.

Erin recognized their destination first and noticed Allie's body tense when she idled slowly through the weeds. Their momentum took the boat to shore. Sophie hopped like a squirrel over the bow, taking the rope with her. She wrapped it around the nearest tree trunk and waited for her auntie to come and help her secure it. The kids were already exploring onshore when Erin held out a hand to Allie, who had not moved from her seat.

"Come on, baby. It's time." Erin said tenderly and Allie stood. The wolf's bite marks had healed to ragged pink furrows on her calf but the emotional scar would persist much longer. Since the attack, Erin had been back with her father to check the site. Scavengers had long since dragged off the wolf's carcass. The only reminder of that horrific night was the cairn of rocks that marked the place where Fiona was buried.

Once onshore, Allie walked directly to that spot and sat down cross-legged on the moist ground. Last fall, Erin had scattered a handful of wildflower seeds into the broken ground and a cluster of Smooth Blue Asters now bloomed at the head of the rock cairn they'd built.

"The flowers are beautiful, honey," Allie whispered. "Thank you." In the distance, one of the girls squealed and Allie leapt to her feet.

"It's okay," Erin reassured her. "That's not an upset noise. The kids are just exploring or something."

Allie brushed a few stray hairs from her face and squatted to open the brown paper wrapped package she'd been holding close. She carefully unwrapped a handmade wooden grave marker with an intricate border of flowers and leaves painted around the name. Fuzzy Fiona, it read. She pushed the stake deep into the earth and stood to contemplate it. Erin circled her waist with her arm and they stood in quiet reflection. It was perfect. Tears freely ran down Allie's face but she made no move to wipe them away.

They were still standing there when the kids emerged from the trees, pursued closely by a small gray and black bird. The bird swooped and playfully dove over the kids' little heads and then perched nearby, tittering with delight.

"This is sure a pesky whiskey jack!" Jimmy exclaimed. "It just won't leave us alone." He surveyed the bird with hands on hips, like a curmudgeonly old farmer.

Erin shrugged sheepishly at Allie. "I come out here sometimes and I like to feed the little gaffer. It's sort of grown on me."

Allie managed a smile. "I think we know this gray jay."

"You know a wild whiskey jack?" Jimmy's face said that this was an absolutely preposterous idea.

"She's right." Erin backed up her girlfriend. "We are friends." The bird hopped onto the grave marker and trilled a long sweet note. "I'm sure she and Fiona would have been good friends too."

"This is where you buried Fuzzy Fiona, isn't it?" Jimmy asked somberly. He surveyed the rock cairn, nodded his approval and then reached inside his pocket for a half chewed stick. "This was her favorite and I brought it so she could have it." The little boy leaned over to place it on the top of the rock pile. Sophie and Victoria nestled onto the ground beside Allie.

"Mama said you fought the wolves and they hurt your leg." She laid her head against Allie. "We miss Fuzzy Fiona too." The tears running down Allie's face multiplied.

"This is a really nice place for her to be. I think she would like it." Sophie pointed to the wooden marker.

"Yes, our friend Gina did a nice job, didn't she?" Allie said. The bird tweeted its agreement and fluffed up its chest feathers. "If you are going to stick around, I think you need a name. Sassy Sarah?" The bird squawked and fluttered to a branch above them. "You're right. What was I thinking? That is so not you. How about Pesky Priya?" The gray jay dove back down and resumed its spot on the marker. "Priya it is!" Allie announced.

"She named a wild bird," Sophie whispered loudly to her sister, shaking her head in disbelief.

"I don't care," Victoria retorted a little too loudly. "When I grow up, I'm going to name my daughter Allie, just like her."

Erin smothered a laugh. Her family was her family, and she could just imagine how this story would be told in twenty years' time. A tiny smirk tugged at the corner of Allie's lips. "Where did you come up with that name?"

"I knew a girl named Priya once." Allie shrugged and the smirk stayed put.

"You named the whiskey jack after your ex-girlfriend?"

Allie shrugged again. "Yes, I sure did."

"Let me guess. Wrong-Way Rachel?"

"Yup, her too. Rachel had a terrible sense of direction and a plastic knee."

"Even Fuzzy Fiona?"

"She had a little tuft of blonde hair on her—"

"I get it." Erin glanced at the kids to ensure they were not listening. "How many girlfriends have you had?" A jealous tone crept insidiously into her question.

"Let me just say, I have a few more pets to name." Allie smiled sadly and put her hand out to touch the rocks. "None will ever be as good as this one."

They ate their lunch on a fallen log and talked about what a great dog Fuzzy Fiona was. Pesky Priya's little belly full, the gray jay began to vanish into the trees to stash what it could not consume. Bread crusts, broken crackers, sausage ends, it all disappeared and by the time they were ready to leave there was not a crumb on the ground.

"Goodbye Pesky Priya," Sophie called and the kids waved from the front of the boat when they departed. The bird followed them through the trees, dark wings flitting from branch to branch before they disappeared.

"See you next time, Priya!" Victoria called. She cuddled up to Allie on the trip back. "Are you ever going to get another dog?"

"I'm not sure. I think I will wait until the right one finds me." Allie pulled a blanket from the storage bin under the seat and all three kids snuggled in with her for the ride back. Both girls were fast asleep when Erin cut the motor and eased back up to the dock. She skipped easily over the side and secured the rope while Allie woke the girls. Hearing the motor approach, their mother met them at the dock.

Liz winked at Erin. "Thanks for taking the kids. They really wanted to go and I sure enjoyed my alone time." She led the drowsy girls up to the house.

Jimmy followed Erin and Allie to the driveway and slid his fingers around the door handle of a shiny red Jeep YJ. He opened it for Allie like a well-trained valet. "I like your new car, Auntie Allie. Your old one was nice, but not good for a Minnesota winter, mom said."

Erin snorted. Her siblings talked way too much.

"Thank you Jimmy." Allie picked him off the ground and hugged him. She whispered in his ear before she set him down. "And thank you for the tip on the blueberry patch. I appreciate it." Red-faced, he

216

fastidiously smoothed his shirt but could not hold in a toothy smile.

"My family loves you," Erin told her when Allie backed her new Jeep down the driveway. "After everything that happened, they were afraid you wouldn't stick around and they are so happy you did."

"I am too." Allie shifted into second gear and dodged a pothole, causing Erin to lunge for a handgrip. She shot her a sideways glance. "We need to do a little something on the way home." Two miles down the road, Allie pulled into a turnout and reached behind the seat for a plastic bucket before getting out. "Come on."

Erin followed her along a short trail lined with low brush and scrabbly weeds until they arrived at a mossy clearing. "Blueberries," she said and helped her girlfriend fill the pail. Two berries in the pail and one in the mouth. Allie shot her a look. A handful of berries in the pail and two in the mouth when Allie wasn't looking, until the pail was full.

The sun was low in the sky by the time Allie turned down the gravel driveway to Gina's house. mud tires crunched loudly when she pulled her Jeep in and parked behind a recently washed Chevy Crew Cab. Erin did a double take. She knew that truck, didn't she?

The two women had no chance to knock before Gina appeared behind the screen. Erin noticed that Gina's skin had a particularly rosy glow and her brown hair was swept up into an attractively tousled twist at the nape of her neck. Allie held out the pail of berries and Gina accepted them graciously.

"I wanted to thank you for the beautiful marker you made," Allie said.

Gina's mouth twitched below misted eyes. "I just wanted to do something nice," she said sincerely. Slow jazz music was playing on the radio and her eyes flicked toward the living room. She self-consciously tucked an errant strand of hair behind her ear. "I know how hard it is to suffer such a great loss. Won't you come in?"

Erin's eyes dropped to the floor where a pair of size fourteen boots stood like sentries at the door. Allie followed her gaze and her eyes widened in understanding. They only knew one man with boots like that.

"I'm sorry, we can't stay," Allie said politely, and Gina breathed a tiny sigh of relief. "But perhaps you would like to come for coffee sometime?"

"Thank you, that would be nice," Gina said. They backed tactfully off the porch to the Jeep.

"Chris Zimmerman and Gina!" Allie giggled like a grade schooler. "I am so happy for them. I knew Gina's garden worms would work!"

"Worms?" Erin grimaced. She'd been excluded from a private joke.

"Gina has been sending little presents over for Chris's pets and I guess he finally got interested enough to come knocking."

"Worms!" The mysterious Tupperware containers marked "CZ" that appeared in the fridge at the police station. "I thought she was baking him sexy cinnamon buns or something!" Erin slapped a thigh like an Old Tyme fiddler after his tune is done. "I have to hand it to her, she really knows what a man wants!" She was glad she hadn't tried to pilfer any of those.

"They both deserve to be happy."

"I never would have figured it, but Z-man is a complex man." Erin segued into the question she really wanted to ask, thumping her heel restlessly on the Jeep's floor. "So, you invited Gina to our house for coffee? Is this a way to overcome your jealousy?"

Allie laughed out loud. "Oh, honey, seriously. One kiss in elementary school? Unlike you, there is not a jealous bone in this body."

Erin squinted a suspicious eye.

"She and I became acquainted when you were both in the hospital. There is much more to Miss Gina Braun than she lets on."

Erin relaxed.

"We talked at the grocery store after—well, after everything happened. She was so nice and genuine. Then when she came over with the grave marker that she had made by hand, I realized she is a really special person. I'm glad she looked after you in school."

"Yeah, I had no idea," Erin said. They rounded the corner and she pointed out the rebuilt convenience store. "Hey, check it out! The new sign is up!"

Allie slowed when they passed the lot. The illuminated sign still featured a big fish but the wording had been amended. It now read Gina's Stop 'N Go. "Gina told me that the store is twice its original size with a row of fridges and tanks in the back. She can sell live bait so all the tourists and local fishermen coming in will improve sales."

"Wow, she's hit the big time! Jimmy and the twins will be happy to hear that. They can spend all next summer trapping minnows and catching worms to earn money. It's the best job ever for a kid."

"I'm sure she will be well stocked with lizard treats for Chris."

"I'll bet." Erin laughed.

Allie parked the Jeep in the driveway and they walked hand in hand to the house. Erin shoved the door open with her foot and, ill-at-ease, hesitated in the hallway. With its absence of wagging tail and toenails skipping on hardwood, the silence was louder than noise. This was the time that she missed Fiona the most and she wondered if the hole in her heart could ever be filled.

It had also been an especially hard year for Allie, with her workouts at the gym stretching to hours sometimes. She pecked Erin on the cheek, scooped the three legged cat up from her hiding spot in the front hallway and wordlessly carried her upstairs to the bedroom.

Erin headed to the kitchen and made herself a decaf. She sat at the kitchen table with The Journal of Forensic Science and her computer tablet. Halfway done her introductory home study course, she was hoping to be selected for training by fall. Since last summer, Dave struggled with his career. His suspension from lab duties in the Forensic Identification Unit had ended but he was not doing well and there was talk of firing him outright. With a possible opening in the Unit, it might be a good move for her.

"I'll be up in just a minute, baby!" Erin called out and there was a grunt in response.

Allie would wind down by reading a Tracey Richardson romance novel. She and Erin had settled into a new pattern since last summer. She knew that 'just a minute' really meant that the grandfather clock in the living room would be striking twelve long before Erin came to bed.

In the kitchen, Erin hunched forward over her tablet's bright screen and rubbed dry eyes. The text of Winnipeg's news headlines flew by when she scrolled down the page and she scanned each local online source for crime reports. The lines furrowing her forehead deepened. TWO KILLED IN HIGHWAY CRASH, one headline read. She clicked on it for the full story. After a few seconds, she returned to her original page and read the next headlines. CHILD INJURED AT DAY CARE and CHARGES LAID IN BOATING ACCIDENT also proved fruitless. Her eyes were bleary and her coffee had long since grown cold when Erin spotted it, buried at the bottom of the page. Her heart thudded in her chest when she clicked the link and read the article.

HOUSE FIRE SENDS ONE TO HOSPITAL

A LOCAL WOMAN IS RECOVERING IN WINNIPEG REGIONAL HOSPITAL AFTER BEING RESCUED FROM A BURNING HOME THURSDAY NIGHT. HOSPITAL SOURCES REPORT THAT BARBARA SCHMIDT, AGE 46, SUSTAINED SERIOUS BURNS BUT IS IN STABLE CONDITION. HER HUSBAND WAS NOT AT HOME AT THE TIME OF THE INCIDENT AND POLICE REPORT THAT A FEMALE TEEN WHO RESIDED AT THE HOME ESCAPED UNHARMED. FIRE INVESTIGATORS ARE EXPLORING THE ORIGIN OF A GAS LEAK SUSPECTED AS THE FIRE'S CAUSE.

"Allie! Allie! It's happened!" Erin's voice climbed to a high pitch and she bolted up the stairs to the bedroom.

THE END.

ABOUT THE AUTHOR

Makenzi Fisk grew up in a small town in Northwestern Ontario. She spent much of her youth outdoors, surrounded by the rugged landscape of the Canadian Shield.

Moving west to the prairies. she became a police officer with experience in patrols, covert operations, plainclothes investigation, communications and forensic identification. Within the policing environment, she transitioned to internet and graphic design. She now works for herself.

In her novels, Makenzi draws on her knowledge of the outdoors, policing and technology to create vivid worlds where crime, untamed wilderness and intuition blend. Her novels' characters are competent women who solve crime using skill and a little intuition.

Currently Makenzi resides in Calgary with her partner, their daughter, and assorted furry companions.

Website: makenzifisk.com

Next in the
INTUITION SERIES

BURNING INTUITION